One Summer at Ril Lake

One Summer at Ril Lake

By Margery Reynolds

A Muskoka Cottage Read Novel

Golden Pencil

Published by

Golden Pencil ✏

Copyright 2022 Dale Margery Rutherford

(aka Margery Reynolds)

All rights reserved.

This book is a work of fiction. Names and characters are the product of the author's imagination and are used fictitiously. The incidents are not real and are not meant to replicate any person living or dead. Some places mentioned exist at the time of writing and the businesses mentioned have given their permission to be used in this series.

Library of Canada Archives and Publication

ISBN 978-1-7386767-1-2

Cover Design With Canva

By Margery Reynolds

www.goldenpencil.ca

Golden Pencil ✏

For Judy,

who has tirelessly read nearly every word I've ever written, who found the cottage at Ril Lake all those years ago, and who has never given up on me, even when I was ready to give up on myself. You will always have my gratitude, admiration, and respect. Thank you.

"We dance round in a ring and suppose,

but the secret sits in the middle and knows."

–Robert Frost

1

Felicity Jefferies did not believe in Fate or Destiny or a Supreme Being who toyed with people's lives or created opportunities for them. But she couldn't deny that when her husband of twenty-eight years died of a heart attack, unburdening her from the obligations of a loveless marriage, for once life was moving in her favour.

Three months after Richard's death, what Felicity needed was some time alone to acclimatize herself to this new unencumbered-by-spousal-duties life. With her intent to spend the entire summer at the family cottage, alone, except for a few weekends when her kids would join her, she set out earlier than usual. There was where she would find the peace and tranquility she longed for, away from the constant reminders of the past, of Richard, and of the secrets of their spurious life.

"Drive safely, Mum." Tom, her eldest, hovering over her, uttering last-minute warnings as he kissed her goodbye. "I know you're an excellent driver, but it's the other idiots you have to watch out for."

"Other idiots?" Felicity had laughed. "What you're really saying is that I'm one of the idiots, too?"

"You know what I mean." Tom brushed a wisp of loose hair behind her ear for her and smiled. He'd been around a little too much lately, worried that after his father's death she might crumble and come apart at the seams. She couldn't possibly tell him how she really felt any more than she could tell him the reason she was relieved that Richard was gone. Especially now, since Tom had become the unappointed man of the family, stepping into his father's role without being asked and sometimes at the frustration of his siblings. He was a man with an instinctual need to take care of those he loved, and she'd given in to his need to comfort and protect her. He missed his father and assumed she did too and by taking care of her, as he thought his dad would have done, he was doing his bit.

Olivia, the nurse who mended the visible wounds, and worried about the ones she could not see, kept her own feelings close to her heart. She had a practical mind and dealt with things in a practical and a forgiving way. Tom lived in a world of black and white, right and wrong, acceptable and not, whereas Olivia's world, when it was not sunshine yellow, was grey. Things needed to be seen from all sides, and nothing was ever as it first appeared.

That morning, Olivia had a shift at the hospital and couldn't be there to say goodbye, but they had talked on the phone. Felicity had not forgotten her daughter's words of reluctance that her mother was going all the way up north, alone.

"I'll be fine," Felicity had said. "Don't worry." But of course, Olivia would worry. It was what she did.

But it was Will, her youngest, who Felicity was most concerned about. Two years ago, he had dropped out of Carleton University, and since, was unable to keep a job. Since university, he'd been floundering, flitting from one job to the next, always searching for the perfect one, the challenge that would lift him out of his funk and make use of his creative talents. None of them seemed to do the trick. Felicity supported his efforts to try new things, but secretly harboured worries he would continue in this vein until he was thirty. But, at twenty-two, he was his own man, and she had to let him make his own mistakes.

Tom stood back with a hesitant smile, still wavering about her going alone. Will stepped in and gave her a reassuring *'you're doing the right thing'* hug and kissed her cheek. "Call us when you get there. I know you'll be fine, but it will put old worrywart here at ease." He flashed a teasing look at his brother.

Felicity had laughed. "Alright, alright. I promise to drive carefully and to call when I get there. That should be about five-ish."

She looked at her boys fondly. "The weekend seems a long time away. Are you sure you can't get away sooner?" On one hand, she wanted the time alone, on the other she knew she'd missed her children's company. They'd been sticking together like wet t-shirts in the rinse cycle since Richard's death.

Will shook his head. "The boss would kill me if I asked for time off. The weekend will have to do this time."

"I know. I know. And Olivia has shifts at the hospital and you, Tom, have a ton of work. As usual." She patted his cheek. "Just don't let your work take over your life, okay?"

"I won't, Mum. Promise." Tom had closed her door when she got in, and leaned in with last-minute instructions again, to drive safely and to remember to prime the generator, just in case. "We'll see you on Friday," he'd said.

"And don't forget Hope's vet appointment on Wednesday before you bring her up. And please be careful when you go inside. Remember how she likes to bolt."

Tom smiled and nodded. Will gave the hood of her car a tap as she backed out of the driveway, and then she was gone, waving until the sight of her boys waving back at her fading into the scenery from her rear-view mirror.

Traffic had been unusually light, even for a Monday, which meant Felicity had made good time, cutting nearly half an hour off her customary three and half-hour trip, even with her stop for a caffeine infusion and some fries to nibble while she drove. In

Baysville, at last, she pulled into Wally's Garage to fill up on fuel. She had a quarter of a tank, but it was always good to have the tank full when heading up into the woods.

Wally came out of the office and waved as she got out and pushed her debit card into the slot to start the pump. One of the two bay doors of the garage stood open, the other closed, with a car on the hoist, just visible through the filmy glass. Wally wiped grease off his hands and shoved a rag into his back pocket as he made his way across the tarmac. His unmistakable lopsided gait seemed more laborious than she'd remembered; the result of a narrow escape with a bear, or so the rumour went.

"Hello Felicity," he said, taking over the pump for her, even though he ran a self-serve station. Wally liked the personal touch, and it was rumoured he knew more about the goings on in and around Baysville than the hairdresser or the lady that ran the secondhand shop. He'd have things to tell her if she let him and he'd want to know how her winter had been. They hadn't been up since Christmas, so Wally wouldn't have known about Richard.

"You're up early this year," he said, lifting a still-greasy hand to shade his eyes from the sun as he peered into the back of her car and saw it was loaded. Wally was what Felicity's mother called a late bloomer. He'd met and married Doris late in life and now had a son younger than Felicity's children, though he was at least a decade older. The weathered skin and his lopsided gait were his only betrayals of that. His sense of compassion and understanding never wavered, nor did his sense of humour. He glanced at her car again, empty of children, pets, or a husband. "And you're alone. That'll be a treat."

"Fewer obligations now. Some 'me-time' for once," she said with a little laugh. "How's the family?"

"Good," he said. "Yours?"

She nodded. "The same. Although, I suppose you wouldn't have heard, Richard died in March."

"I'm sorry," he said, leaving it at that. Felicity knew Wally and Richard hadn't liked each other much. More than once they'd come to loggerheads about some car matter or other with Richard mumbling under his breath that backwoods mechanics didn't know what they were talking about. Wally wouldn't have said anything negative about anyone, but he'd always cast a woeful look to Felicity that suggested he felt sorry for her. Felicity had complete faith in Wally's abilities with their car, and she liked him. She liked his wife, too, though Doris was a shy woman, which people often mistook for self-importance. Nothing could be further from the truth. And then there was Adam, their son, who was the image of his father in his youth, but with his mother's temperament. They were a nice family, and if Richard had ever taken the time to read the certificates on the wall inside the office, he would have known that Wally had done his apprenticeship and training with a big shop in Ajax. Wally might live in a tiny village with a population of less than two hundred now, but his knowledge about cars wasn't *small-town* at all.

Felicity was telling Wally how much she liked Olivia's new boyfriend, Eric, when a blue Subaru Impresa pulled up to the other pump and a man, dressed in blue jeans and a pale-yellow golf shirt, got out and looked toward them. He ran a hand through a thick crop of dark hair and pulled his wallet out of the back pocket of his jeans. "Afternoon," he said. "Beautiful day, isn't it?"

With a reassuring smile, Wally left Felicity to finish pumping her own gas, and went to talk with his other customer. "Fill her up?" he asked.

"Sure, but you're busy. And isn't this a self-serve?" the man asked, bending to undo his gas cap.

"Never too busy to help a customer," Wally replied, already lifting the handle on the pump. "Where you headed?"

"Family cottage." He glanced toward the road ahead and lifted his chin in that direction. "Just up the road a bit, according to my GPS."

"First time up here?"

"It is." The man took in the view surrounding them and cast a flashing glance toward Felicity. "I'm beginning to see what all the hype is about. It's so quiet up here."

As if to prove him wrong, a jackhammer started up in the distance, where a construction crew was digging up the road near the bridge. It made them laugh.

Wally shrugged. "It usually is," he lifted his voice over the noise. "You know, Baysville isn't big, but we've got a little grocery store over there if you need anything." Wally nodded toward a single-story brick building next door to the garage, with stacks of firewood and propane tanks set on either side of the door. "And there's the liquor store, over there, and over the road there's the library and a couple of shops. And the bakery is something you won't want to miss." He tugged a little on his belt. "Doris keeps telling me to stay away from there."

Felicity pointed down the road. "And then there's Yummies in a Jar where they make the best jam and maple syrup you could ask for. You just passed it a couple of clicks back."

A wide smile crinkled the corners of the man's eyes as he leaned against the car, while Wally filled the tank. "Sounds like I have some exploring to do."

He certainly didn't look like a man who ate a lot of pastries, Felicity thought as she watched them from her side of the pump island. She admired the distinguished look of a man in his early fifties, especially one with a little grey at the temples who wore their clothes like a perfect sized mannequin in a men's wear shop window. She looked away when she felt him watching her too and fed the last bits of gas into the tank, topping it up to an even dollar amount. She smiled when he commented on her overstuffed car.

"You look like you're here for the long haul."

She laughed. "Yes. The summer, at least. If you're looking for serenity, this is the place for it." She reset the nozzle into the pump, pushed the button for a receipt and twisted her gas cap back on. "All set, Wally," she said as she climbed back into her car. "Say hi to Doris for me." She gave a quick glance over her shoulder, started the engine, then waved out the window as she pulled away. Wally and the man in the yellow shirt waved back.

Felicity's generations old family cottage was exactly twelve point two kilometers out-of-town once you crossed over Baysville Narrows. At the bridge, she came to the construction they'd heard moments before and found the traffic condensed into one lane for both directions. She waited until the flagman waved her on, negotiated the tight single lane over the bridge, and then she turned right onto Echo Lake Road. Just past the six-kilometer mark, she heard a thumping sound and felt an odd vibration at the back of her Santa Fe. As she pulled to the side, she felt the rear passenger side of the car sink.

"Damn," she said out loud. "A flat. Out here. Why couldn't this have happened when I was at the garage?"

2

Felicity shut off the engine and got out to investigate. The waning light from the afternoon sun, this deep in the woods, did not escape her as she rounded the back of the car and spotted the passenger side rear tire. Flat, as she suspected. She lifted her cell phone out of her pocket, already knowing reception was spotty along this road. Half a bar was not enough to make a call, confirmed by the no-service warning blaring up from her screen.

She considered filling her backpack with things from the cooler that would spoil, but it would be a long arduous walk up and down the hills that made up the rest of the journey. From there, should could call Wally and get him to come and fix the tire. She glanced at the time on her phone and calculated that by the time she reached her cottage, Wally would be home and eating one of Doris's delicious suppers. Walking back to town would take just as long and produce the same result. Maybe she could change the tire herself. She'd watched the Roadside Assistance guys do it once or twice. How hard could it be?

First, she had to unearth the jack and the spare from beneath the boxes, suitcases and two coolers. She piled them at the side of the road, as neatly as possible, out of the way of traffic. Not that many cars ever came up this way, unless, of course, you lived up here or were renting. She surprised herself by getting the jack into place and lifting the back of the car enough to get at the offending tire. and was just about to loosen the lug nuts when she heard the crunch of gravel; a car was coming up the road. She stood up just as a blue Impresa pulled up behind her piles of stuff, and the man in the yellow golf shirt from Wally's garage got out of his car.

"Need a hand?" he asked, hovering near the front of his car.

"I'm okay, here," she said. He looked safe from a distance, and when she'd had Wally around it was okay, but out here, alone, Olivia's warnings from earlier this morning came back to her. *'You shouldn't be going up there alone, Mum. There are stalkers and creeps everywhere. You're open prey for the weirdos. You have to be careful.'*

Felicity glanced up at the man with his hand extended to hers. "Ben Pierce," he said. "I've changed more tires than I care to count. Really, I'd be happy to help."

She shook his hand but did not give her name. And then she turned back to the tire. "I can manage," she said, squatting beside the car. "You must have somewhere you need to be." She watched him out of the corner of her eye, her hand gripping the jack handle so hard her knuckles turned white.

He shrugged. "Not really. Who'd want to be in a hurry to do anything up here? And I don't mind. I could do it in less than five minutes."

"I'm fine," she said. "Honestly, I know what I'm doing… I just need to…"

He leaned around the back of her car, just close enough to view the tire and her. Then he rubbed a finger over an almost invisible scar, just above his right eye, as he surveyed the situation. "Ah, you might want to…" He reached out a hand. "May I?" He took the jack handle from Felicity and turned it the other way. "It's easier if you use this end," he said, with a half-smile. "But I wouldn't want to get in your way. If you're sure you can manage on your own." He turned and headed back toward his car.

Was he being smug? She couldn't tell. Felicity cranked the lug nut. It shifted and loosened. She stood up and shielded her eyes from the sun. "Thanks, but I'm good," she called out, as the sun glinted off his windshield and threw a beam of light across his features. He should have been a movie star, Felicity thought, with those devilishly good looks and the overconfidence, both of which seemed to be prerequisites for Hollywood. Still, he wouldn't be the first handsome *creepazoid*, as Olivia called them. If Tom were there, he'd have done this in no time. But he wasn't, and she had to get used to doing things for herself.

The man flashed a brilliant smile her way, gave a nod and a little two-fingered, boy scout salute. Then he opened his door. "Okay, then."

Idiot, Felicity whispered to herself. *You just cost yourself the chance to let someone else fix this problem.* If she was honest with herself, she wasn't sure she could do it on her own. She should stop him. *Stalker*. Olivia's voice popped into Felicity's head as Ben Pierce's car door closed, and he sped away. Dust spun from the gravel his tires kicked up, and it occurred to her that Ben Pierce, or whatever he'd said his name was, could have tried a little harder to convince her. But then, she could have accepted his offer, couldn't she?

"It's your own fault," she whispered, half to herself and half to the rabbit sitting at the side of the road staring up at her. "I know. I should have let him do it, shouldn't I? Maybe you'd like to help instead?" The rabbit blinked, and then with complete disinterest scampered up the hill and into the woods.

"Thanks for nothing," Felicity called after it. And then she bent to her task. She broke two fingernails, bruised her right knee, and worked up a fountain of sweat that dripped down her back in the time it took her to loosen exactly three nuts. She stood up to wipe her brow with her forearm, when the sound of another car approaching made her glance toward the road. She knew by now she could not manage this on her own and if this person stopped and was willing to help, she would accept it and be grateful. Even if he was a creepazoid.

An orange Jeep pulled in just ahead of her. Another fifty-something man, this one in a dove grey suit, his tie loosened at the neck, stepped out and came toward her. She whispered a word of thanks to the gods for the muscles that bulged beneath his sleeves. "Problem?" he asked, already taking his jacket off and handing it to her. He ran a hand through his hair, then rubbed his hands together and squatted down by the tire.

"Flat tire," she said, watching him survey the problem.

He reached for the tools and set about loosening the remaining nuts, while Felicity hovered nearby, watching the speed at which he worked.

"Terrible place for a flat," he said. "Looks like you picked up a nail. See here?" He pointed to the metal head of what seemed more like a spike than a nail to her. "That construction by the bridge," he went on. "I noticed a lot of debris around there. Maybe that's where you picked it up."

"Could be," she said. "I'm grateful you stopped. I thought I was going to have to walk the rest of the way and get Wally up here tomorrow."

"Where's your cottage?" he asked, spinning the handle around the nuts like a professional tire changer.

"Ril Lake. I'm on Ril Cove Road," she answered.

"Ah. My dad's on the opposite side of the lake. Just at the tip of McGregor Road."

"I kayak through that channel all the time." Of the hundreds of cottages nestled into the woods around these lakes, what were the chances this man's cottage would be so close by?

"Well, you've probably seen my dad then. He sits on the back porch all day, watching the lake. He's too old to take up a hobby or and too stubborn to find anyone to keep him company." He lifted the flat tire off the axle, set it easily into the well in the trunk, and reached for the spare. He smiled from a half-head height above her. "I'm Cameron Meyers," he said, wiping his hand on his trousers, then extending it. "Or just Cam. It's easier," he added, when she shook it.

"Felicity Jefferies," she said. "Your father will probably know our place as The Bailey Cottage. My grandfather built it back in the thirties."

"I know the one," he said. His eyes fell to her hands, where her wedding band still burned a ring around her third finger. She would have removed it the day after Richard's funeral, if not for her children. But a bare finger would have required an explanation and how could she tell them the only thing she'd felt when their father died was relief?

"Baily cottage. But you're a Jefferies. Too bad your husband isn't here to help." It was more of a question than a statement, and Felicity knew he was fishing for personal details.

"He passed away a few months ago." And that was all he was getting.

"Oh. I'm so sorry. That was callus of me." Cam began tightening the nuts, colour flushing his cheeks as he gave it everything he had. The muscles in his back strained against his shirt, his forearms bulged, and Felicity knew what she'd suspected; she could never have managed this on her own.

"It's alright," she said. "Really. Things were not great between us for some time."

"Then I really am sorry. I have a little experience in the bad marriage department myself," he said, giving a grunt as he tightened the last nut. "There. All done."

As Cam straightened, the jack handle dangling in his left hand, she noticed the permanent impression a ring that was no longer there had left. She wondered how long Cam had been single, as she picked up the rest of the tools and put everything back into the well of the car while Cam handed her the boxes and things she'd unpacked earlier. When it was all inside and the hatch closed, she dusted her hands on her jeans, then looked up to thank him for his help.

"Oh, no!" she said, seeing dirt smudges across his thighs and grease marks on his white shirt. "Please let me pay for the dry cleaning. It's the least I can do."

Cam shook his head. "No worries. I've got all summer to sort this out, and I'm not worried if I don't. Might be time for another sabbatical year."

"You're a teacher, or professor?" It was not at all what she'd expected, though she couldn't say why. Her first thought was the financial industry, banker or investment broker or something like that.

"I teach history at the Barrie Campus of Lakehead University. I'm spending the summer with Dad, helping help him with a few things around the cottage. Actually, I'm trying to get him to consider a nursing home, but he won't hear of it. Stubborn old goat." Cam grinned.

"Well, if I can't pay for the dry cleaning, at least let me bake you and your dad a pie. Another couple of weeks and strawberries will be in season."

His smile was bold and so was his response. "I wouldn't say no to a pie. And strawberry is Dad's favourite." He reached out to open her door for her and watched her get in. "It was nice to meet you, Felicity. I'm sorry it wasn't under better circumstances. Maybe you'll stop by sometime, when you're kayaking by our place."

"Maybe I will. Thank you again," Felicity said, as he closed her door.

Not a stalker. Not a creep. Just a nice neighbour, she thought as Cam climbed into his Jeep and sped off down the road.

3

She lowered her window for the rest of the drive and listened to the whisper of the trees as if they were answering the birds calling to one another in the hedgerow. The sounds of nature, the tranquility, life without stress; that's what she had come for. Here was where she breathed deeper, slept more soundly and let the little things wash over her. In a day or two, she would drive back into town and see Wally about fixing that tire, but for now all she could think about was unpacking the car, and settling onto the back deck with a cool drink while the sunset over the lake. She wasn't even hungry, though it was well past supper time when she arrived.

The first thing she did, even before parking the car, was call Tom. Arriving more than an hour later than she expected to be, he would have been climbing the walls with worry. Her call went to straight to voice mail so she left a message.

"Had a flat. A neighbour stopped to help me change it. Just arrived. I'm fine but call me when you get this."

The engine ticked as it cooled down, the only sound around except for the scurrying of nearby squirrels. Felicity glanced toward her neighbour's place, a cottage only slightly smaller than her own, but set deeper in the woods and marginally closer to the water. It was owned by Alice Styles, a widow in her early sixties, was a piano teacher from Burlington. When she'd bought the place three years earlier, it direly needed renovating and, for the first summer, it had been mostly the repairmen Felicity had seen coming and going. But by the summer, she and Alice were enjoying drinks on the dock at sunset, or a hot chocolate around one or the other's campfire pit. They even had a few shopping trips to Huntsville and went to the occasional concert together, although once Richard and the kids joined her, Alice kept t herself to herself. Apparently, she wasn't fond of Richard either. And since Alice was childless and without a partner, Felicity sometimes wondered if the chaotic life at her cottage when everyone was there was too much for her neighbour. Alice's custom was to escape the city just after the July first weekend, which meant it would be a few weeks before she and Felicity could catch on their news.

But just then, as she peered through the woods, Felicity spotted a car in Alice's laneway. Either Alice had a new car since last summer or someone else was in her driveway. Felicity stepped out for a closer look around the trees and then her jaw dropped. It was a blue Subaru, not unlike the one that the man from the gas station who'd first stopped to help her had been driving. Ben something.

"You're kidding," she mumbled, half under her breath. Ben something-or-other was to be her neighbour? Hadn't he told Wally he was going to a family cottage? Was he related to Alice, she wondered, or her late husband? Just as she reached for the hatch to open the back of her car, he came out of the woods between their two cottages. Had he been tramping through her backyard?

"Hey," he called out to her. "What a co-incidence." He stopped at the edge of the woods and looked down at her tire. "I guess you didn't need my help, after all." He stepped easily between fallen logs, rocks, and other forest debris. "What are the chances my sister's cottage would be right next door to you?"

"Yeah. How about that?" Felicity said, not sure she wanted to talk to the man who'd left her on the side of the road. Then she reminded herself that she had refused his help. She opened the back of her car and pulled out as much as she could carry.

Ben reached up to help.

"Don't trouble yourself. I can manage," she said, as he reached for her cooler.

"I know you can, but wouldn't it be easier if I help, won't it? It will go faster, and you could relax on that beautiful deck I saw behind your place much sooner."

"I can't argue with that. But I don't want to put you out." She didn't argue when he put a few lighter things on top of the cooler and followed her to the door. Felicity unlocked it, pushed it open wide, and jammed the doorstop in place. "Just put it there, on the kitchen counter."

"As you wish," Ben said, setting the cooler where she asked him to. And then he returned to the car for more things. And she did the same.

When everything was inside and Felicity had locked the car up, Ben stood in her kitchen, arms crossed, leaning against the counter, watching her unpacked groceries, a perpetual friendly smile glued to his face. Three times she had to pass him, in the narrow galley kitchen as she put things in cupboards, the fridge or set things on the counter. She felt his eyes follow her with every move she made, and soon she found his smile contagious, and she smiled back.

"Is there something else?" she asked, at last.

"No," he shook his head. "Unless you need help with something else?"

She watched his mouth form the words. A nice mouth, she thought. No facial hair hiding his full lips or casting shadows over his jawline, just that tiny pink scar just over his brow, which from time to time, he rubbed as he thought about his answers to her questions.

She handed him a crock pot and pointed to a cupboard. "Can you put that up there, please?" And when he did, she asked, "Are you related to Stan or Alice?" unsure of what to say next. He didn't seem like the stalker type; too helpful, too smiley, too friendly.

"She's my sister." He took cans from her and put them in the pantry cupboard she pointed to.

"I see. Are you staying long?" She handed him boxes of tea.

"I don't know yet. It depends on a few things. That was clever to bring all that food up with you. I'll have to find a grocery store. I didn't bring much."

"Go to Bracebridge or Huntsville. That little shop by Wally's has essentials, but at a ghastly price."

"I'll remember that. Thanks," Ben said, as she closed the last cupboard and folded the last paper bag. "Well, I suppose you don't need my help anymore, do you?" It was a rhetorical question; one she did not answer. But looking at him, she sensed he still wasn't ready to leave. *Stalker? Creep?* No, just Alice's brother, who she might have misjudged earlier. Maybe he was just a nice, friendly guy who liked to be helpful.

"I was going to make a cup of tea and sit outside. Would you like to join me?" she finally relented.

"Oh. Ah. I don't want to interrupt. You've probably got things to do or you're expecting someone…" His gaze fell to her finger, just as Cam's had. "I really should go."

"Ben," she said. "It's just a cup of tea. Besides, I feel a little bad about being rude to you earlier. If I'd known you were Alice's brother…"

"You would have let me change your tire?" He flushed then, a sweet innocent shade of pink dotting his cheeks. "I just wanted to help. I've always been the good Samaritan sort. Honestly, I'm sorry if I gave you the wrong impression." He sighed. "But… I should go."

Felicity shrank inside, knowing how badly she'd misjudged him. "No, it's me," she said. "I'm to blame. I'm a little strong-willed sometimes. Too independent for my own good. I think I can do things by myself and usually I can, but sometimes, this time, in particular, I needed help. I shouldn't have been so stubborn."

"But you did it. You changed the tire."

"No, I didn't. A fellow from the other side of the lake happened by while I was struggling. When he came along, I knew better than to say no. I would have been there all night or, worse yet, forced to walk the last five kilometers with the contents of that cooler stuffed into a backpack. I was the fool, Ben. I should have let you help. Stay for tea and let me apologize, please." Felicity reached for the kettle and filled it with water. "Pick whatever kind you like, and I'll have the same. I like them all."

They sat later, on the lower deck behind Felicity's cottage, where the gazebo netting kept away the early bugs, and gave them shelter from the cool breeze off the lake. As the sun sank behind the trees, it cast pink and lilac shadows across the sky and woodsy shadows across the lake. It was breathtaking, as Ril Lake sunsets always were.

"How is your sister?" Felicity asked after a moment or two of contented silence.

Ben shrugged. "I assume she's fine, but truthfully, I've been out of the country for over a decade, so I'm a little out of touch." Felicity felt herself relax in his at ease and friendly manner. There was something about the way his entire face smiled when he laughed, the way his eyes wrinkled at the corners, and the way he let their pauses stay silent, content not to talk sometimes but to listen to the sounds of natural all around them, that softened her earlier suspicions.

"Where have you been, if you don't mind me asking?" She asked.

"I don't mind at all," he said. "My company rebuilds villages in third world countries after natural disasters. Or sometimes we're in war-torn areas. We build houses, schools, libraries and other community buildings. I'm an architect, but I've learned to do a lot of things, too."

"It sounds interesting, and challenging, I'm sure. And you've been away for ten years?"

"It is more rewarding than anything I ever did working in an office." His face lit up with passion as he spoke. "It has opened my eyes to a world I'd only read about or seen on television. It's given me a very different outlook on life. Some things just aren't as important as they used to be. You know?"

"I do, but obviously not in the same way you do. I've never been to a third world country or seen the devastation you have. But I've always thought we depend too much on material things, and that we should learn to live a simpler life. This place is a constant reminder of that." She tilted her head to one side and thought of the city and traffic and children she'd left behind. "Maybe that comes from age, or from seeing things like you have. I have three children who don't quite agree with me. They think recycling and cutting down on single-use plastics is all they need to do to save the planet. They like it up here, but I'm afraid they like their toys a little more."

His smile broke into a wide grin. "I didn't get it when I was young either. How old are they?"

"Tom is twenty-six. He's an engineer who's always had a passion for the sort of life you've led. I'm sure he'd love to talk to you about it if you're going to be around for a while."

"I'd love to meet him. There are always openings for engineers with the group I work for. What about your other children?"

"My daughter Olivia is twenty-four. She's a nurse hell-bent on taking care of the entire world, and me, now that I'm on my own.

And then there's my youngest, Will. He's twenty-two. He went to Carleton to be an architect. He didn't get past second year, though."

"That's my alma mater. It's a tough course. A lot of students don't make it. I'm ashamed to say I sneaked through by the skin of my teeth. What's he doing now?"

"Building websites, if you can believe it. I don't think he's happy, but it's a pay cheque."

He nodded. "Sometimes you just *gotta do what you gotta do* to pay the bills." If only Will was paying his bills, Felicity thought, as Ben continued. "And then one day, you get old like me. The big five-0 comes along, and you realize how much time you wasted trying to get ahead and how much better off you'd have been if you'd just done what makes you happy." He raised his hand. "Sorry. I'm preaching. I didn't mean to."

"No. it's fine. You're absolutely right. I've thought the same thing myself, many times. It's the reason I love coming up here. I can disconnect and do what I want to do, not what I'm obliged to." She took a breath, wondering if her next question was too personal. She asked anyway. "Are you home for good now, or is this just a stopover between projects?"

"I really don't know yet." He smiled without looking her way, his eyes fixed on the shaft of moonlight, from a clear night sky, lighting a path across the water. "I should go. It's getting late, and a little chilly. You probably want to go inside. Thank you for the tea and the visit." Ben set his cup on the table between them and stood up. He was almost at the door to the gazebo when he turned back. "I should apologize for something. I should have insisted on helping you earlier with the tire. It's just that you seemed set on doing it yourself. I recognized that look of determination. I also realize that being a stranger, you might have thought I was some kind of creep or something. So, I get it, but I want you to know if you ever need help with anything, you only have to ask."

Felicity nodded, a flush of embarrassment at her own ridiculous notions creeping up her neck. "Actually, I just might need a hand with something. Do you know anything about generators?"

"I sure do. Got a problem with one?"

"I'm supposed to prime it or something, get it ready in case we need it. No one's been up here since Christmas."

"Where is it?"

"Along the path, just at the side of the cottage. But it's too dark to see anything now."

"Tomorrow. First thing in the morning, then. It will give me something to do. I like to be useful." He smiled, gave a little nod in her direction, and then headed into the woods between their properties. She heard the crunch and crackle of his footsteps as he picked his way through the undergrowth, heard his footfall on the steps that led to the deck and finally, there came the slap of the screen door against the frame. His porch light snapped off, leaving Felicity in the dark, except for that single beam of moonlight dancing on the water.

She took a few moments to enjoy the quiet and the solitude, kicking herself mentally for being so silly about Ben and letting Olivia's warnings cloud her better judgement. He was a nice man. He seemed to want to be friends. What was wrong with that?

She gathered their mugs and went inside, deciding she should try calling Tom again. He hadn't called her back yet, and she wanted him to know that everything was okay. This time, Tom answered before the first full ring.

"Where are you? What happened? Why didn't you call?"

"Relax. Goodness, you sound like an old mother hen. I left you a voice mail hours ago."

"I know, but Mum, I was ready to call out the National Guard."

"This is Canada. We have the RCMP and I'm almost certain there isn't an office in Baysville." He huffed and grunted something unintelligible into the phone. "Tom, I'm fine. I had a flat, that's all, and you know what it's like up here. No reception at all."

"You just took the car in, and had it all checked over, and I'm sure I saw a bill on your desk for new tires."

"I picked up a nail or something. Don't make this a big deal. I'll take it to Wally's later in the week. The spare is fine for now."

"You didn't put the spare on yourself, did you?"

"No. A neighbour helped. Don't worry. It's all good here. I just wanted to let you know I'm fine and that I'm here."

"Well, I'm glad you're alright. Wait. Who's this neighbor? Not that old man Grandpa used to play darts with. No, he's too old to change a tire. Is it the one with the big dogs he lets out every time you walk by his place?"

"No. Neither of those. Stop fussing over me. I'm fine. Listen to me. There are lots of casseroles and other stuff in my freezer. I hope you boys took some of them with you. If you didn't bring some of them with you on the weekend. And what about Hope? Did you get her to Olivia's?"

Tom ignored her question and droned on. "Mum. Whoever this guy is, don't let him into the cottage. He could be a stalker or something."

Felicity laughed. "Tom, you watch too many horror films. Love you. Talk later. Bye."

4

It was nearly nine when Felicity showered and changed into a pair of navy pinstriped capris and a favourite pale blue t-shirt. Time to get things in order, she thought as she unlocked the garage and, one by one, took the canoe, and both the kayaks down the hill to rest near the dock. Her last trip to the garage brought her back to the dock with the paddles and her lifejacket, which she put on and zipped up. Time for a quick paddle around the cove, she thought, climbing into her grandfather's old wooden kayak. *The Old Gal*, as it Grandpa Bailey had called it, had seen better days, but it was lightning fast, and Felicity preferred it over the red fiberglass one.

The water was so clear she could see down to the reeds and plants on the bottom as she paddled the shoreline. Her strokes were even and true, and the boat glided silently through the water. The only other sound was a dove cooing for its mate. She rounded the bend, stopping to touch the side of Abby's Rock as she'd done every trip out these last years, and then she turned to follow the north shore. Tomorrow she would do the entire lake, but as this was her first time on the water since last fall, she just wanted to feel the cut of the paddle, the glide of the boat, and the water beneath her. So, she didn't go beyond their own little cove. The Lawson girls waved as she passed by their dock. She waved back and called out good morning to them and carried on her way. No sign of life at the Carters place yet, she thought, passing the Lawson's neighbour.

Finally, back at the dock again, she tipped the kayak to drain the water and hung her lifejacket on the line. Refreshed and revitalized, she went inside to start the spaghetti sauce for dinner. Next door, the blue Impresa was not in its parking place under the pines, and she had no idea if Ben had seen the note. He might have used the back door when he went out or stepped over it without seeing it. Or he might have noticed it and set it on the table, inside the door where she knew Alice kept her keys and things she wanted to deposit the minute she got inside. If he had found it, what had he thought? He might have already made plans, she thought. A note like that, from someone he barely knew, might put him off. On the other hand, he might consider it the simple friendly, neighbourly gesture it was. That was what she intended, wasn't it?

She looked at the amount of sauce she was making. Her grandmother's recipe was meant for a houseful of people, not a quiet dinner for two. Still, she could freeze some for when the kids were here and spaghetti was just as good the second day, maybe even better.

Half an hour before the time she'd suggested they have dinner, Felicity added a pinch of salt to the sauce and stirred it for the hundredth time. One eye was on the driveway next door, which was still empty, the other cast a critical glance toward the table she'd set in the dining room. Were dim lights and candles too intimate? What would he think? What was she thinking? Oh, God! She hurried to turn up the dimmer switch and put the candles back in the cupboard.

Dinner was one thing, but candlelight suggested something entirely different. Ben was her neighbour. He was a kindhearted and generous man. He built houses for flood victims, for goodness' sake. Of course, he was the sort of man who would help someone with a flat tire or offer to look at their generator. A neighbour and a friend. Then why was she so nervous about this dinner and why had she ironed her nicest summer dress and taken the time to do her hair and make-up? Stir the spaghetti, she told herself, and stop fretting. He might not even come.

She had all but given up when she heard a stirring on the porch outside the front door and then a knock. Three raps, as if it were a code. He stood there, a bottle of wine in each hand a complete surprise since she hadn't even heard his car come down the lane.

"Your invitation said spaghetti. I'm not sure which goes better, which goes better with pasta. They say red, but doesn't white go with everything?"

He came, Felicity thought, pushing the door open wide. "Come in. You didn't have to bring anything." He followed her into the kitchen and set the bottles on the counter. As she passed him in her narrow galley kitchen, to get glasses out of the cupboard Felicity was so close she could smell his aftershave and knew by its scent that it was the same brand she'd bought for Tom last Christmas. It was masculine and a little spicey with its hint of cinnamon. She flushed, knowing he watched every move as she reached up to get glasses out of the cupboard. "Shall we have the white, since it's chilled?" she asked. "The red should breathe, shouldn't it?"

"Should it?" he laughed. "I confess, I'm not much of a wine connoisseur."

"Oh. I just assumed since you brought it, you'd want some. There's some beer in the fridge or if you'd rather have something without alcohol, there's plenty of pop and sparkling water."

"You know, if you have a sparkling water, that would be great."

"Twist of lemon?" He nodded. "Coming right up. Make yourself at home." She nodded toward the archway, directing him to the living room, where two leather couches flanked a bay window overlooking the lake. At the end was a comfy armchair. A fireplace took up one corner of the room, with a mantel above, boasting pictures of her family, most of them taken at the cottage or places nearby. Her grandparents, her mother and father, and loads of her children. On the walls, there were paintings too, some poor attempts by her mother to capture the view from the deck, which she despised, but her father insisted should be on display. They were both gone now, but Felicity didn't have the heart to table them down.

"That view really is a spectacular." Ben was standing between the couches, admiring the shimmering water below. It glistened like the glass of a thousand shining chandelier crystals, the light reflecting in all directions. "I could get used to living in a place like this."

"Me too," Felicity said, handing him a glass tinkling with ice cubes and a slice of lemon floating on top. "My grandfather built this place nearly a hundred years ago. It was just this room, the bedroom, and the kitchen then. Not even a bathroom in those days. There was an outhouse where the tool shed is now."

"Really? Your grandmother was okay with that?"

She waved him toward one couch and took a seat opposite. "They were so in love she didn't care about anything. Whatever Grandpa did was fine with her. I've never known two people to be as in love as they were."

A silence fell between them, and Felicity struggled for things to say. What was okay in polite conversation these days? It had been so long since she'd made small talk with anyone, especially a man, she'd almost forgotten how. "Does your sister enjoy teaching piano?" she asked, eventually, hoping the common ground of Alice might give them something to talk about.

"I think she does," Ben said. "But honestly. I really am out of touch with family. She'll be up sometime later in the summer. It will be the first time I've seen her in ten years. Good thing she has pictures over there or I wouldn't have recognized the white-haired old lady she's become." From the tone in his voice and the grin on his face, she knew Ben meant no harm by what he said. "Don't tell her I said she was old, or she'll kill me," he added.

"Your secret is safe with me. Weren't you in contact while you were away?

He cocked his head to one side and gave a little shrug. "The internet was pretty sparse in a lot of places. There were some letters, now and again, but they were mostly obligatory. The usual, how are you? Dad's will has gone through probate and here's your share, that kind of thing. The longest one I had from her was when she asked if we should put Mum in a home. Someone saw her squatting over a pail by a tree in the backyard. They live in the middle of nowhere. The nearest neighbour is a half a mile down the road."

Felicity grinned. "Alzheimer's?" she asked.

"Severely clogged toilet," he said with a laugh. "I'd probably have done the same thing if I'd been in her shoes. Sometimes Alice overreacts. She worries about what other people think, but then someone had to take care of Mum. I haven't been much help."

"Is your mother getting on in years?"

"She turned eighty-two in April. But she still goes to Euchre nights at the community center once a week and to church every Sunday. She even puts on her kilt when the Fergus Highland Games are on."

"Good for her. And if you ask me, she's not old. She's just middle age. She must be. Aren't you and I still teenagers?"

"Tell that to my knees when I'm jogging," Ben said, instinctively rubbing his knee.

They both laughed. "But when he and Melody talk about getting married, it's hard not to feel old."

"Do you like his girlfriend?"

"I do. She fits in, just like she's one of us. If she has a fault, it's that she's too organized. She likes to shuffle things around in my cupboards when she visits, but usually the changes are for the better. Anyway, that doesn't matter. What does is how they are with each other, and I think she's good for him."

A timer buzzed in the kitchen, and Felicity shifted to the edge of the couch. "That'll be the pasta. I'll just drain it and then we can eat."

"Can I help?"

The question surprised her a little. Richard liked to barbeque, but he had never been one to help in the kitchen. "Sure. You can monitor the garlic bread. I always seem to forget it's under the broiler and let it burn."

"Glad too." He followed her to the kitchen and while she drained the pasta and poured the sauce into a tureen, Ben manned the broiler. The garlic bread came out perfectly.

"Voila!" he said, setting it on the table with a tea towel draped over his arm, as if he were a server at a posh restaurant. And then, with the same flair, he pulled out her chair for her. "Madam," he said, waving his hand for her to sit.

"Thank you," she said, when she was settled. She might be an independent woman, but Felicity appreciated good manners and a man who still did the little things, like a door hold open, or seat a lady at the table. She smiled as Ben seated himself and surveyed the table.

"This looks delicious," he said. "And to think, I would have eaten something for that local food truck by Wally's garage if you hadn't invited me. Thank you for rescuing me from what was probably a case of food poisoning."

"Oh no. Their food is good. No worries there. And you might not want to be too hasty in your choice. My kids tell me I'm not much of a cook. But this is an ancient family recipe Grandma Bailey got from an Italian neighbour in Toronto. I've never heard them complain about this when I make it." She passed him the spaghetti noodles and watched as he put a generous portion on his plate and then, before he ladled on the sauce, he held it under his nose, savouring the aroma.

"Smells just like Nona used to make," he said.

"You have Italian roots?"

"No. Nona was a neighbour when we were growing up. Alice and I used to sneak over to her house now and again and she stuffed us so full of food by the time we got home for dinner, we couldn't eat another bite. Mum always knew where we'd been."

She laughed. "I'll bet your mum was angry."

"More likely, she was jealous. She hated cooking, but she sure loved Nona's. I think Nona and your grandmother's neighbour in Toronto must have been sisters. This tastes just like Nona's sauce."

She bit into a piece of garlic bread. "Mmmm. Why doesn't it taste like this when I make it?"

"Apparently you burn it." He teased, reaching for another slice.

"I do. It's the only thing I do well," she said, laughing.

"Somehow, I doubt that is true."

They ate in silence for a while, sipping wine, enjoying their meal. Eventually, Ben wiped his mouth with his napkin and declared he could eat no more.

"There's dessert," Felicity said. "Nothing too exciting, just pie from the bakery, and coffee, if you like."

"What's the lake like?" he asked, when they had settled on the deck with their dessert and coffee. "Deep? Shallow? Can I fish?

Can I swim out to that big rock without getting my toes nibbled by piranha?"

"It's shallow until you're in the middle of it, but there is a drop-off about ten feet out from the shore. It's about twelve feet down. We call that rock Abby's Rock and I'd say you have a pretty good chance of making it there and back."

"Good to know. And the piranhas?"

She laughed. "Maybe a trout or two. I don't know what Alice has over there in the way of watercraft, but we have a canoe and two kayaks if you want to borrow something."

"That's kind of you. I haven't found the key to their garage. I was going to call her tomorrow and ask about that."

Ben finished his pie and set his plate on the table. "That was delicious, Felicity. Thank you for inviting me."

"My pleasure. It's nice to get to know your neighbours."

"Is it the dinner that's so special tonight, or is it the company that makes this all so wonderful?" He looked across at her and smiled.

Felicity's cheeks spotted with rosy colour, and she lowered her gaze to her lap. "Or the atmosphere," she redirected after a moment. "I've been coming up here for as long as I can remember, and it never loses its charm." Except that one winter, she thought, but she would not talk about that tonight. "I keep thinking I might move up here, now that Richard is gone and my kids are on their own, more or less."

Felicity relaxes into her chair with a sigh. How long had it been since she'd had such an easy evening, with laughter and fun, good food and great wine? She couldn't remember. Years, she thought as she listened to Ben talk about Africa and a remote village he'd lived in for three years. He could have been talking about ink spots or planets or the chemical compound of margarine for all she cared. His voice was like a velvet caress on her soul; soft, tender and soothing.

"I'm monopolizing the conversation. Sorry. It's easy when someone doesn't stop me. But what about you? What do you do for a living?" He was watching her, watch the tree line in the distance, holding her breath as the last bit of apricot disappeared from the sky and the lake and everything before them fell into the shadows. She turned, and a look flashed between them, an understanding, a simpatico of minds and in their appreciation of the surrounding beauty.

"Oh, well. I used to work in a bank, but now I…"

"Wait, let me guess." He set down his cup and shook a thoughtful finger at her, squinting. "You work for CSIS."

"The Canadian Secret Service? Hardly. No. I'm a genealogist."

"A genie what?"

"A genealogist. I help people trace their family tree, learn more about their ancestors, who they were, what they did, and the history of their time and place. I do a bit of writing, documenting historical findings mostly, as they relate to people's ancestors."

"Gosh, I've never thought of doing something like that. How would someone even start?"

"You just get a piece of paper and write everything you know about the people who came before you. Parents, aunts and uncles, cousins, siblings, grandparents. I've got some charts you can fill in, if you're really interested."

He shrugged. "It might be fun to root out the skeletons. I'm sure there are a few. Like my great aunt who was a lesbian, which in her day was scandalous. She moved to Florida when she was in her thirties, met someone there and they apparently lived happily ever after, although she was cut off from the rest of her family. I didn't even know she existed until I found a box of her old letters in my grandmother's attic. They were the only two of six sisters to keep in touch."

"I'll bet those letters tell a lot. You know, if you're really keen to do this, I'm teaching a beginner's workshop next Wednesday at the Huntsville library."

"So, you're not just on vacation up here. You're working."

"To be honest, I love doing this so much I don't really consider it work."

"Alright then. You're on. I'll take a stab at my ancestors. Alice might remember more than I do. She's nearly ten years older, so her memory of the old folks has always been better than mine. And something tells me there's a family bible kicking around somewhere. I'm sure she has it."

"You can get a lot of information from old bibles. I'll put together some blank charts you can fill in."

At the same moment Ben set his coffee cup on the table between them, Felicity put hers down too. Their hands met in the middle, touching ever so slightly. He looked at her and smiled. She flushed, grateful that the living room light behind them was dim and cast shadows over the deck. She had no wish for him to see how embarrassed by his touch.

Perhaps he'd sensed it too, as he reached out to caress her hand. ", when Alice offered the cottage for the summer, I was grateful for a place out of the city to unwind but, I was worried I might get bored."

"And now?"

"Not a chance."

For a micro-second, Felicity thought Ben might kiss her. She wasn't sure how she felt about that just now. She might like it, but then again, she might not. At least, not yet. "There's loads to do up here in Muskoka country," she said. "I could never be bored."

"I'm sure that's true." She felt the squeeze of his hand as he let hers go. "Perhaps you'll show me some of the best places."

"I'd love to." It would be a pleasure, she thought, feeling absolutely at ease now, in Ben's company.

"Well, it's getting late." He rubbed his hands over his thighs and pushed out of his chair. "Thank you for a lovely dinner and for the conversation. And if I can't find that key for the garage, I just might borrow a kayak in the morning. If the offer is still there."

"Of course." Felicity stood too and walked with him down the steps and across the lower deck. "Do you want a flashlight?" she asked, peering into the darkness.

"There's one on my phone." He produced it from his pocket and held it up. "Thanks again, Felicity. This was… really nice." He was so close she could feel his breath on her face. He hovered there a moment, and she was sure he was going to kiss her.

Not yet, she thought. *I was ready for dinner, ready for quiet conversation, but I'm not ready for that.* As if sensing her hesitation, or perhaps he was hesitant too, he reached for her hand and let his fingers hold hers for a moment. And then he was gone, into the woods, the light from his phone, like a bouncing firefly, lighting his way.

5

The next morning, Felicity woke to the tap-tapping of a woodpecker outside her bedroom window, followed by the squawk of a Blue Jay somewhere in the woods, and the scampering of squirrels on the roof overhead. The sounds of the busy woods stirred her to get up too, though she was sure it was no more than six o'clock.

She got up and open the window, remembering with fondness her grandfather's words. *The whispers of nature are so much better than the shouts of civilization.* She could listen to crickets and croaking frogs all night if it meant not hearing the traffic rolling by or the whine of a lawnmower, or her neighbour revving the engine on his new sports car, before taking off to work.

Coffee was her first thought after a bathroom visit. In the kitchen, while Grandma Bailey's percolator chugged and slurped away, she beat eggs and chopped vegetables for an omelet. Outside, the morning was fresh, and the sun began to climb into a brilliant and cloudless sky.

When it was ready, Felicity took her breakfast to the Muskoka room, and settled in her favourite chair, facing a wall of windows overlooking the lake. To her right, the patio doors led to the top deck, which was their outdoor dining area and the home of the built-in barbeque and the pizza oven she'd added two years ago. The lower deck spread the entire length of the cottage and led to a well-worn path to the beach on one side, and a trail to the dock on the other. In between was the firepit, where many nights of roasting hotdogs or marshmallows had been a family favourite.

Will's words from a few days ago came back to her. "I can't believe Dad will never spend another Christmas at the cottage. He was so happy there."

Olivia had scoffed at him. "Are you kidding? He hated it up there. Especially after Abby died. He only went because we wanted to go."

Tom settled it. "There will never be another Christmas with him, whether it's at home or at the cottage."

There was no disputing the death of Tom's twin sister had eaten away at Richard, and he hadn't wanted to go back to the cottage. Ever. Eventually he did, but he was restless there, and

Felicity knew it was because he was never been able to work through his grief. She wasn't sure he'd even tried. Maybe he'd just shoved it all into the back of his mind, the same way he'd pushed her out of his life and into the recesses of his memory. If he'd been able to talk about things, maybe they could have fixed what was wrong with their marriage. Maybe he wouldn't have drunk so much. Maybe he wouldn't have needed other women. Maybe he would have seen how much she'd wanted to help him, to be there for him. But he hadn't, and she'd given him space to do what he needed to do.

"Oh, Abby," Felicity whispered, her gaze now drifting to by the big rock sprouting out of the water, its tip painted white with bird droppings. This was Abby's Rock, because for the first time in her life, at the age of ten, Abby had beaten Tom at something. A race to the Poop Rock, as they used to call it, and back to the dock. Tom's challenge and Abby had won. No one questioned whether Tom has let her win because she was so overjoyed. The smile on her face was priceless, and she never let her brother live it down. And so it had become, and always remained, Abby's Rock.

From the moment she popped into the world eleven minutes after her brother, Abby was constantly playing catchup with Tom. When Tom took his first steps, Abby watched from the sidelines for less than a day. Then, with almost no thought of caution, she let go of the coffee table and staggered across the room. Three years later, Tom raced into nursery school on their first day and Abby followed right behind him, even though she was inherently shy around other people. She did everything just to keep up with Tom, content to live in his shadow, but never to be left behind. Tom was Abby's hero. Not Richard. Not Batman or Superman or even Wonder Woman. Tom.

A distant banging pulled her from her reverie as she scanned the lake, looking for the source of the sound. There was nothing there but gentle ripples of water. But there it was again. And then she realized it was the screen door at the front of the cottage, banging against the frame. Who could that be? She wondered?

She carried her plate and empty mug to the kitchen and, with a quick glance out the window, noted there was no car in her lane except her own. But when she got to the door, there was Ben, looking helpless on the other side of the screen and holding up an empty mug. "I forgot to buy coffee," he said. "Do have any to spare?"

Felicity laughed. "I do. Do you want grounds, or do you want to join me for a cup?"

He opened the door and stepped inside. "I can't even find a coffee pot over there, so if you can spare a cup, that would be great." He leaned on the door frame, a helpless look on his face. His hair was still damp from his morning shower, and a layer of stubble shadowing his chin. "I don't want to disturb you, though."

"You're not disturbing me. Come in. We can sit outside and enjoy the morning. I'll get to the chores later."

"Chores? What are those?" he teased, waving away the sugar she offered to add to his coffee.

"I have some things to do in town and Will is going to send me a YouTube video to tell me what to do with that generator." Felicity handed Ben a cup, refilled her own, and motioned for him to follow.

"About that generator," he said. "I did that for you already. You shouldn't have to do anything more to it."

"Oh. I didn't even realize. Thank you."

On the lower deck, she picked up a Muskoka chair and said, "Grab another one and come with me." She balanced her coffee in one hand, her chair in the other, and made her way to the dock.

"This is lovely," he said, kicking off his sandals and setting his chair up beside hers.

Just then, two bikini-clad teenage girls on paddle boards came around the bend toward them. "Hello, Mrs. Jefferies," one of them called.

"Hi girls," she called back. "Are you here for the summer now?"

"Yes. Dad's only here on the weekends, but Mum's off for the summer. When we saw you yesterday, we thought Will was here, too."

"He's coming up on the weekend. I'm sure he'll be over to say hello. Tell your mum I said hi."

They turned toward home amid a round of overly zealous giggles, copious amounts of splashing, and hilariously balancing acts as they paddled away.

"The Lawson girls live directly across the lake," Felicity told Ben. "See the dock with the big Canadian Flag sticking up from the end of it?"

Ben nodded. "I noticed it this morning. An enormous dog came bounding down the dock and dove in after a stick or something."

"That's Zeke. He's big, but he's harmless. The girls both have an enormous crush on Will, but he's too old for them. He's only interested in their media room in the lower level of their cottage. The kids have always been back and forth to watch movies or play board games."

"Do they really like it up here all summer? I'm betting the hit and miss internet cuts into their social media time?" He sipped his coffee and instinctively lunged forward when one of the girls toppled from her board into the lake. She righted herself with a giggle and was up and away in no time.

"They don't seem to mind it. Neither do I, actually. Tom says I need a better router, but I rather enjoy unplugging from the world now and again."

"For most of the past ten years, I've been off the grid, and I rather like it."

"I worry about this generation of teens. They almost don't know how to have fun without their phones." She looked at him and wondered. "Do you have kids? You haven't said if you have any, I just…"

His faraway look over the lake left Felicity feeling as if she'd hit a nerve. "I'm sorry if I've said something wrong."

"No. No. You didn't. I have a daughter. She's turning twenty-one soon. She's part of the reason I came home. I was hoping to see her for her birthday. Twenty-one is still a special birthday, isn't it? Or am I really out of touch?" A pained expression pulled at his features, and he let his gaze drop to his hands.

"Absolutely not. Twenty-one is every bit as important as it always was. The rite of passage into adulthood and all that. Have you made any plans with her?" The expression on his face grew more intense, and Felicity was instantly sorry she'd brought up the subject of children. Clearly, it was a touchy topic for Ben. "I'm sorry," she said. "It's really none of my business. I shouldn't have pried."

"You weren't. It's fine. It's just a long story. Maybe one for another day." He gulped the last of his coffee. "I should get back. I have some projects I need to stay on top of and you have all those chores." He said with a forced laugh. "Good luck with that." He put his empty cup on the table. "Thanks for the coffee. And if the offer is still good, I might borrow a kayak this afternoon."

"Sure. Help yourself. We have an abundance of life jackets, too. I'll hang them on the clothesline."

"Thanks for that, and for the coffee. I'm eternally grateful for the infusion of caffeine."

Felicity's gaze followed him as he passed the firepit and headed up the slope toward his cottage. She was sorry now that she'd asked him about kids. She hadn't meant to ruin the mood of their morning and wondered what he had not wanted to tell her. A long story could mean a lot of things. A divorce and she got custody of the child, or he might still be married but estranged, which might have made life difficult. No matter what Ben's story was, it wasn't any of her business unless he made it so. She would not ask again. Not because she didn't care, but because of the obvious pain it caused him.

She spent the rest of the morning washing sheets and towels and airing out the bedrooms, getting things freshened up and ready for the kids' arrival on the weekend. She remembered to hang the rest of the lifejackets on the line to air out and filled a wheelbarrow with firewood and stacked it by the firepit. It might be a good night for a fire, if the weatherman's promise of a clear night was to be believed.

By mid-afternoon, a growl in her stomach reminded her she'd missed lunch. But she also wanted to go for a paddle before evening set in on to the lake. Even when the days were the longest, it could get dark quickly in the woods. Grabbing a couple of apples and her water bottle, Felicity headed for the boats just in time to see Ben in her red kayak rounding the bend by Abby's Rock.

She could have pushed and caught up to him, but she didn't wish to disturb his serenity, nor did she wish to share her own, just now. Sometimes alone was better. Felicity paddled across the cove and blew a kiss at Abby's Rock on the way by.

6

Felicity didn't see Ben again on the lake that day. Ril Lake was not large, but there were coves tucked here and there, where a small craft could slip undetected while another one passed by. When she arrived back at the dock, the red kayak was tipped over to drain and the lifejacket Ben had borrowed was drip-drying on the line. When she glanced toward Alice's cottage, he was nowhere to be seen.

In the kitchen, wondering what to fix for her supper, Felicity had a clear view of the laneway next door. The place where Ben had parked his car was empty. Something inside Felicity felt empty, too, though she couldn't say why, exactly. She'd enjoyed her time on the lake, felt refreshed and energized after giving her muscles a good workout. But a sense of loneliness tugged at her just the same and she wondered, just for a moment, if Ben was avoiding her. Perhaps he was tired of small talk. Perhaps she'd pushed a little too hard when she'd asked about children. It was obvious he hadn't wanted to talk about his daughter, at least not then. Still…

Leftovers for supper, she thought, pulling the spaghetti sauce out of the fridge. She'd enjoyed spending time with Ben last night and again this morning. She liked Ben; at least, what she knew of him so far. He seemed to fill a room with his presence, but in a gentle way, unlike the way Richard domineered a room. Ben had an easygoing, unassuming way about him. He seemed relaxed, comfortable, what her mother would have called a down-to-earth man. Even his clothes were casual and to Felicity, blue jeans and a button-down shirt that exposed just a bit of chest hair, never looked better on anyone. It had been a long time since she'd thought of Richard looking sexy in anything. But then Richard would never have worn jeans. Even on weekends, a pair of tailored trousers and an expensive brand of golf shirt were as casual as he'd got.

Beyond the clothes and the good looks, though, was Ben's truly generous heart. His stories at dinner last night had kept her spellbound and wanting to know more about him, his life, and how he'd become the man he was. She admired the passion with which he spoke about his work. It was contagious, and she was sure she could listen to his stories all night long. He had more than ten years of them, and each one told her something more about his work and his life. Humble and always giving credit to the rescue workers before himself, he'd been in the thick of it all when disasters struck.

He wasn't just the clean-up guy, which would have been enough to endear him to her. This man who rebuilt everything was also the rescuer and the clean-up guy. He carried pictures in his wallet of people he'd met and helped, and in them she could see that he was obviously loved and admired.

But something still niggled at her. For all that seemed wonderful about Ben on the surface, she could not understand how he could be away from his family for ten years and hardly talk to them. By his own admission, he hadn't talked to Alice much and had left her to deal with their parents. And what was this long story for another time, surrounding his daughter? Had he lost touch with her, too? And where was the girl's mother? Was Ben still married? Divorced? Felicity couldn't imagine not being in her children's lives, but then, she wasn't a sought-after architect with a dream of saving the world. She reminded herself that it was none of her business and that she should be content with sharing a coffee or two with her new neighbour and leave it at that.

Supper, Felicity thought, that's what I need to focus on just now. She dumped a portion of sauce into a pot to warm it and set water to boil for the pasta. She decided to forgo the garlic bread. It wasn't worth heating the broiler for a single slice, and she'd probably burn it, anyway.

While her pasta rolled and bubbled in the pot, she surveyed the contents of the fridge, thinking about the weekend and five more mouths to feed. Even with the things she'd brought from home, it was sparse, barely more than the essentials. Tomorrow, she would take all Richard's things to the secondhand shop in town, drop the tire off at Wally's and while he repaired it, she would get groceries, stop at the liquor store and visit the garden centre. It wasn't too late to put in some annuals and make some big flowerpots for the corners of the porch. She pulled a notepad and pen out of a drawer and started making a list, beginning with the groceries and their favourites.

Cooking was never her strong point, but now she had less desire than ever for it. She'd always said that if she could have any hired help in the house, it would be someone to do the cooking and the cleaning. She loved gardening and liked doing the laundry. There was something truly satisfying about seeing it neatly folded and put away again. But cooking and cleaning she could easily give over to someone else.

She surveyed her list, knowing Tom would do most of the barbequing, Melody was a whiz in the kitchen, and Olivia always brought the ingredients for at least one supper. No pressure for Felicity to perform. She could tantalize them with desserts, all of which she would buy. Key-lime pie, tiramisu, and cherry cheesecake, all her kids' favourites.

She ate in front of her laptop, preparing additional notes for her upcoming workshop. The talk was lodged in her memory by now, but she liked to stay sharp in case someone had questions she hadn't thought of. She always asked for a review from her attendees and hoped that if she showed them professionalism, they might become regular clients. A review wouldn't hurt.

A stack of handouts to give her attendees lay on the hutch. Reaching for one of them, she noticed the folder she'd prepared for Ben. They hadn't taken time to fill in any of his information, though he had sounded keen to learn more. There was one name she could add to his chart, though she didn't know where it belonged. On the inside of Ben's arm was a beautiful tattoo of a heart, with the name Emma across it. It wasn't as if she'd snooped or come by this information in some unscrupulous way. It was just there, when he'd rolled up his sleeves. She hadn't wanted to pry, and if he had noticed her glancing at it, he didn't offer an explanation.

Felicity penciled *Emma* with a question mark beside it, on the top of one of Ben's blank charts. Emma might be the daughter he didn't wish to talk about. Emma might be his mother, or she might be a wife, the mother of his child. He wore no wedding band and had not mentioned a wife in his stories. Whoever Emma was, she had, quite literally, earned a place in Ben's heart.

When she'd eaten and tidied the kitchen, Felicity went downstairs to put the last load of laundry into the dryer and found she was out of fabric softener sheets. In the storage cupboard where she kept spares of everything, she found another box. Right beside it was a drip coffee maker she'd forgotten about. Since she'd discovered Grandma's old percolator, this one had gone into storage. She decided to clean it up and give it to Ben, since she had no use for it now.

While running a vinegar and water bath through the machine, she ground up some beans from the stash she'd brought up with her and sealed them in a freezer bag. Evening shadows accompanied her as she gathered the coffee maker, coffee and the folder of blank genealogy charts for the short walk through the woods to next door. There was still no car in the laneway, but as the porch light was on, she assumed he was probably going to be late. She knew where Alice kept a spare key, so she could have put everything on the kitchen table. If it was Alice, she might have. But it was for Ben and somehow, going inside felt like an intrusion. She left everything on a chair by the door. No need for a note, she thought. He'll know where they came from.

And then Felicity returned to her Muskoka room, with a cup of jasmine and honey tea, to watch the sunset over the lake and the evening mist swirl and float and coax its way around the bend and into their little cove. Abby's Rock cast an ominous shadow in the light of the three-quarter moon, and with the swirling mist, it created an eerie, bog-like vision in the distance. It was almost as if Nessie or some other lake monsters were about to rise out of the water. She actually laughed out loud at the way her imagination had gone a little off kilter. Maybe she could she write a novel; The Monster of Ril Lake, she thought.

"I could certainly do a better job than this guy." She looked down at the unopened book in her lap. Three quarters in and she already knew who the murderer was and nothing exciting had happened beyond the opening chapter, when they found the dead body. Talk about a slow burn. But once she'd started a book, Felicity always finished it, even if she didn't like it. It was a challenge she'd set for herself years ago, in her never-give-up-on-anything phase. She opened it to where she'd left off. Somehow, she managed not to fall asleep while the detective questioned his suspects, and the story approached the so-called crisis moment. She read on, and on, and on.

"How does a book like this sell?" she said with two chapters to go. She slapped it closed and set it on the table, ready to call it a night.

Getting up to shut off the lights, she heard the crunch of gravel in the distance, and the headlights of a car flooded the laneway next door, then winked out. She couldn't see him, but in the stillness of that late hour, the sounds of a door opening and closing echoed across the cove and she knew Ben was home and somehow that felt satisfying to her.

Felicity went through the cottage, dousing candles, turning out lights, and locking doors, just as she did every night. And then she went to bed, exhausted, and ready for sleep. She had just pulled the covers up when another set of tires crunched over the gravel, followed by another pair of headlights, this time sweeping across her side of the cottage. This car was in her laneway.

Probably a lost renter, she thought, getting up again and pulling on her housecoat. She shoved her feet into her slippers and went to the kitchen, where she had a clear view from the window above the sink. The car pulled slowly down the lane, then turned and parked beside hers. When the engine shut off and the headlights went out, Felicity's heart pounded. Olivia's warnings about creeps and weirdos came back to her as she held her breath. The driver's side door opened and someone tall and lanky stepped out.

Melody's car, Felicity realized, letting go of her breath and the grasp she'd had on her housecoat. It was Tom who had been driving, and Melody got out of the passenger side. Her heart slowed to an easier pace as she reached over and flipped on the porch light.

"You scared the life out of me. I thought you weren't coming till Friday?" she said, unlocking the inside door and pushing the screen door wide for them. Melody came up the step after Tom, rolling a suitcase along behind her.

"We were worried about you, Mum," Tom said, pushing himself and his own suitcase through the door and setting it aside to give her a hug. And then Melody pushed past Tom and gave her a hug, too.

"But why didn't you text me to say you were coming?" Felicity stooped to grab the handle of one of their bags.

"Leave all that, Mum," he said. "They're too heavy, and I'm too tired to fight with them tonight. I'll just get the food out of the car, but the rest can wait till morning."

"The rest. Are you staying the whole summer?" Felicity said with a grin as she led Melody into the kitchen. She was still in office clothes; a hunter green jacket and skirt Felicity had seen before and complimented her on. It suited her and filled in her almost too thin body. Tom, she knew, would have driven to Toronto, left his pickup truck in Melody's underground spot at her apartment building, and then they would have driven her newer, fuel-efficient car here rather than his gas guzzler.

Melody stretched her long arms over her head in a yoga mountain pose, and then dropped them at her sides. And then she covered her mouth with the back of her hand to stifle a yawn. "Sorry. Long day. I told him you were fine. It's just a flat tire, I said. People help other people up there."

"Yes, they do. It isn't like the city where everyone's afraid to stop and help."

"Tom's worried the guy is some kind of weirdo or something."

Felicity laughed. "Tom has always had an overactive imagination. I know how he worries. I tried to tell him everything was okay up here. You must be exhausted. Shall I put the kettle on? We could make some hot chocolate, or tea. Are you hungry? What would you like, I can warm up some supper for you, if you like?"

"I'd really like a bed. But tea sounds nice, too." Melody grabbed her suitcase. "I should get this out of the way. Can we take the room with the queen-size bed this time? I've gotten used to my own now, and a double seems so small."

"Sure. There are fresh linens, but the bed isn't made yet. I'll help you make it up in a minute."

Melody was already halfway down the short hallway when she called back. "I'll do it. I don't mind."

"Okay then," Felicity called back. Of course, Melody would prefer to do that on her own. She was particular about many things, and no doubt she had a specific way to make a bed. Felicity would only get in the way. She filled the kettle and switched it on, while Tom lumbered in first with grocery bags of food and then a cooler full of beer. "Basement fridge?" he asked, still holding the cooler.

Felicity nodded. "But put a few in here so you don't have to go down every time you want one."

When he came up a few minutes later, he leaned against the counter, watching her pull containers of tea out of the cupboard. She reached up to caress his cheek. "You didn't have to come up here tonight. I'm perfectly fine."

He took her by the shoulders and spun her around, checked both her arms and her jaw and then, with a laugh, he announced her unscathed and declared her to be fine.

"Didn't I tell you I was?" she said, pushing away and giving him a playful slap on the arm.

He nodded toward the cups she was setting tea bags into. "Got anything to put in that?" he asked. "A little brandy or some Forty Creek or something?"

"You know where everything is. Help yourself." Felicity poured hot water over the bags of tea; ginger and honey for Melody, her favourite; chamomile for herself, not that she would need help to fall asleep tonight, and a cinnamon rooibos for Tom. It would go well with anything he brought back from the cupboard.

"So," Felicity said, when they settled on the couches in the living room and sipped their tea. She looked directly at Tom. "Did you really think someone was going to attack me or something? I mean really, Tom."

He fidgeted, rubbing his thumb over his cup and flitting his gaze between Melody and his mother. "We were worried. Not just about the tire or the guy. What's his name?"

"Cam Meyers."

"Right. Cam. But you know you came up here all on your own and it's so soon after Dad died and... I just thought maybe you shouldn't be alone. Not yet anyway. So, I called Olivia, and Will, and we decided..."

"You decided," Melody interrupted him. "Olivia and Will told you to... what were Olivia's words, *'stay the f home'*, I believe." She arched a single brow in Tom's direction.

"Alright, yes. Olivia said I was being an idiot." Tom fidgeted with a thread on his sleeve and avoided his mother's gaze.

"What else?" Felicity asked, knowing that Tom was hiding something.

"Nothing. That's all. I was just worried about you."

It wasn't all, but Felicity wouldn't press him. Eventually, he would tell her the rest. "It's sweet of you to be concerned, Tom, but I'm fine. Really, I am. And I'm sorry you had to rearrange your plans, but I am happy to see you both. You work much too hard. The rest will do you both a world of good."

She'd barely finished talking when Tom blurted out. "But you've never even cried for Dad. Not a single tear."

Felicity set her teacup down on the table. "Is that what's bothering you? You think I haven't grieved for your father and I'm going to have some kind of meltdown up here? Oh, Tom." She paused and rested her hand on his. "And just how should I have grieved? By making a public display in front of everyone at his funeral?"

"Well, no I suppose not, but…"

"Darling, you don't know what's in my heart or what I think about when no one else is around. He was my husband for nearly thirty years. They weren't all roses and sunshine, but there is much about him I miss. So, my love, don't misjudge my feelings just because you think I didn't cry enough. There have been more than enough tears and many sleepless nights. I just don't trouble you with them."

"It's just that I remember when Abby died. You were a basket case for weeks. But this time. I don't know. It's like you were glad he was gone."

She took a moment to gather her thoughts. Did she want to get into this with him now, at this late hour, and with his emotions obviously high? How could she explain the gaping hole in her heart that Richard's indiscretions had carved out years ago? He'd left her devoid of anything close to love. All she'd felt for him lately was sadness for a wasted life. How could she tell her son that all she felt now was relief? Relief that she no longer had to tolerate a man she'd grown to despise. Relief that people who knew his secrets wouldn't look at her with sympathy and pity. Relief that she didn't have to wonder if he was going to disappoint his children with the truth about his life.

She reached deep for words that would explain herself, without hurting her son. "We were all devastated by Abby's death, but the death of a child is very different, Tom. When you have children of your own, it will become clearer to you."

"Are you saying that you loved Abby more than you loved Dad?"

"It's a very different kind of love. And…"

"And what? What aren't you saying, Mum?"

Her eyes found his and overflowed with tears. "I can't," she whispered. "I just can't."

"You can't what? For crying out loud, stop treating me like I'm still twelve years old."

Where was this coming from? Her children didn't talk to her like this, nor did she speak that way to them. They weren't harsh, and they didn't make demands like this. But he was still grieving the loss of his father, and that brought back memories of Abby. Of course, he was upset, but where had this judgmental side of him come from?

"No, you're not, but you're pouting like you're still a child. Still, maybe it's time you knew some truths about your father and I." A trace of anger welled in Felicity. She didn't like being probed about things she'd hoped to keep secret, had never thought her children had to know the truth. Perhaps they'd been wrong to hide things from them, especially now when Tom was considering marriage himself.

"Okay," Felicity began. "Our marriage has been difficult for a long while, but more so since Abbey died."

"You mean his drinking? That's no secret."

"No, I suppose it wasn't. And you're right, he'd been drinking himself to death for years. He wouldn't accept help. He wouldn't listen to anyone. In all honesty, I'm surprised he lived as long as he did. And it shocks me even more that it was his heart that failed him, before his liver."

Tom nodded and shrugged one shoulder and she knew her words were not news to him. "He wouldn't listen to me either when I suggested he get help. But that doesn't explain why you seem almost happy he's gone. He didn't hit you, did he?"

"There are more kinds of abuse than the physical kind, Tom. But no, I'm not suggesting he was abusive." She paused to consider her words. "I'm not happy you've lost your father, Tom. But he was unfaithful, Tom. With many women and almost from the first."

"You're making that up," Tom snapped.

Felicity shook her head. "You know me better than that. I might protect you from the truth, but I wouldn't make up lies. Your father and I have been living separate lives for a long time now. Living in the same house was a convenience, and it meant we didn't have to put you guys through all the trauma of a divorce." She threw a glance at Melody, who had been sitting quietly, hands wrapped around her teacup. Did she, at least, understand? Felicity wondered?

Tom's eyes filled with tears. "Why didn't we know?"

"You don't even want to hear it now. Imagine if we'd told you years ago. Although I have questioned our decision to keep it from you for a long time now. Even now, I'm not sure telling you was the right thing to do."

Tom reached for Melody's hand, his voice low as he said, "You were right." He looked at Felicity. "Melody said there was more to this than we knew."

Melody kissed his cheek. "I didn't need to be right. I just wanted you to understand. And if coming here early to get answers helps, then I'm glad we did." She turned to Felicity. "I tried to tell him couples don't sleep in separate rooms or celebrate separate Christmases, if they are happy and still in love. I think Tom just needed to hold on to the memory of how it used to be."

Felicity nodded. "I get that. We tried to keep things as normal as we could. But it was getting more difficult all the time, especially after Abby died. Your father went to pieces then. And after that…" She sighed. "I guess I always hoped we might fix things someday."

"But you still loved him, right?" Tom asked, a desperation to cling to a memory in his voice.

"I loved the man he used to be, Tom. I loved the man I met thirty years ago. Sadly, he wasn't that man anymore. Abby's death, too much stress at work, too much alcohol, the women who really meant nothing to him. It all took its toll and somehow the Richard Jefferies I knew disappeared and was replaced by a man I no longer recognized."

Tom got off the couch and sat down beside Felicity. And then he pulled her into his arms. "I'm sorry Mum. I'm sorry I doubted you. I'm sorry… I'm sorry I took Abby away from you…" His tears soaking her shoulder.

"Wait. Wait a minute," Felicity said, pushing him away to see his face. "You didn't take Abby away from us. Do you think her death was your fault?"

He shrugged. "I miss her. So. Much," he said through great gulping sobs. "I guess Dad's death brought it all back for me. It just doesn't seem fair. I did try to save her, you know."

"I know you did. I know. There was nothing more you could have done. And if I'd lost you both that day, I don't know what I would have done." She rubbed his back and kissed his cheek. "I do miss your dad. In my own way. And I hope he's with Abby now and the two of them are having a whale of a time in heaven, or wherever it is we go when we die."

"I'm sorry. I shouldn't have assumed," he said.

"It's human nature to assume things. And you were right to ask for answers. I'm glad we talked, Tom. I will always want and need you, all of you." She reached for Melody's hand to include her in those words.

Tom grinned and swiped his tears away. "I'm guessing you haven't figured out how to prime the generator, have you?"

7

Felicity was the first one up the following morning. Dawn at the cottage was always spectacular, unless it was a dull, rainy day, which it wasn't that third day of her summer. She took her coffee down to the dock and tipped her face to the east as the sun kissed the horizon and began its climb into the morning sky. Behind her, the resident woodpecker and squirrels were already busy with their day chattering and tapping and scurrying about. A chipmunk raced across the sand, stopped long enough to note Felicity's presence, deemed her to be safe, and then scurried off again.

Ah! Serenity, Felicity thought. She really could make this her permanent home. Winters weren't bad. She had the snowblower, and she could always buy a snowmobile if she wanted to get about without taking the car somewhere. With a little modernizing, the cottage would suit her just fine. But maybe she'd add that second floor she'd been thinking about.

As her mind floated over the possibilities of working from here, she heard the slap of a screen door and turned to see Ben on his dock, a cup of something hot and steaming in his hand. He gave a nod to her, held up his cup and called out across the trees. "Thank you."

"You're welcome," she called back, glad to see he'd found the things she'd left for him and wondering, for no more than a second, when he'd come home and where he'd gone. And then he went inside, without another word, or a nod in her direction. Again, Felicity could not shake the empty feeling and wondered if she'd done or said something to make him keep his distance.

There was rustling behind her, and the dock shifted as Tom, still pajama clad on the bottom but shirtless, carried a deck chair in one hand and a coffee in the other.

"Morning," Felicity said, as he settled the chair next to hers. "How did you sleep?"

"Surprisingly well. I never liked that room, because the squirrels start chattering at about four in the morning, but this morning I didn't hear a thing. How about you?"

"I always sleep well up here. It's so peaceful."

"Yeah, a little too quiet, if you ask me."

"You might change your mind when you've raised a family and fought traffic every day of your life."

"Never happen," he said. "I work from home now, remember? About the only decent thing to come out of the Covid pandemic was that." He took a long sip of his coffee. "The kids, mind you, might come along one of these days."

"Is there something you haven't told me?" Felicity eyed him with a curious smile.

Tom's face broke into a sheepish grin. "We're making some plans, but we haven't set an official date or anything yet." He looked at her. "We don't want to disappoint anyone, but…"

Something in his look made her wonder. "Go on. Whatever it is, you can tell me."

He shrugged. "We don't want a big flashy wedding. We just want a small civil ceremony, maybe on the beach somewhere, you know, Jamaica or… maybe St. Lucia."

"At your grandparents' place?" Felicity bit back the disappointment in her voice. It was up to Tom and Melody, but a wedding at the Jefferies' estate in St. Lucia meant she wouldn't be there, though Tom couldn't possibly know that.

"I know you always wanted us to get married in a church, but we just don't do the churchy thing, you know. Neither of us. So…"

"It's your wedding, darling. You and Melody must decide what you want. Not what I want or anyone else." She took a long pause and considered what to say next. Last night had been difficult enough, for her and for Tom: weddings should be happy times. Did she want to have to tell him everything about his father's side of the family, and force him and Melody to choose between her and Richard's family? She couldn't do that. Richard's parents loved her children as much as her own parents had, and they were his grandparents.

Before Felicity could find the words to speak, Melody, fresh from her shower, her dark hair still damp in tight dark curls around her face, came down to the dock.

"Good morning, everyone." She looked at Tom. "You told her?" It was a half whisper to Tom as she settled into a chair beside him. He nodded, and she turned to Felicity. "I didn't mean to eavesdrop. I only heard him say St. Lucia, so I assumed Tom told you his plans."

"He did." Felicity sucked in air and tried desperately to keep her voice even. "It's up to you two. It's your wedding. If your grandparents agree to it, then I'm sure St. Lucia will make a lovely wedding destination." It came off a little smug, despite her attempt to keep things neutral.

Tom went on the defensive. "Mum, you know how beautiful the island is. Surely you can see why we'd want to get married there."

Melody tugged on his arm but spoke to Felicity. "We've had a bit of a tiff about this. I don't really want to get married in St. Lucia. It's Tom who is insistent about it." She flashed Felicity a smile that said, *if he loves me, I'll get my way.* "We haven't decided yet."

Felicity's nerves were stretched to within an inch of their limits. Last night's conversation with Tom's judgmental attitude about her grieving process and now a wedding in St. Lucia she would not be able to attend. She was on the edge of her seat, about to go inside, when Tom dumped the dregs of his coffee into the lake.

"Don't do that," Felicity snapped, a little too sharply.

"What? It's just a little coffee."

"You know we don't dump stuff into the lake. People have spent years doing everything they can to keep this lake clean." Felicity pushed out of her chair, grabbed the cup out of his hands and stomped back toward the cottage.

"What was that all about?" Tom's question to Melody echoed across the water and reached Felicity as she stepped onto the lower deck.

"Shh," Melody replied. "Your voice carries on the water."

Felicity reached the top deck, just as the Lawson girls came around the curve and into view. "When's your brother coming up?" they shouted when Tom waved to them. The girls giggled and nudged each other, then both toppled into the lake.

Teenagers, Felicity thought, as she climbed the stairs. But wasn't that the same infatuation she'd felt for Richard all those years ago? And look where that took me, she thought.

Felicity got ready for errands in town, putting her hair into a sloppy bun, adding a little make-up and choosing a flowered sundress, since the weather network promised a hot day. She fished two of her mother's rings out of her jewelry box, one for each hand,

and grabbed a light wrap, just in case it turned cool, or the stores had their air conditioning cranked.

Tom and Melody were still sitting on the dock, so she scrawled a note: *Gone to Huntsville. If you need anything txt me,* then stuck it on the fridge with a magnet from the Dorset look-out tower. She rinsed the coffee cups and put them into the dishwasher, her thoughts turning to what really upset her. It wasn't coffee dumped into the lake. What she was upset about was all the Thanksgivings and Christmases for the last twenty-six years, when the Jefferies had her children, while she sat home alone. And the fact that a wedding at their family estate in St. Lucia meant she would not be there. This was just one more knife in her back from Richard's family. She wondered if Tom had spoken to his grandparents about their plans. Naturally, they would be delighted, but they would never tell him that she wasn't welcome there. They would get that dig into her personally. Her morning errands would give her time to cool off and hopefully Melody would win the battle for their wedding location.

At the *New To You* secondhand shop, Felicity unloaded Richard's things into the donation bins at the back of the shop. A girl the age of the Lawson twins came when she rang the bell and was excited to see some of the novels Felicity had added from the shelves in the Muskoka room.

"You like mysteries?" Felicity asked.

"Oh yes. But I like romance even more. Makes me think that someday my prince charming will come." She giggled and rolled her eyes. "Corny right? But you never know when your true love might appear. Sometimes we just have to trust the universe to work its magic."

Felicity smiled at the girl, who didn't seem to know just how lovely she was. "I'm sure your soul-mate is just around the corner," she said, handing her the last box of Richard's things.

"I hope not. I look a fright today." She giggled again. "Would you like a coupon for the store?"

"That's okay. Give it to the next person. Maybe it will be your prince charming."

The girl flushed and waved as Felicity pulled out of the parking lot. Cute, she thought of the girl and her idea that the universe was organizing someone's life to align with hers. It was the stuff romances were made of and it was every young girl's dream. Too bad life wasn't really like that.

A few moments later, Felicity pulled into the parking lot at Wally's garage, noticed the bay doors were open and that there were already two cars on the hoists. She found an empty spot, shut off the engine and went inside.

Even sitting behind his desk, Wally filled the small office with his presence. She was used to Doris sitting there in the past, and her absence took Felicity by surprise.

"She keeps busy doing other things now," Wally said, when she asked about Doris. "At least that's what she says. I think she just needed a change, and I don't blame her. Some days it's pretty bleak around here. But enough of my blathering. What can I do for you?"

"I wondered if you could take a look at my tire."

"Sure. You pick up a nail or something?"

"I think so. Cam Meyers helped me put the spare on."

"Ah yes. Slim's son. Cam's a bit of a local hero. Wrote a book a few years ago. You can get it in the library."

"Did he? I should check it out."

"Want to give me your keys? I'll send Adam out to get it."

"Goodness, is he old enough to work now?"

"Fourteen last September. If you can believe it."

"I can't. I remember when Doris was sitting behind this counter, complaining about being pregnant in the heat of the summer. Seems like yesterday."

"It does to me too."

She handed over her keys. "Thanks Wally. I'm going to run some errands. Do you think a couple of hours is enough time? If it isn't, I can leave the tire with you and come back another day."

"Should be plenty of time."

Felicity turned her gaze to the shop door as it opened, and a string bean of a boy dressed in grease-stained jeans and a steel-grey Wally's Garage t-shirt appeared out of the back. "Something for me, Dad?"

Wally handed him Felicity's keys. "Get Mrs. Jefferies' spare tire out of her SUV. The red one out there."

"Sure," Adam said, taking the keys from his father and smiling at her, his lips spreading over a row of perfect white teeth. And then she recalled the last time she'd seen the boy and the mouthful of metal he'd had. Those braces had really paid off.

"Morning, Mrs. Jefferies." Adam didn't wait for her reply before heading out to the parking lot.

"Polite boy," Felicity said with a smile.

"He damned well better be, or he'll get a cuff around the ear." Wally was grinning with pride. "Nah. I'm all talk. He's a chip off his mother's block, not mine."

"Well, a good chip whatever block he came from."

She left Wally and Adam to assess the tire and headed for Huntsville. As she got closer to town, she noticed several new subdivisions lining both sides of the road, with active building going on; a sign more people were moving out of the city. The additions changed the landscape of the town, but never seemed to alter the atmosphere of the people. She always got the same small-town hospitality in the shops and restaurants.

She turned onto the main street, noticing more than a few *for rent* signs and boarded-up windows. Not unexpected, she thought. The pandemic left no one untouched, and certainly not these smaller independent businesses.

Her first stop was Cedar Canoe Books. Any bookstore was a delight to Felicity, but this one had its own charm. The long wooden counter, polished to a glossy shine, the smell of old paper and leather mixed with lemon oil, the creak of the wooden floors beneath her feet. A chair here, and a chair there, to sit and read, and the library-like quiet, all wrapped her in its familiar and unwavering warmth.

She bypassed her usual historical fiction genre and went straight to the shelves of summer romance. Something about a casual beach read appealed to her. Sometimes she wanted to be taken away to the past, to worlds her ancestors might have lived in and sometimes she just wanted to be entertained by something light and fun and, if she were honest, just a little cheesy.

An hour later, with four books she couldn't say no to, including Cam's memoir, Felicity felt a rumbling in her stomach and remembered she'd skipped breakfast this morning. At eleven-thirty, her favourite restaurants would be open. With half an hour to spare, she went to kayak and canoe shop to look for a new kayak paddle.

Standing at the display, measuring the balance of one paddle over another, Felicity had the distinct feeling she was being watched. She replaced the paddles in their rack, and glanced up, wondering if there were cameras and some shop attendant was watching her. As if she could steal one of paddles. What was she going to do? Fold it up and stick it in her purse? The thought of it made her smile as she turned from the display, deciding the paddle she already had would last the summer until some of these went on sale.

She rounded a pillar with a clearance bin of toques and winter gloves in front of it and nearly sent it toppling to the floor, as she ran headlong into another customer.

"I'm sorry," she said, without looking up, as she saved the bin from complete disaster.

"Well, this is a surprise," said a man's voice.

Felicity looked up. "Ben! I'm so sorry." She slid her purse strap back up over her shoulder. "You startled me." Had he been watching her?

"I came in to buy a kayak," he said with a hesitant smile. "I can't keep borrowing yours."

"Oh, but we don't use them all the time. You're welcome to them."

"That's kind of you, but I would like one of my own. Even when I leave here, it would be something I'd use again, so…" He shrugged and lifted his hands in a *what-can-you-do* kind of motion. "I've already chosen one, and I bought a car carrier too. I just have to pull up out back and they'll set it all up for me."

"Oh, then you're on your way, soon?" She did her best to hide her disappointment, still unsure whether she was the reason he'd kept his distance this morning.

"As a matter of fact, I haven't eaten yet, and I saw a restaurant that looks interesting. *The Little Place By the Lights*. I was going to have some lunch there. Are you free or do you have to get back? I noticed you have company, so I don't want to keep you."

"Company?" Ah, he'd seen the second car in her driveway. Was that why he hadn't come over this morning? "It's my son, Tom, and his girlfriend, Melody. They came up late last night. A couple of days ahead of schedule. So no, I don't have plans and I don't have to get back. I'd love to have lunch and how did you know that's one of my favourite places?"

"I think you might have mentioned it the other night, and I wanted to try it."

One of the things Felicity had loved from her dating years was when a man placed his hand in the small of her back to lead her somewhere. Richard had never done that. Maybe that should have been a sign. And maybe it was a sign when Ben's hand went to that place, and she felt a familiar warmth and intimacy she craved. She let that warmth and the flow of his energy move through her and felt something stir inside.

"The food is delicious there. You're going to love it," she said, as he opened the door, and they went outside.

"I hope this isn't an intrusion. You seemed a little preoccupied," Ben said as they walked.

"Oh, I'm sorry. I don't mean to be. I guess I'm just a little frustrated, that's all. Children stuff, you know?" The moment she said it, she wished she could take it back, remembering the way he'd reacted the other night when she mentioned children. But Ben just nodded in agreement and followed her into the restaurant.

Over delicious chicken and meatball paninos, Felicity found herself telling Ben about Tom and Melody's plans for an island wedding. It explained her preoccupied manner earlier. Yet, the moment she said it, she realized it was a mistake. Now she would have to tell him everything, or it would seem unreasonable for her to want them to get married somewhere else.

"St. Lucia is lovely, but I sense you're opposed to it."

"It's complicated."

He grunted and set down his wineglass. "That's a bit of a copout." And when he saw her face fall, he quickly added, "Sorry. I'm sure you have your reasons. It's really none of my business."

"No. It's alright. It's just that…" She paused. It was too personal, and she was angry with herself for bringing it up. She should have stuck to small talk. She could leave it a little vague. "Let me ask you this. Am I wrong to think that there are some things children don't need to know about their parent's relationships?"

Ben wiped his mouth with his napkin, set it on the table, and then he pushed his plate away. "I agree with you entire so no, you're not wrong. There are certain things within any relationship that should stay in the bedroom, so to speak. But I get the impression this is more than that."

There was something about Ben and the way he looked at her that made her want to tell him everything. He was a like a warm blanket she could wrap up in and feel her worries fade away. But what would he think of her if she told him about this strange arrangement between her and Richard's family? Would he wonder why she'd tolerated it and them and think less of her for having allowed it? When she talked to her friend Carrie about these things, Carrie sided with her, but maybe a man looked at things differently. Knowing Ben's thoughts might help, but it meant she would have to tell him at least some of the awful truth and what good would it do to oust the Jefferies as the cruel people they were? She'd rather it all stayed buried with Richard.

"You're hedging," he said softly. "I'm sorry. This is uncomfortable for you, and I don't mean to pry. I just thought if you could talk about it, you know, adult to adult, it might help."

"It might," she admitted. "But I'm not sure I'm ready, and I can't really tell it in part. It's an all-or-nothing kind of thing."

He reached out to cover her hand with his. His thumb caressed the back of her hand. "We all have scars, Felicity. Some deeper than others. Sometimes it helps to talk to them, but sometimes it doesn't. Only you can decide that, but I'm here, if you ever want to talk, okay?"

"Thank you, Ben. I appreciate that. More than you know." He pulled his hand away, and hers felt suddenly cold by its absence.

He sat back and rubbed his stomach. "You're right, the food here is great. I am stuffed. But I want to try one of those desserts." His phone buzzed and slid around on the table. He glanced at the screen but ignored the caller.

"Take that, if you like," she urged. "I don't mind."

He shook his head. "I can call her back. It's my daughter."

"Oh. You mentioned you had one but…"

"Yeah, to use your words, it's an all-or-nothing kind of story."

She reached for his hand and met his gaze. "I'm sorry," she said. "You're right. We've all been through things. Some we can talk about, some we can't. Forgive me?"

"There's nothing to forgive," he said with a half-hearted smile. "I understand your reluctance to talk about things, because I've got things I don't like to talk about too. So, there you have it. We are a couple of middle-aged people with baggage. Nothing extraordinary about that, is there?"

Felicity shook her head. "No, but you know something. When I am ready to talk about it all, I know you would understand. I don't know why because I hardly know you. But I know that."

His smile was quick and gentle, his manner more like that of the man who'd brought wine to her place the other night, not the one who seemed to need his own space. He reached into his pocket for his wallet. "Let me get this," he said. When she tried to protest, he said, "If it makes you feel better, you can pay next time."

"Okay. Next time." Felicity liked that idea.

8

When she arrived back at the cottage, it was mid-afternoon. Felicity hoisted grocery bags out of the car and set them by the door, then called out to Tom, who she could see at the kitchen window. "Can you bring those in while I get the rest?"

"Sure, Mum," he replied. "What's all this? Potting soil? Plants?"

"I'm going to do some pots later. You can just put that stuff by the garage."

Inside, when the grocery bags were emptied onto the counter, Melody appeared ready to help. "Where do you put these?" she asked, holding up some canned goods.

"Pantry cupboard, over there," Tom told her. "And these too." He pushed more cans toward her. "I spoke to Olivia while you were gone," Tom told Felicity.

"Did she say if she's bringing Eric on Friday?" She stepped back to survey the groceries. "I hope I've got enough food." Then she edged her way past Tom to put things in the fridge.

"Yes, Eric is coming, but that wasn't exactly what I called her for."

"Oh. Well, I suppose there's enough. We can sort out the sleeping arrangements when they get here. They won't share, will they?" Tom was about to say something, but Felicity raised her hand. "Never mind. Don't answer that. I should know better." Her children were adults now, and she knew Olivia was not one to wait before sleeping with men. Felicity didn't ask questions, as long as her children were happy.

Long ago, she'd vowed she would not be the disapproving parent her own mother had been. It would have killed them to know that Richard hadn't been her first. They were strict churchgoers until their dying day. Felicity felt they held unrealistic expectations in today's world and was of the mindset that what they didn't know wouldn't hurt them. She kept her personal life a secret most of the time.

It was her parent's values, though, that had been the bar by which she'd measured everything in her life. Perhaps if she'd taken a step back to honour her mother and father's wishes, she might have thought harder about marrying Richard, especially when his parents forced her to sign the prenup. There should be trust in a marriage, her father had always said. Without trust, there is nothing. The Jefferies trusted no one, especially a young girl they were convinced was only marrying their son for his money.

For Felicity, it wasn't about his money. It had never been. She'd signed the prenup to prove a point. She was in love with Richard. If a prenup was the only challenge in having him, then bring it on. She wanted Richard, and she got him and maybe, just maybe, she'd made his life as miserable as he'd made hers. Tom thought she hadn't grieved, but not a day went by when she didn't wrestle with the guilt and the question that had been haunting her for years. If he'd married someone else, would Richard have been a different man? Maybe their unhappy life was all her fault.

Tom was holding two bags of potato chips. "In the pantry, dear," Felicity told him.

"I know where they go. You weren't listening. I said, Olivia said something I wish you'd either confirm or deny. Something about you and Dad and our grandparents."

Felicity set a loaf of bread by the toaster and turned to look at him. "Do you have to do this now, Tom?"

"When then? Tomorrow? Next year? A decade from now?"

"She doesn't have to tell you anything, Tom," Melody intervened. "I keep telling you, it's none of our business."

"But why can't she tell me?" His voice nearly screeching, his hands in the air in a *don't get it* gesture.

"Because there are things that are private within a marriage," Felicity said. "And because your father isn't here to tell you his side of things. It isn't that I'm keeping things from you, personally, Tom." Felicity pushed past him to put things in the fridge, desperate to deflect this conversation to another time and place. She closed the door and looked at her son. "You and Melody will have things that only the two of you talk about. Things you don't discuss outside your marriage. Things that are no one else's business."

"But why does Olivia know?" Tom asked.

Felicity threw up her hands. "What is it that Olivia thinks she knows?"

"She knows something about St. Lucia. She said you've never been there. She says there was some sort of rift between you and Dad's family. Is that true?"

Felicity pursed her lips and curled her fingers at her sides. "Olivia is right. I have never been to St. Lucia. In fact, I have never been to any of the Jefferies' homes." She saw Tom's face work itself into a grimace. "They had their reasons."

Tom rolled his eyes. "Well, that's about as clear as the muck in the bottom of the lake. Can you be more specific, Mum?"

Melody flashed a concerned look at Felicity and stepped between them, placing a hand on Tom's chest. "Really, Tom, if she doesn't want to talk about it, she doesn't have to. Stop pestering her. I think it's obvious whatever happened, it's now in the past, right Felicity?"

Tom pushed Melody's hand away. "Melody, I love you honey, but this is between me and Mum. I wish you'd stay out of it. Obviously, there are things she's been keeping from us. Maybe for years." He looked at his mother. "Right Mum?" It was a challenge, again. Just like last night, and Felicity didn't like being challenged this way.

"Why can't you just let this stay buried with your father?" Tears burned in Felicity's eyes and her throat tightened around her words. She knew she had to get out of the cottage, get away from Tom, and this line of conversation. Why couldn't he just let this be? She pushed past him and slid her feet into a pair of sandals by the door. "I'm going for a walk." She waved her hand toward a package of sausages still on the counter. She could barely see them for her tears. "We'll barbeque tonight, if you don't mind."

"Sure, Mum but… Mum? I'm sorry…" Tom's voice faded into the distance. The screen door slammed shut behind her, echoing like a gunshot through the woods and across the lake. The sound made her jump, her nerves taught, her mind whirling as emotions surged through her veins. "Damn you, Richard, for leaving me to deal with all your shit." She took a deep breath and let the woods bathe her in serenity as her heart slowed and gave up its threat to burst out of her chest.

As she came to the end of the lane, she saw Ben's car, with his brand new neon green kayak mounted on top of it, turn off the main road. As he came closer, he waved, and lowered his window and then he rolled to a stop. "Hey, you beat me back. Did they fix your tire?"

"Apparently it's a right off, so no. I had to buy a new one," she said. There was a little residual anger in her voice. The tire would have been something Richard should have looked after. Just one more way he'd let her down. But it wasn't Ben's fault, and she regretted it the moment she spoke.

"Ouch. Sorry I asked." He pulled his head back inside the window and put up his hands, pretending to ward off a blow.

"I'm sorry," she said, trying to disguise her frustration with a smile. She blew out a big breath of air. "I'm frustrated, that's all. It's this baggage we carry around with us. I'd like to unpack it all and throw those old suitcases into the lake."

"Say no more. I get it." He nodded toward a bakery bag on the passenger seat next to him. "I've got butter tarts," he said. "I went to that place in town. I could have bought one of everything." He patted his belly and grinned. "I only bought a half dozen of these, though. Gotta keep my trim figure." She laughed at that, and Ben seized the opportunity to invite her in. "Come, enjoy a guilty pleasure with me. We can sit on the dock and watch the Lawson girls topple over on their paddle boards."

"Alright. But only one butter tart. You're not the only one watching their waistline."

He grinned and his eyes drifted over her figure. "Nothing wrong from what I can see."

Felicity felt the heat rise in her cheeks. "Oh, go on," she said. "I'll catch up with you and help you get the kayak off your car."

"Deal," he said, then drove on, turning into his lane and finally rolling to a stop by the garage.

After they'd set the kayak around the back by his dock and laid the paddle across it, all ready for its maiden voyage, they went inside. Ben waved her to a bar stool at the island and filled the kettle. "Your tea choices are raspberry, mint, ginger and honey, or plain old English Breakfast. Or I could fix you something stronger if you like."

"Hmm, is it that obvious?"

"I don't want to pry, but when I see a woman walking with her fists balled up ready to punch something, or someone, I have to assume something's up."

"That bad, eh?" Felicity's eyes fell to the tea containers Ben set in front of her. "Ginger sounds lovely and it will settle my nerves."

He moved easily about the kitchen, taking down cups, arranging four of the butter tarts onto a small plate and putting napkins out. When the kettle boiled, he filled their cups, then settled onto a stool next to her. He nudged her shoulder and pulled the butter tarts a little closer, nodding that she should take one. Felicity did. They were irresistible, really, as anyone who'd ever followed the great Canadian Butter Tart Trail would know.

"You look very comfortable in the kitchen," she said, catching a drip of syrup sliding down her chin.

"Years of living alone," he said, savouring his own tart. "And I'll have you know, I can cook, do laundry, even the ironing. And I do windows." He nudged her shoulder again. "I'm a great catch."

"Indeed," she said with a laugh. She might have asked why there was no ring on his finger, or why he was alone, if that was the case. Or was he hinting that he'd be a great catch for her? Maybe he would, she thought. He certainly wasn't Richard, or anything like him. But he reminded her of someone she'd dated years before, someone gentle, kind, and not so self-absorbed.

"You don't believe me." He put his hand over his heart. "I'm bruised by that."

"Oh stop," she laughed. "I was joking."

"Honestly, I owe all my kitchen skills to Gordon Ramsey and Jamie Oliver. Tell you what. Why don't I cook something for you? What's your favourite meal? Any allergies?" He slid off the stool and went to open the freezer to survey the contents.

"Wait, slow down. I've got Tom and Melody here, remember? Another time, though, when they go back." She saw disappointment in his eyes and wanted to remedy that. "Why don't you join us instead? I told you Tom has always wanted to do something in the developing countries, so I know he'd been interested in your work. And you'll love Melody. She's wonderful."

"Oh, I don't know. I don't want to interrupt family night or anything."

"Trust me. The only thing you'll be interrupting is a conversation I'm not ready to have."

"Oh right. I'm to be the buffer, am I?" He put a hand over his heart as if she'd just stabbed him. "Gosh, just what every man wants to hear." He grinned when she rolled her eyes. "It's okay, I get it. It's about that suitcase you aren't quite ready to unpack." He looked down at the tattoo exposed by his rolled-up shirt sleeve. "I know just how you feel."

"I don't want to pry. But it's hard not to notice. It's really a lovely tattoo. Is it for your daughter?"

"You're not prying. It's rather obvious, isn't it? I can't really hide her." He returned to his stool and wrapped his hands around his cup. "Yes, Emma is my daughter. I've already told you we haven't spoken in years, but I didn't tell you why."

Talk about opening suitcases…

9

Suddenly, Felicity felt guilty for asking. "You don't have to…"

"I know I don't, but I want to. We build friendships on trust, and I consider you a friend. Hopefully, a good friend. So, this is something I'd like to share. It's a rather long story, so I hope you're not in a hurry."

She shook her head and put her hand over his. "I'm not going anywhere."

He smiled. "Okay then. Here goes. I'll have to start at the beginning. Sorry, but like I said, this is a long one. I met Nancy, that's Emma's mother, when I was at Carleton. It was in my final year, and I was cramming for exams and working like a madman to complete my last assignments. I'd been at it for days and finally my roommate, Jerry, convinced me to take a break. I knew I needed a break, but in hindsight, I should have gone for a bike ride instead of the pub."

"But you went for a drink instead."

Ben nodded. "We picked up a couple of other fellows along the way and by the time we got there, Jerry's car and the pub were packed. We found a booth near the back, crammed into it, ordered a couple of pitchers, because whatever was on tap was always the cheapest. Didn't matter if it tasted good. We couldn't afford anything else."

"I remember those days," Felicity said, smiling at memories of university life.

"There was a table of girls next to us, business students, they said." Ben laughed. "I'm sure their major was How to Win a Rich Husband. My family didn't have any money. I worked two part-time jobs while going to school to pay my way. I'd been wearing the same jeans since grade nine, and my two favourite t-shirts came from secondhand shops. They were radio giveaways, advertising a 1970s rock concert. I didn't even know the name of the bands. I just liked the shirts because they were black and cheap. Most of my classmates had parents helping them. A couple were really well off, but most of them were better off than me. Anyway, these girls knew who had money and who didn't and before long, everyone paired off. The next thing I knew, they'd all left except for me and one girl.

She looked at me and I looked at her. I said, 'see ya later,' and headed for the door."

"Oh dear. Not even an offer of a lift home?"

"Jerry took his car. Anyway, I was too drunk to drive. Walking was already a chore. She wanted to come back to my dorm room, said she'd make it worth my while." Ben grinned. "God, I was stupid back then. She kept pressing herself against me, whispering in my ear." He shook his head, a boyish grin spreading across his face. "How does a young kid with raging hormones say no to that? Especially when she tells him it's just sex, and no strings attached."

Felicity grinned. "So, you took her back to your place?"

"I didn't live on campus, so we went to her place. An hour later, I went home with little more than my finals and a splitting headache on my mind. I never thought I'd hear from Nancy Jenkins again. I graduated with honours, took a summer internship at a firm I'd done some of my practical work with, and dug in my heels. About a month into my first paying position in that same firm, Jerry came home with Nancy tagging along behind him. She smiled and looked up at me with those Bambi eyes of hers and opened her jacket to reveal a round belly."

"Let me guess. She said the baby was yours."

"She did. But I wasn't that naïve. I knew she'd been with others. And I'd used a condom, not that they are a guarantee. I insisted on a paternity test after the baby was born. If it was mine, I agreed to support them, but if it wasn't, she'd have to find the real father and sort it out. In the meantime, her parents had kicked her out and no one would hire her for work because she was pregnant. And she was a bit of a mental mess. So, I gave her my room, and I took the couch in the living room. And that's how we lived until the baby was born."

"Emma?"

"Emma," he said, caressing the tattoo on his arm. "When she was born, we had the test done. Emma wasn't mine, but I felt so sorry for Nancy I couldn't bear to ask her to leave. And I confess, I got caught up in the whole baby thing. I'd already bought a crib and a highchair, blankets, clothes, diapers. God, the diapers." He ran a hand through his hair. "You had three of them. How did you ever manage it?"

"It was very generous of you to let her stay," Felicity said. "But I would expect nothing less, from what I know of you already."

"Well, where was she going to go with a tiny baby? She got some financial aid for a while and eventually she took a night job cleaning offices. It meant I could take care of Emma while she worked. She didn't make much, but she helped with the bills. After a while, Jerry moved out, claiming it was too crowded and he couldn't live with a crying baby unless it was his own. I really couldn't blame him."

"What happened with the biological father? Did she ever look him up?"

"Apparently, he was married. I never knew his name or much about him. She said he was some guy up she'd met in a bar during a convention. When she contacted him, he refused to acknowledge knowing her, let alone anything more than that. Bastard. Taking advantage of her like that."

Ben didn't notice Felicity flinch at that. She kept her emotions out of her voice. "So, they stayed with you."

"Right. Before Emma was three, I'd asked Nancy to marry me, more than once. Not because I loved her. I didn't even like her much. In our own crazy kind of way, we'd grown accustomed to each other. I did it for Emma's sake. If we'd gotten married, I would have adopted her and taken care of her, no matter what Nancy did."

"But she turned you down?"

He nodded. "And we argued, a lot. The place was too crowded for the three of us, so I started taking out-of-town jobs so I could be away for a while, give them some privacy. I'd fly to British Columbia. Down east. To the United States. My boss was eager for me to go, and I was eager to learn and to make connections. One day, when I came back from a three-month trip in Edmonton, Nancy was pregnant again. I have no idea whose baby it was. I didn't even ask her. I just knew it wasn't mine because we never… well, you know." Ben looked at her, his face in a twisted sort of smile.

"Her son was born a few days before Emma's eighth birthday. But she wasn't good at keeping track and she never went to a doctor, but I was sure her labour was too early. How would I know? By the time we got to the hospital, it was obvious that something was horribly wrong. They rushed her in, did a C-section. But he was born way too early, and had only half a brain, and a multitude of other deformities. Poor little thing. He didn't live more than a few hours."

"I can't imagine how that must have been for her, for all of you."

"Devastating. And he wasn't even mine. Emma took it in stride, as kids do. She had tons of questions and she had to work through her anger and disappointment and a few other things. But Nancy. From the moment she looked at that baby, something snapped. She was never the same. She slipped into a world where no one could reach her. I brought her home and took care of her for a few days, then got a woman from a government organization who helps families that are grieving. I had to go back to work. Someone had to pay the bills, and it was obvious she couldn't do it. With the woman's help, Nancy seemed to rally. She made promises to get herself straightened out, for Emma's sake. And she did for a while. But after a couple of months, she started doing weird things, like putting Emma's slippers in her lunchbox instead of food. Or forgetting to pack a lunch at all. Sometimes, she forgot to pick Emma up from school. She stopped taking care of herself, too. She didn't shower or wash her hair or do her laundry. And she didn't take care of Emma either.

"Eventually, the school called Family and Children's Services. I tried to explain our odd living arrangements, but they insisted that because Emma's birth certificate listed me as the father, I must be lying. Nancy put my name down as the father. I'd never even seen the birth certificate, but it was clear why FACs were blaming me."

Tears rimmed his eyes as he continued. "Once they got involved, things got uncomfortable for everyone. They agreed to let Nancy's aunt came to live with us. I thought it would help too. If nothing else, she would take care of Emma and she could vouch that our relationship was not what everyone FACs thought it was. I gave up my room again and slept on the couch. Nancy's aunt was supposed to stay a couple of weeks, but it turned into a year."

He looked at Felicity when she gasped. "I think I would have moved out."

"I wanted to. But my name was on the lease and if Nancy didn't pay the rent, I'd still be accountable. Maybe I could have tried harder to get out of that, but there was Emma to consider. I didn't really care what happened to Nancy anymore. The apartment reeked of her body odor and unwashed clothes and the aunt's horrible cooking. But I couldn't put them on the street. In the end, the aunt finally conceded that Nancy needed psychiatric treatment. She agreed to sign her into a facility for assessment. She took Emma to her house with FAC's blessing, of course, despite my wishes to take care of her."

"That must have been difficult for you."

"It should have been a relief. I was free of my obligations, of the mess of it all, but I missed Emma and when I tried to see her, the aunt wouldn't allow it. I called, I sent emails, I even tried FACs, but they said Emma was better off with the aunt. So, they moved to Huntsville."

"What did Emma think about all this?"

"I don't know, and I doubt they ever told her the truth. They wouldn't let me talk to her. So, after months of no success, an overseas job came up and when my boss asked if I wanted to go, I said yes. There was nothing keeping me in Ottawa anymore. I tried to keep in touch with Emma, wrote her loads of letters, but I never heard from her. My emails to the aunt went unopened. All my phone calls were ignored. Until now."

"What's happened now?"

"The aunt died about a year ago, and I got a letter through my lawyer, saying I owed an enormous bill at the institution where Nancy lives. It was nearly three years of back payments. Of course, I called them and argued that I wasn't responsible, but they said the records listed me as her husband, and it was up to me to pay the bills. They couldn't understand why I'd paid them before but hadn't kept on paying them. Of course, I hadn't paid any bill so none of it made any sense at all."

"What did you do?"

"I did what anyone would do. I got my lawyer to dig into it. Thanks to digital copies of everything, we now know that the aunt had forged my signature on the admission documents and had a fake marriage certificate made. It must have been the aunt who was paying the expenses, but at some point, she stopped. Now they are threatening to kick Nancy out if someone doesn't pay up. So, the shit has hit the proverbial fan."

"And Emma? What does she think of all this? Does she know the truth?"

"She has the documents from the lawyer now. She knows what her mother and her aunt did. But she won't talk about it. She still thinks I abandoned her and left her mother to rot in an institution."

Felicity was silent. There were no words, not a single sentiment, to make this better. She reached for her his hand. "I'm so sorry, Ben."

Ben took a deep breath and nodded. "Thank you. It's just that Emma is so angry with me. She thinks I just left her. I wouldn't do that. I could never do that. That job was supposed to be for a year, but when there was no response from her and the aunt refused to take my calls, I gave up trying. I thought maybe she was better off not being pushed between the aunt and me. I didn't have any legal right to ask for visitations, despite what that birth certificate said. At least I didn't think I did."

"But you still call her your daughter," Felicity said.

"To me, she is my daughter. I changed her diapers, I fed her. I read to her, went to PTA meetings. I sat in the audience at her ballet recitals. I took her shopping for Halloween costumes. I kissed her scraped knees and laughed at her silly jokes. I was her father. No, that's not quite right. I am her father."

"I'm sorry Ben."

"Yeah. Me too, but maybe one day, she'll come around once she comes to terms with it."

"I hope she does, because she's missing out on a chance to know a great man, biological father or not."

"That's kind of you to say. You asked me, when we first met the other day, if I was going to stay and I told you I hadn't decided yet."

"I remember."

"Well, I have now. I'm not going back. I won't let Emma think I'm abandoning her again. If there's a chance that she and I can have some kind of relationship again, I don't want to miss that. I listened to you talking about your kids and how excited you were with their achievements and how much you were looking forward to them joining you up here. I'd like that with Emma, or something close to it. I can't change what's in the past, but I can do something about the here and now."

"Why don't you invite her to spend some time here?" Felicity suggested. "This weekend when my other kids are here, too. She might feel more comfortable with people her own age around. A buffer of sorts."

"I think it's too soon for that. For her, at least. We have made progress, though. We met for dinner the other night. It's a start. I don't want to push her, but if things go well, next time we talk, I'll ask her about coming here."

"Have you told her everything? That you and Nancy weren't really, you know, a couple?" Felicity asked.

He fixed his gaze with hers, a grim smile on his face. "As much as she needs to know," he said. "And don't give me that look."

"What look?"

"Remember what did you ask me in the restaurant? Should kids know everything that goes on in their parents' lives? No. They shouldn't. So don't judge me for not telling Emma everything unless you're prepared to tell your children everything about their father. Like his infidelity and his drinking?"

"How did you know...?"

"A hunch," he said. "The way you turned down my offer to help with the tire, as if it were a more than just an offer to help or you were still wondering what he would think of it. And a few little things you've said. Then there's the way you sip wine but never finish a glass of it." Felicity's cheeks blushed with colour. But Ben continued. "And then, there's something you're not saying about St. Lucia, though I haven't figured that one out yet."

Felicity's gaze fell to her lap. "I wish I could say I don't know what you're talking about, but I can't." She looked up at him again, wondering if she could sort out everything she felt, or at least enough to tell him. "It isn't all just my dead husband. Richard's family, like Nancy's, did awful things. My kids love their grandparents. How can I tell him the truth?"

"I get that, Felicity. But things must be faced, eventually. I've got the chance to do that with Emma, if she'll let me. I won't tell you what to do. You have to work that out for yourself. But maybe, don't wait ten years, like I did, to fix this."

Felicity reached for his hand. "I won't. I promise. And I hope you work things out with Emma. They say the teen years are the toughest with girls, so maybe if you had to miss some, those were the best. There were a few trials with Olivia, but I wouldn't change it for anything. We're closer now than we ever were."

Felicity looked up at the clock over the sink, ticking away the minutes as the afternoon wore on. "Goodness, look at the time. I should get back before Tom sends out a search party. Thank you for the tea and the butter tart and for the talk." She slid off the stool and put her cup and plate by the sink. "Please come tonight. You'll love Melody, and Tom would love hearing about your work."

"Is that the only reason?" His smile held a hint of flirtatious hope.

"No," she felt heat rising in her face as he came to stand close to her by the sink. "I want you to come, but I don't think that's much of a secret, is it?"

"If it's a secret, then it's mine, too." He laughed then and walked her to the door, his hand on the small of her back again. They lingered a moment at the door, she not quite ready to leave, he not yet moving his hand. "What time shall I come over?"

"Five? Four-thirty? Now?" She said, wondering if he would kiss her. She could reach up and kiss him, she thought. No, much too forward.

His hand stayed on the small of her back when he reached out to open the door, the intimacy of the touch sending chills up her spine. "Shall I bring more wine?"

"We didn't even open the red you brought the other day, and Tom prefers beer and Melody likes coolers."

"If you're sure," he said with a contented smile. "Thanks for hearing me out. There is something to be said for unpacking all this baggage. I feel lighter somehow. And no pressure, but when you're ready…"

"I will tell you, Ben. I promise."

He lifted her chin, so she met his gaze and cupped her face. "You can tell me anything, Felicity. I mean it. No judgement. No sage advice or words of wisdom. Just an ear. That's all, or a shoulder if you want to cry on it." He nudged one shoulder into hers and she laughed. And then he pushed open the door. "See you in a while."

No kiss then, she thought, wishing she'd gotten the nerve up to rise on her tiptoes and drop a kiss on his inviting lips, instead of being the good girl her mother raised her to be.

"Yes. See you."

At the bottom of the porch steps, she turned to wave and found his eyes following her. He grinned and waved, then scratched at the stubble on his chin. She could almost hear him thinking, *just enough time for a shave* while she was thinking, *damn I wish he'd kissed me.*

10

Felicity loved their barbeques and the way they brought everyone together. It was the one thing even Richard had enjoyed, here or at home. Maybe because, as head chef, it was his chance to outshine everyone else. He revelled in the compliments of a perfectly cooked steak or burgers cooked just right.

Now, it was Tom's turn to take over as head chef at the barbeque and he did it in his fun-loving, good-natured way. By the time Felicity delivered a tray of drinks out to them, he and Ben were deep in conversation about Ben's work, while the sausages sizzled behind them. In the background, Ben's phone was playing old country tunes through a speaker Tom had brought outside. She was glad to see Tom was in good spirits, and it was clear he and Ben were getting along famously. Melody had fixed the rest of their dinner and done herself proud, as usual.

A warmth of friendship filled Felicity as she looked at the faces around her table. They ate and laughed and let go of their worries and Felicity lifted her eyes to the sky, whispered goodbye, again, to those who no longer sat at her table.

Just as dusk gave way to night, they were rewarded with a spectacular display of Aurora Borealis. When they went down to the docks to watch the show, others around the lake did the same. Quiet murmurs of ohs and awes drifted across the water as the shimmering lights danced in the sky.

"I've never seen it so vividly," Melody whispered, as if saying it out loud might break the magic.

"Me either," Felicity said, feeling Ben's breath as he came to stand behind and put his arms around her.

"Is this, okay?" He whispered in her ear.

She nodded. "Very okay." She put her hands over his arms in reassurance.

After the light show, Tom suggested a fire and S'mores for dessert. When Ben said he'd never had them and didn't know what they were, Melody couldn't believe it.

"You never went to Boy Scout camp, or had campfires with friends?" Tom asked.

Ben shook his head. "Nope."

"Well, you're in for a treat," Melody assured him. "You guys get the fire going, and I'll help Felicity in the kitchen."

Inside, Felicity put on the kettle for hot drinks while Melody rummaged in the pantry. "I think I put the marshmallows in here. Ah, here they are." She set them on the counter, alongside the graham wafers and chocolate bars.

Felicity felt Melody staring at her. "What is it, Melody?"

"Nothing, really. Except what a lovely man," she said, her brow lifting in a question she didn't ask.

"He is nice, isn't he?" Felicity agreed.

"Is there something going on between the two of you?"

Felicity looked at her future daughter-in-law. "Can't two people be friends without something more being insinuated?"

Melody raised her hands and backed away. "Okay, sorry. I was teasing, kind of, but I guess I hit a nerve." She reached for the napkins. "Look Felicity. I'm on your side here. I only meant if there were someone in your future, Ben seems like the kind of man who would treat you right."

Felicity stepped back and looked at Melody. "As opposed to…?"

Melody flushed, the colour filling her face all the way to her hairline. "Okay, look. You realize I work in the same office as the Jefferies' lawyer, don't you?"

"I thought they were with Harrison and Associates?"

Melody shook her head. "Not anymore. Shortly before Richard's death, they moved over to us. At the time, I think it was because they expected Richard to inherit, so it made sense to have everything under one roof. But they aren't about to change back now. So, all the family deals with Gerard." She gave a little shrug and said, "I probably should have declared a conflict of interest, but I didn't put two and two together until I was sorting the third box of papers. That's when I came upon your prenup. It should have been in Richard's file, but for some reason it was in his parents' files instead. All I'm saying is, as prenups go, it was pretty brutal. And it seems to me, after hearing what you said to Tom earlier, that you've had a really rough deal. I'm so sorry."

Ah, the infamous prenup was still haunting her. "Don't be, Melody. It's water under the bridge. And besides, it was mutual. I made him sign one too. Believe it or not, I married Richard because I loved him. I couldn't give a fig about his money."

"I know, but the letter that was attached to it." Melody gave a shudder. "It's… it's just so… cruel and coldhearted."

"What letter?"

"You don't have a copy of it?"

Felicity shook her head.

Melody chewed on her bottom lip. "Maybe I shouldn't have said anything."

"You might as well spill it all, my dear. Whatever is in that letter hasn't really mattered for a long time."

"Alright then. I suppose it can't hurt. Richard's parents offered a bribe to your parents if they convinced you to break off your engagement."

"Hmm, well, they didn't so I assume my father told them what they could do with that offer. What else?"

"St. Lucia. It's in the letter too. The trespass order which states that you're not allowed to come within a hundred feet of any Jefferies' property."

"Does Tom know any of this?"

"Not from me, but he is putting things together. The reading of Richard's will, which didn't include you and this St. Lucia business, he spoke to Olivia about. And then there was the condo that was left to his Uncle Alan."

"Yes, Richard kept a suite in Toronto for nights when he worked late. I cleaned it out before the will was read."

"You don't have to beat around the bush with me, Felicity. I've met several of the women he carried on with. More than one of them work in my office." Her hand covered Felicity's on the counter. "I'm really sorry. It isn't fair."

"No one ever said life was going to be fair. There were times when I was sure things would change and we would be happy again. That's how naïve I was."

"Don't say that. How could you have known you wouldn't have another twenty or thirty years to work things out? I know it's really none of my business, but I think you should talk to your children."

"It seems they know more than I thought, but not everything, for sure." Felicity ran a hand over her hair. "But if I do, it will ruin their impression of their father and his family. How can I do that?"

"It would explain a lot."

"Maybe."

"Whatever you decide, we are not getting married in St. Lucia. After you left this morning, I told Tom, I want a small garden wedding at my parent's house so we can put the money we would have spent on a destination wedding toward a down payment on a house."

Felicity nodded. "Your father's rose garden would be the perfect place for a small wedding. But you shouldn't let me get in the way. If you want St. Lucia, you should have it."

Melody shook her head. "Not if you aren't there to share our day. We could always go there for our honeymoon."

"Yes, you could. Maybe that's the solution to this." She put the last of the things onto a tray and lifted it. "Thank you, Melody. I appreciate your discretion."

"No problem. But I'll just warn you that after his conversation with Olivia this morning, Tom is not going to settle for silence forever. And neither will the others."

Felicity nodded. "Point taken. I will think about it." And then she smiled and kissed Melody on the cheek.

"And I meant what I said about Ben. You deserve to be happy, Felicity, so if he makes you happy, then why not?"

"It's too early to say. We've just become friends. But thank you for that."

Outside, Tom tossed another long onto the fire and it crackled and sputtered, shooting sparks of orange like fireflies dancing in the night air. "There you are," he said, taking the tray from Felicity. "I thought you two had gone to bed and given up on us."

"And miss S'mores?" Felicity said. "Not on your life."

"Okay," Ben said, peering at the tray as Tom set it on the table between them. "What goes in these things?"

Melody speared marshmallows with a roasting stick. "Let me make one for you and you can tell us what you think. I can't believe you've never had one."

"I guess I just never had the chance. I guess it's true that life starts at fifty. What a great experience…. At least I hope it is." He accepted a S'more from Melody and turned it over in his hands. "Interesting. This looks good."

"I can't believe your kids haven't made you make these, Ben," Melody persisted. "You do have kids, don't you Ben? Are you divorced? Separated?"

"Really Mel," Felicity said. "It's none of our…"

Ben patted Felicity's arm and cast a reassuring *I-got-this* look at her. "I'm not married and never have been. I have a surrogate daughter, Emma, who I consider my own. She works in a shop in Huntsville. I don't know if she'll have any free time, but trust me, if I can lure her here, I will. And maybe we'll make some more of these S'mores. Who would miss these?" He took a generous bite and with his mouth full said, "How have I missed having one of these all my life?"

Felicity flashed a glance at Melody, who was looking at Tom and did not see the daggar Felicity threw in her direction. Ben was being gracious, but she wished Melody hadn't forced him to talk about his personal life. Especially when it was none of Melody's business and especially when Ben was walking on tender ground with a daughter who believed things about her father that weren't true.

She wanted to tell Melody she'd gone too far, but instead she said, "I'm sure Emma would fit right in with our gang, wouldn't she, Tom?"

"The more the merrier, as you always say, Mum."

11

Felicity woke the next morning, the smell of campfire, the night air and chocolate still lingering in her hair and her room. She was too tired last night to shower before she went to bed since it was after midnight when Ben crept off through the woods to his cottage and they had gone inside.

She smelled coffee brewing in the kitchen; the wafting scent of it enticing her out of bed, into her housecoat, and down the narrow passageway. Tom stood at the stove, a whisk in one hand, a bowl filled with eggs in the other.

"Morning," she said, reaching past him for a mug. "Smells great in here. Omelets?"

"Scrambled is my specialty. There will be lots, so I hope you're hungry."

"Starving. I'll set the table."

"Set it for four," he said, not taking his eyes off his whisking. "I invited Ben. He seems to think his eggs are better than mine, so we're having a cook-off. He's bringing over his version of scrambled eggs and I'm making mine. So, like I said, I hope you're hungry."

"Oh. I should get dressed if we're having people over," Felicity said, tugging the sides of her housecoat together and cinching the belt. "And a shower," she added, running a hand through her hair. She set down her cup without filling it. "What time did you say he was coming?"

"Soon," Tom said, throwing her a curious look as she headed back the way she'd come. "I thought you were going to set the table?"

"I will. After I shower. Or Melody can do it," she thought.

By the time Felicity had showered and changed into a pair of jeans and a short-sleeved shirt, added a little eyeliner and blush and fixed her hair, Melody had the table set in the dining room. Apparently, Melody approved of Ben's marital status as revealed last night, and thought they needed to have an intimate meal. She'd taken the leaves out of the table so that now it was square with just enough space for four to sit comfortably. The places were set two on each side, with Felicity's linen tablecloth and napkins and a candle in the middle. Tom and Ben leaned against the hutch, arms crossed, comparing notes on how they'd made their eggs. Neither seemed to give any thought to the seating arrangements or the setting of the table.

"The key is in taking it off the stove," Ben was saying. "So the eggs don't get too hot. They come out fluffier that way."

"Ah, here she is," Tom said, when Felicity walked into the dining room. "Finally, we can eat."

"This all looks delicious," Felicity said, accepting the chair Ben pulled out for her, right next to his. "Much better than my usual toast and jam." Felicity accepted a dish of eggs from Tom and put some on her plate. "Whose creation is this?" she asked.

"Ah, no." Tom said. "You and Melody cannot know who cooked which eggs. You have to tell us which you like best first. And then we'll tell you."

She handed the bowl to Ben after serving herself a portion. "Okay. Are you ready for this, Melody?"

"There's something about being in the great outdoors that makes you hungry, don't you think?" Ben said. He put a generous portion of eggs onto his plate and passed the bowl to Melody.

"Mmm," Tom agreed through a mouthful of food. "You know, Ben, I don't often admit to this, but this time I must. My eggs bow to yours. They are definitely better than mine."

Melody howled. "That's a first. Tom never gives in to anyone about anything."

"Hey, I do so."

"Uh. No, you don't," she said, patting his hand. "But I love you, anyway."

"What's your specialty, Tom?" Ben asked.

"Mushroom risotto," he said with a wide grin. "Right Mel?"

Melody flicked her gaze between the two men. "Hey, you guys should have a risotto cook-off, don't you think, Felicity?"

"Oh. I love risotto," Felicity answered.

Tom's eyes lit up, his head filling with an idea. "Alright. Whatdya think, Ben? Care to take the challenge?"

"Just name the day," Ben said. "No wait. It would have to be Saturday. That way, the rest of your family is here to help eat it. Plus, it will give me time to shop for what I need."

"Or time to buy some already made from the store is more likely," Tom joked.

"I have never bought readymade risotto in my life, unless it was in a restaurant, for my supper."

"Okay then. But just to keep you honest, we'll prepare it together, side by side. Mum and Melody can supervise."

Ben nodded toward the kitchen. "But not in there. There isn't enough space for both of us to work. You'll have to come next door. The kitchen's bigger and the ladies can sit at the island and watch."

"You're on."

"Saturday night it is," Ben said, clinking his orange juice glass with Tom's. And then he looked at Felicity and winked at her. He was loving this, and she was, too. She was glad Melody's prying hadn't put him off because Melody was right. She was sure she could find happiness with Ben. He fit in with the rest of them, as if he was meant to be there all along.

After their huge belt loosening breakfast, Ben headed to Huntsville to do some errands, and Tom and Melody opted to drive into Dorset to climb the tower and visit Robinson's General Store. They asked Felicity to join them, but she declined.

"You don't want me tagging along. Besides, I can go there anytime," she said. "Go, enjoy the view and have fun. The only thing I want is a puzzle. We've done everything in the cupboard, and they always have such a nice selection at Robinsons."

"Mum's favourite pastime," he said to Melody as they got ready to go.

"I love doing puzzles, too," Melody said. "I'll find a good one, Felicity."

Once the kitchen was tidied, Felicity decided to take advantage of the clear sky and warm temperatures to go for a paddle.

The wooden one, her favourite, lay waiting for her by the dock. *The old girl*, or sometimes *The Wooden Wonder*, according to her father, had made thousands of trips around Ril Lake and had the scars to prove it. She'd scraped bottom a few too many times, and more than once, Felicity's father had patched her up. But there was life in *the old girl* yet which made Felicity reluctant to put her out to pasture, or sea, or whatever you did with old wooden kayaks when they were no longer seaworthy.

She zipped up a lifejacket, climbed in, and pushed off from the dock. A good paddle would wear off some of that enormous breakfast and give her time to consider what she should tell Tom. Ben and Melody were both right. She couldn't avoid his questions forever and she wasn't going to wait ten years to work this out. However, she still harboured a great resentment toward Richard for leaving her to deal with this.

The lake and the air were both calm. Unless you counted the autumn when the leaves were in full splendor, June was the best month on Ril Lake. Temperatures were moderate, the water was usually calm and almost always warm enough to swim, because the lake was so shallow. No matter what season, it was the quiet she liked best. In a few weeks, school would be out, and all the renters and regulars would send their music reverberating all around their little cove. That was also when a couple of motorboats came out of their winter hibernation. There were only a few on Ril Lake and they usually kept to the wider, more open places, away from their little cove, but not always. But just then, that morning, there were no other boats, not even a canoe as far as she could see.

Felicity heard nothing other than the cutting of her paddle in and out of the water, and a distant loon calling to his mate. Even the kayak glided silently as it made its way across the water. Pure heaven, she thought as a lone hawk circled overhead. She recognized the slight tilt of his wing and the missing tail feathers. Lawson's Hawk, as the locals called him, had lost those feathers when the Lawson girls' grandfather mistook him for a wild turkey and thought he'd make an excellent supper. Grandad Lawson suffered from dementia in those days, and probably several other undiagnosed illnesses. After that incident, his guns were confiscated. No one ever asked why he kept them in the first place. Maybe he feared bears would come calling in the early days up here.

Felicity kept her eyes forward, level with her task as she rounded the point by Abby's Rock. After all these years, the memories still haunted her, and though she knew they always would, to some extent, she was grateful that each time she rounded that bend, and stopped to say hello to Abby's Rock, the pain lessened. More than once, in the past couple of summers, she was sure she'd seen Abby sitting on the rock, smiling, happy and carefree, waving to her as she passed. Felicity had to stop herself from waving back, telling herself it was only her imagination.

These days, she gathered her resolve and pushed happier memories of Abby to the front of her mind; Abby in her little pink tutu at ballet class; Abby at the Y learning to swim; Abby and Tom cuddled together on the living room floor, with Hope watching cartoons on Saturday mornings. It was the only way she could deal with the horror, the guilt, and the blame.

The blame.

Tom was right when he'd said she was a basket case back then. It felt like ages before she could even come here, and put a boat into the water again, and still more before she could paddle anywhere near the rock. To this day, she had not forgiven God for taking her daughter away from them. She clung to the hope that there really was an afterlife where all is forgiven, and all souls lived happily ever after. She hoped, too, that her parents and Abby, and now Richard, were together. And if Richard was with them, she hoped now he could forgive himself because he'd never managed it while he was alive. Truthfully, neither had she. She'd blamed herself, sure, but mostly she'd blamed him. If he'd just put down his drink when they'd asked him to, and put on his damn skates, Abby might still be alive.

As she rounded the bend and left the serenity of the cove behind her, she came into the open water and faced a strong headwind from the east. The wind pushed back at Felicity as she increased the depth and intensity of her strokes. Paddling back would be a cinch, she thought. She wouldn't have to do much more than steer. But now, staying within thirty feet of the shoreline, she had to work hard.

With her eye on the wide-open expanse of the lake, Felicity felt a familiar urge to challenge the wind and paddle full-out to the other side. "You're on," she said to the wind. The old girl was a bit of an eyesore to her kids, and they never wanted to be seen in it, but she was light, and she responded well to every stroke. Now as Felicity dipped her paddle, one side, then the other, pulling hard against the water, straining her arms, her back and her stomach, *the old gal* did not let her down. It was as if she'd hoisted a sail as she picked up speed, shifting the water, faster and faster, until her arms ached and the muscles in her stomach pinched under the strain. She welcomed the pain. It felt good, cleansing somehow. She pushed harder still, focusing on her strokes; right, left, right, left, until halfway across the lake a great surge of hot tears welled up, blinded her momentarily, and then spilled down her cheeks. Suddenly, as she thought her arms were about to give out, Felicity felt a rushing release of emotion.

Still, she paddled on, every stroke summoning the demons that haunted her. She tugged at the blame first, wrestling with memories of long-ago arguments, of things said in the heat of their anger, and finally the deadly silences Richard inflicted on her. Did she blame him for that, too? What does it do to a man's pride when he can't provide for his family? And how many hits to that pride could a man take? Is that what had driven the wedge between them? His damn pride? She'd always thought it was Abbey's death, because things were so much worse after that, but maybe she'd been wrong.

This time, when her thoughts turned to blame, it was with a certainty that nothing was served now by blaming anyone for what happened to Abbey. She understood Richard's grief. She'd suffered too. But no good had ever come from the blame they'd laid at each other's feet. In her mind, she opened a suitcase and dumped the contents it over the side of the kayak. Gone, she thought, the blame, and feeling guilty for blaming him. I'm done with it, she thought as the imaginary suitcase tumbled in after and sank to the bottom of the lake.

Almost instantly, her heart softened, and she found forgiveness at its core. There was so much she hadn't been able to forgive; the lies, the cheating, the anger Richard lashed on her, and the way she always questioning her part in everything. It was an ugly nest of secrets they'd kept from their children, thinking they were sheltering them, doing what was best. And now that Richard was gone, and she was left to deal with everything, she knew she would tell them the truth; all the truth.

"I forgive you, Richard," she shouted into the wind. It threw her words back into her face and it was Richard's voice she heard. *"For what? Maybe if I'd never met you, my life would have been different."*

"Would it?" she asked. "Or would you have just made someone else as miserable as I've been?"

Felicity opened another imaginary suitcase and dumped her guilt into the lake. "I cannot carry this burden anymore," she told the wind. Richard is dead. There is no changing that. It's time to tell the children everything and let them sort out the pieces for themselves. No more secrets. No more hedging around the truth.

None of it mattered anymore. What mattered was the future; hers and her children's. Tom and Melody would get married and give her grandchildren. Will would find a purpose for all that creative energy that burned inside him. Olivia would go on being the wonderfully nurturing, loving soul she'd always been, and maybe she and Eric had a future together. But for Felicity, a second chance at happiness, at a new life, and whatever that might bring, was waiting for her. Did she really want to let her past rule her future?

"Goodbye, guilt. Goodbye blame. Goodbye Richard. I won't let you hurt me any longer." Her words floated on the wind and this time there was no response.

She slowed a little then, as she came to the narrow spot between the points of Mac Arthur Road to her left and Watson Road on her road. Her arms ached yet, as she slowed to navigate the opening of the channel, there was a lightness to her stroke now, born of a freedom she had not felt in years. Wisps of her hair flipped about her face and fluttered the water before her, flutter into miniature ripples of the wind's liquid breath. She was still moving too fast, a reckless speed almost, and she knew it, but she kept on determined to make the end of the narrows before quitting her challenge against the wind.

Crossing into the narrows, she did not see the boulders that lay beneath the surface just a few feet off the end of Keating's dock. The sound of wood scraping rock was ominous in the quiet all around her and jolted her out of her thoughts as the kayak jerked to a stop and water instantly began seeping in. Felicity set her paddle across her lap and peered over the side.

"What on earth…?"

She'd paddled this lake a million times, been over every inch of surface water, knew where every rock and boulder sat, where to avoid the reeds that would tangle your paddle and the shallow spots to steer clear of. The two times she'd been out this summer, she had not been on this side of the lake, but she knew well enough that these rocks were not here last summer.

"Shit," she said, as the leak in the bow became a stream. Bailing was little use, not that she had anything to bail with. She had to get out of this area and away from the rocks. Rocks in the plural, she thought, counting six huge boulders laying just below the surface. She turned the boat as water sloshed around her feet and headed for the opposite side of the channel where she knew Cam Meyers was staying with his father. If she hurried, she might just make it before the kayak completely washed out. She had her lifejacket on, and she was a good swimmer, but she wouldn't need it. The water wasn't deep here. The problem was her arms ached so badly she wasn't sure she could swim. If she could just manage another twenty feet, she could get out and walk the rest. For certain, she would never find the strength to swim all the way back to her cottage. She cursed her ridiculous race against her own emotions that made her arms ache with pain. She knew better than to go all out by herself, like that. It was foolish and she would pay for it, was indeed paying for it now.

The water was shin deep in the boat, when she pushed up onto a bit of sandy shore beside a crumbling old dock, grateful she'd made it without sinking. She got out and dragged the kayak out of the water and flipped it over. The sight of the damage made her heart ache. "Sorry Grandpa," she said, more to herself than out loud.

"Ahoy there," someone called from a deck above her. "Run amuck, did she?"

Felicity looked up to see an elderly man peering through a deck rail at her. She whirled around to see his view of the lake and realized, as she squinted into the afternoon sun, he must have been watching her for some time, and had probably seen her come into the channel at a reckless speed. What an idiot, she whispered under her breath. And then she turned back to him. Exhausted and breathless, she lifted her paddle and pointed. "I hit some big rocks over there," she said. "I don't remember them being there before."

"Weren't," he said, leaning forward to rest a pair of bony elbows on the railing. He pulled his cap down over his eyes to shade the sun and squinted into the distance. "Somebody bought the Keating place. Brought in a dozer and moved them rocks out of the front and pushed them into the lake. Just last week, or maybe it was the week before that. I lose track of time sometimes."

"Can they do that?" Felicity set down her paddle and made her way to the steps of his deck.

"Nobody stopped them, so I guess so. They shudda put a flag up or a buoy, to warn people away. You're not the first one to hit 'em."

"I wonder how they'd feel if I knocked on their door and asked them to replace my kayak." She only half meant it, but she also knew it was the end of her grandfather's pride and joy. There would be no patching *the old gal* this time, and she'd like the new owner to take some responsibility.

"You want help to get that one home?" he called out.

She didn't want to trouble the man. "If you don't mind, I'll leave it here. I can walk home. Get my car, come back and pick it up."

"You're Felicity Bailey, aren't you? Frank Bailey's daughter. I thought I recognized that kayak. Built it himself, didn't he?"

"My grandfather did, actually. But you probably saw my dad paddling it. Are you Mr. Meyers?"

"That's me. Your dad and I used to play darts now and again, in Baysville, and sometimes we'd do a little fishing together."

"Well, it's nice to meet you, Mr. Meyers. Is it okay if I come up?"

"Course you can. And you can call me Slim. I've been Slim to everyone since I was knee high to a grasshopper."

"Because you're so thin?" Felicity smiled coming up his stairs.

"No. Because I liked to eat Slim Jims. Remember those?" He waved her into a nearby chair.

"Do they still make those?"

"They do, as a matter of fact. And I still eat 'em. Can you fix the boat, or is it a gonner?"

"To be honest, I think it's toast. Firewood now."

"Well then, best you leave it right where it is. I'll burn it for you. Unless you really want to lug it all the way back to your place."

"Heavens no. I just didn't want to leave you with a mess. If you can burn it, you go right ahead. I'll take the paddle, though. It's seen better days, but it still works."

The afternoon was wearing on, and she didn't relish walking home in the dark. "I suppose if I'm going to walk, I'd better get moving. It's at least four k from here on the ring road, isn't it?"

"Now just sit a minute. You must be exhausted. I was watching you go across the lake. Figured you must be training for some race or something the way you were goin' flat out," Slim said with a grin. "Either that or some demon was chasing you." He waved a hand as if he was swatting a fly. "No, don't answer that. Haven't we all got a few of them on our backs?" He pushed out of his chair. "I'll get my son to run you home. He's got one of them new Jeeps. It's a gaudy orange colour. I think it looks like a giant pumpkin, but he likes it."

"Oh, I know your son. He changed my tire for me the other day. Cam, isn't it?"

"That's right. Now don't go anywhere. I'll be right back." He hoisted himself out of his chair, leaned heavily on a cane and made his way inside, one thump of his stick at a time.

Moments later, Cam came out of the cottage and peered at her over the top of a pair of black rimmed reading glasses perched on the tip of his nose. A three-day stubble, peppered with grey, clung to his chin. "Ah, it's tire gal." He smiled down at her. "You seem bent on getting yourself into disasters. Dad says you smashed up your kayak." His gaze went to their stretch of the beach, where her kayak lay, the bow cracked open. "You need a ride home?" He dropped a textbook thick and weighty, and undoubtedly full of laboriously gathered facts, onto the table. What else would a history professor be reading?

"Honestly, I can walk if it's putting you out."

"No trouble at all," he said. And then he waved an arm, beckoning her toward the door.

"I'll just grab my paddle." Felicity pushed out the chair, her arms instantly caving in as if they were made of jelly.

"I'll get it," he said. "Sit tight." He sprinted down the steps, pulled her paddle from the wreckage, and returned before Felicity had even gotten to the door of the cottage. He reached past her and opened it. "It's Felicity, right?"

It was only a few days ago. Had he really forgotten? "Felicity Jefferies, yes."

A door from a mudroom off the kitchen led to a small, square porch, facing a patch of gravel where Cam's Jeep was parked. He opened the passenger door for her, put the paddle in through the back hatch, and climbed into the driver's side.

"Thank you for doing this. It's a relief not to face the long walk after being out on the water most of the afternoon."

"No problem," he said. "It's Ril Cove Road, right?"

He remembered that much, she thought, nodding that he had the right place. They pulled onto the ring road and Felicity remarked how odd it was that their families had owned cottages all these years, just a few miles from each other, yet they'd only just met the other day.

"Isn't that what this place is all about?" Cam suggested. "The seclusion, the isolation? Somehow, socializing with everyone around the lake defeats the purpose." He flashed her a smile that suggested he wasn't minding their current socializing situation.

Felicity flushed with embarrassment. "I rather like the sense of community here. The small-town atmosphere or Baysville, the neighborliness of people on the lake. Which reminds me, by the way.

Strawberries will be in season next week, and I still have to make that pie for you."

"I was looking forward to that." He grinned at her. "Now it will have to be something more. Like an entire dinner, I think."

"Oh, I bake, but I'm not much of a cook. How about two pies?" He seemed to be relishing in the awkwardness of the situation. The last thing she wanted to do was cook for him and his father, and he seemed to sense that.

"Tell you what. I'll let you off the hook, but only if you agree to let me take you to dinner."

Felicity's heart began to thump. She hadn't expected this. She should have just made the damn pie in the first place. She didn't mind paying a debt, and it was just a gesture, really, but dinner with Cam was not something she'd considered. She looked across the car at him.

"Well, if you're too busy, then…" he began with a shrug.

"I'm not too busy. It's just that I…"

"Alright. What are you doing tonight?"

"I uh. Well?"

"Good. I'll pick you up at seven?"

"Oh, I don't know…" she hedged, and then she looked at him. He had fixed her tire, and he was helping her out now. What harm was there in a dinner? And there was that book Wally had mentioned. Maybe they could talk about that. She didn't really like the way he was pushing her, but he wasn't a creep, or at least not the kind Olivia warned her against. She thought of Ben and wondered what he would think of this. And then she realized it was just dinner, and she had no obligation to Ben.

"I'm divorced," he said, suddenly breaking the silence. "I didn't want you to think I was married or something. I'm not perfect, but I'm not that kind of guy."

"I didn't think you were," Felicity said.

His fingers tightened around the steering wheel, and Felicity saw his jaw stiffen. "I was faithful to her for thirty-two years. She couldn't say the same."

"I'm sorry. It was the same for me. It's unpleasant to talk about."

"I had my chances, believe me. If I'd wanted to, I could have…" His head did a funny wobble then, and he looked at her. "Oh, who am I kidding? I would never have never dared. With my luck, someone would have seen me. Then my kids would have found out and I would have been the bad guy."

Felicity couldn't believe that Cam was saying exactly what she'd felt all her married life. "Children don't know what goes on in their parent's lives," she said. "They're in their own worlds and maybe that's how it's supposed to be."

"Maybe for some. But mine knew the truth, and they still sided with her."

Felicity didn't want to speculate why that might be. She had enough trouble sorting out her own children's feelings and loyalties. She was not one to give advice on the subject, so she stayed quiet.

When they rounded the bend onto Ril Cove Road, she sighed, grateful the conversation didn't have to go any further, at least for now. "Just there. See the scarecrow by the tree? That's me, Uh, us." Cam pulled the Jeep into her laneway and rolled to a stop behind her car. "Thank you, Cam. I appreciate this."

"No problem. See you in a couple of hours." As he reached into the back to retrieve her paddle, his hand brushed her shoulder. He left it there for just a moment, the heat of it seeping through the fabric and into her skin. As their eyes met, his brow lifted in what Felicity was sure was a question. *Can I kiss you*?

Her eyes flitted to Ben's car in the driveway next door and a pinch of worry crossed her face. No, I don't want you to kiss me, she thought. "Thanks again. And I'm sorry about leaving the kayak for you to take care of. I could send my son around to pick it up."

Cam frowned. "No need. It's really alright." He slid out of his seat and opened her door for her. She felt the full height of him as he stood next to her, the strength of his arm guiding her around the back of the car toward her front door and the warmth of his hand across the back of her shoulder blades: not in the small of her back where she liked. He set the paddle by the door and smiled. "You like Italian food?"

"Yes, but do you mind if we have something else? Seems I've eaten a lot of pasta lately. Is the Pub on the Dock, okay? That way you can have your pasta if you like and I can get something else."

"Sure."

She watched as Cam backed the Jeep back down the drive and pulled onto the road. The potting soil and trays of flowers sat nearby, and she regretted not taking the time to do that this afternoon instead of spending it on the water. They would have to wait another day and she would have dinner with Cam Meyers, though she knew already she was going to regret that, too.

She went inside to find her kitchen clutter free, and everything put away and wiped down, her living room vacuumed, the couch cushions straightened, and the coffee table polished to a gleaming shine. In her bedroom, which she'd left in an *I'll-deal-with-you-later* state, the bed was made, without a single wrinkle in the quilt cover and a little bud vase of wildflowers, stood on the nightstand. It all confirmed what she'd already suspected. This was Melody's doing. An apology, perhaps, for pushing Ben as she had last night? Tom cleaned up after himself, but not like this. She would thank her for all she'd done, but just now she was glad she and Tom were somewhere else, so she didn't have to explain where she was going, with whom, or why.

She showered, changed into a skirt and summery blouse and went to the Muskoka room to sip tea and wait for Cam to pick her up. She reached for her book, determined to finish the last chapter, but her arms were so sore she could barely hold the book on her lap. Still, she managed it and when she finished and came to the end, she snapped the book closed and hurled it onto the table. "What a stupid way to end a book."

12

Felicity pouted in disappointment for exactly three seconds longer, then looked out over the shimmering lake where she saw a familiar neon green kayak disappearing around the bend by Abby's rock. She followed the rhythm of Ben's strokes, strong and even, and felt herself wishing she was out there too, matching stroke for stroke, her kayak alongside his. Why was she going to dinner with Cam when it was Ben she wanted to be with?

She glanced at her watch, then wandered to the kitchen, picking up the discarded book on her way and tossing it onto the coffee table. Melody might enjoy it, or Olivia, or she could take it down to the Thrift Shop in town and let someone else be completely disappointed by its ending.

And just then, Cam's orange jeep pulled into her lane and parked. He was dressed in perfectly iron jeans, a button-down shirt, open at the collar and a sweater tied around his neck, like a tennis player, or a professor, she thought. He smiled when she opened the door.

"You look great," he said, leaning in to kiss her cheek.

She pulled back to avoid his kiss, then stumbled over her words and his kiss, not knowing what to say or how to feel. "Thanks," she managed, and then closed the door behind them.

"Doing some gardening?" he asked as they passed the collection of plants and soil by the garage.

"Yes. I like it. Gives me a chance to think. And I like the way the place looks, with lots of flowers blooming."

He nodded and opened her door. "Me too, but I'm not much of a gardener. I don't know a daisy from a pansy. I just like looking at them."

On the way into Huntsville, while Felicity's knees shook and her stomach knotted and unknotted itself as if she was a teenager on a blind date she had no wish to be on, Cam asked her about her work and how she'd come to do what she did.

"I liked learning what I could about my own family so I thought why not do it for other people? It's almost as if by learning about them we give them credibility, and their lives have meaning."

"How so? I mean, if they lived, isn't that enough?"

"When I learn about my ancestors and their hardships and the things they lived through, they become real to me, not just names on a page or faces in a photograph. It's as if I have taken their burdens, recognized them for what they were and said thank you. Because they did that, my life is better now, and if I acknowledge it, they will not be forgotten."

"I get it. A healing of sorts."

"That's it," Felicity said, surprised that he actually did.

"I went to a physic woman once who told me if I found ways to heal myself, my descendants would be better off. It spooked me at first, but I get it now when you say it." He drummed his fingers on the steering wheel, then grinned. "So, you're kind of like that woman. You spend all your time with dead people."

"The way you say it, it sounds awful. Let's just say I do my best to bring their memories alive again."

"Right. That does sound better."

They arrived at the restaurant, were lucky enough to find street parking out front and waited at the door to be seated. Outside, on the patio, they had a beautiful view of the water and the small boats that plied the river to and from the nearby docks. Seagulls soared overhead, then landed and searched for scraps along the waterfront. A soft breeze lifted Felicity's hair and the edge of the shawl she wore over her shoulders. In the background, soft music kept time with the flapping of rope against the masts of sailboats in the harbour. Felicity lifted her nose to smell the delicious scents emanating from the kitchen.

"I love this place," Felicity said, when their wine was poured and they had ordered their food.

"It has a certain charm, that's for sure." Cam's eyes found hers and he reached for her hand. "Sometimes it's the company that really makes a place, though."

Felicity smiled, but pulled her hand back. She wasn't ready for this yet. Dinner conversation, sure, but touching, intimately as he had, was too much, too soon, like the attempted kiss at the door, earlier. "You mentioned kids," she said, changing the subject. "How old are they?"

"Gary is twenty-nine, married with three daughters. All delightfully bright and full of p and v." Felicity cocked her head to one side and Cam leaned in to whisper. "Piss and vinegar," he said.

"Oh!"

"And Marilyn is twenty-six. Married to her job. She's VP of sales at a marketing company in Barrie. No time for kids or men… or even women, for that matter. She doesn't even belong to a book club. Go figure." He grinned. Teasing, at his daughter's expense.

"Marriage and children aren't for everyone," Felicity said.

"Sounds like you have regrets," he said.

"That's not what I meant. I have three beautiful children and there will be grandchildren one day, probably sooner than I am ready for, but I certainly don't regret having them. I love my children. I just meant that it's not the life for everyone. Some people don't want children, or marriage for that matter."

"I didn't imply you regretted the kids. It was him, I meant. Your husband."

Felicity felt a twinge of anger rising in her. She didn't want to talk about Richard, especially not to Cam. She'd dumped this baggage into the lake and didn't want to bring it up again. Did he expect her to feel as badly about her marriage as he did about his own? She refused to share his indignation.

"My husband is dead, Cam. I'll thank you for leaving it at that."

He held up his hands. "Hey, it was just an observation. I didn't mean anything by it."

Their food arrived, and they ate in grateful silence, except for Cam's intervals of praise for the cook.

When she'd had her fill of food and of Cam's phony platitudes, she picked up the conversation again. "What do you do for fun when you're not studying or teaching history?"

Swallowing a mouthful of food, he looked out at the water and nodded toward a sloop just docking below them. "Well, I like to sail. I've got a little fifteen-footer in the marina by my place in Barrie. I like outdoor concerts, movies, a play or two. What do you do when you're not digging up bones or gardens?"

"Oh goodness. That sounds awful," she said. "I read. I write a little, but nothing anyone would want to read. And I've always had a desire to learn photography."

"And you like to kayak, obviously."

"Yes, I do."

"I'm a great admirer of the arts, but I'm no painter or photographer. I heard there are some classes at the Baysville library this summer."

"Maybe I should look into that," she said.

Their waitress removed their plates and asked if they'd like coffee or dessert. Felicity watched Cam, the way he was with the waitress, a little flirty but not entirely indecent, and the way his cheeks dimpled when he smiled. Both might have been endearing, if he weren't so obviously fake in the way he talked to the girl. It was almost the same way Richard used to be, but, she realized, it was nothing like Ben.

Ben. She looked up at Cam as he was about to order dessert for them.

"I couldn't eat another bite," she said. "If you don't mind, Cam. It's been a long day and I'm exhausted."

"Sure. I get it," he said, unable to keep the annoyance from his voice. He ordered cheesecake to go, for himself, when she refused any. And then he turned to the waitress and said, "She's been on the water all afternoon and the sun has made her a little out of sorts."

And that was enough for Felicity to realize that even if she could have overlooked some of Cam's idiosyncrasies, this was something she could not forgive. He'd made her look like a fool or weakling, small and imperfect in his eyes. It was something Richard would do. There was too much of Richard in this man, she realized.

And she realized, too, that never would there be another date with Cam. His teasing was too close to the things Richard used to say. His flirting ways, too familiar, and it made her cringe when she saw the ease with which he slipped a twenty-dollar tip into the waitress's hand and the sly smile he gave her when he did. Just like Richard.

It was only eight o'clock when they pulled into her lane. The sky was darkening, but there was still time for her to enjoy the evening's sunset. Cam got out and came around to open her door and there he braced himself between the door and the frame. When he leaned in to kiss her, Felicity slipped under his arm and hurried toward the cottage.

"Thanks for the dinner," she called out as she stepped onto the porch.

"Sure. It was no trouble at all."

Her whispers to the heavens were answered when he didn't follow her to the door. Instead, he stood by his Jeep and watched as she unlocked the door and went inside. Then he got in his car and drove away. Felicity flipped the deadbolt in place and leaned against the door. She gave a little shiver then. Cam might not have been the creep her daughter described, but he was a little too creepy for her.

His book lay forgotten on the table. She'd meant to bring it along, to have him sign it with something cheeky about changing her tire for her. Now she was glad she hadn't. She might give the book away as a gift to someone who might appreciate it. She was no longer curious about anything Cam Meyers had to say.

13

Before she went to change, she found Tom and Melody in the living room, watching a movie. They were curled up on the couch together with a small furry ball between them.

"What on earth?" she said when Melody presented a small orange and white tabby kitten.

"We thought you might like someone to keep you company. And it's a girl, so you won't have to worry about the disgusting spraying business of a male cat."

Felicity held the kitten up, nose to nose, to look at her face, then nuzzled her against her neck. "Aren't you just the cutest thing?" And then she looked at Tom. "But Olivia is bringing Hope with her.

You know how she chases all the neighbour's cats. She'll hate this little one."

"About that," Tom said. "I got a call from Olivia this morning, before we went to Dorset. Hope… Well, she…" He couldn't meet Felicity's eyes.

Felicity shook her head. "No. Oh, please don't tell me something's wrong with my little Hope." She let the kitten down and she scampered away to explore her new surroundings, while Felicity sank into a chair. Tom's face told her everything she needed to know. "How did it happen?"

"After you left on Monday, Will and I went back inside to lock up and to take Hope to Olivia's place. But… she bolted, Mum. She knew you were gone, and she just made a beeline out the door and right into an oncoming car. She was still alive when we took to the vet. He thought he could save her, and she lived a little while. But when Olivia called earlier, it was to say Hope was gone. I'm sorry Mum. I'm so sorry."

"Why didn't you say something sooner? Why didn't you call me when it happened?"

Melody sat down beside her and placed a hand over hers. "If it helps, she wasn't alone. Olivia and Eric were with her at the end."

"Well, that's some consolation, at least. Oh Tom, I wish you'd called me when it happened." Felicity shot him an agonized look. "I would have turned right around."

"You would have done exactly what we did. Sat and waited. There was nothing to be gained by all of us sitting in the vet's waiting room."

"But I should have been there. Hope has always been there for me."

"I know she was a great comfort to you. But she was getting old, and Hope was a lot of work. That's why we thought a cat would be better. They take care of themselves. Pretty much." And as if agreeing with him, the kitten peeked out from under the couch and began pawing Tom's pant leg. "There you are," he said, scooping her up.

Felicity stroked her, too. "I don't know what to say. In one way, I know you're right. Hope was a lot of work, but she was the best friend I ever had. I always thought I'd be with her when her time came." She looked into the kitten's eyes as it curled itself into the warmth of Tom's lap, purring and nudging his hand for more pats. "I suppose there's nothing to be done about it now. I'll miss her. And you're right, I didn't want another dog. I hadn't planned on any more animals, really."

"But look at her, Mum. She's so cute." Tom held the cat up and turned her to face Felicity. "How can you resist that face?"

"I can't." Felicity reached out to take the kitten into her own hands and stared at the big green eyes, staring back at her. "So, what will we call you? We can't keep saying 'the kitten' or 'her'."

"She reminds me of the caramel swirls in butterscotch ice-cream. Maybe we should call her Butterscotch," Melody offered.

"Scotchy, for short," Tom suggested.

"Or we could call her Mac. Remember the boxed MacIntosh toffee we used to buy? You kids loved that stuff. She could be MacIntosh, but Mac for short."

"But she's a girl. You can't call her Mac," Tom said.

"Why not? What do you think, Mac?" Felicity stroked the kitten's ears, who mewed and nudged Felicity's hand. "See. She likes her name. Mac it is."

"I set up a litter box downstairs in the laundry room while you were out." Tom got out of his chair and bent down to kiss his mother. "I'm sorry about Hope, Mum. Really, I am."

Felicity patted the hand he'd laid on her shoulder. "I know, Hun."

"Maybe she's found Richard and is curled up at his feet," Melody suggested.

At that, Felicity and Tom both laughed. "Not likely," Tom said. "Dad hated that dog."

"I didn't know you knew," Felicity said.

"We all sort of figured it, even though you never said for sure. Kind of like other things you've never told us about," Tom said, with a hint of this morning's frustration still lingering. "But only when you're ready." He gave his mother a weak smile, squeezed her shoulder, then headed for the kitchen to refresh his beer. "Want one?" he asked Melody.

She shook her head. "But if there's popcorn…"

Later, when Tom and Melody returned to their movie, Felicity could not settle in to watch it. She had no interest in the movie they'd chosen, which was not unusual. But that wasn't the only reason for her unsettled feeling. Her dinner with Cam gnawed at her. Why had she agreed to it? Because he'd been so insistent, she told herself. But you could have said no, her conscience argued. And so went her thoughts for the first half hour or so until she finally decided she needed some air.

"I think I'll go for a walk," she said, shifting Mac off her lap and onto Melody's. "It's a beautiful night and if I hurry, I can catch the sunset."

"Take a flashlight with you," Tom reminded as she headed for the door.

"Yes, Grandpa Bailey," Felicity teased. It was exactly the kind of thing her father would have said if he were there. Although Grandpa Bailey would also have gone with her and, in his own unintrusive way, would have eked out what was troubling her. She missed him. She thought of calling Carrie, and even had her phone in her hand, when she cut through the woods between her place and Alice's.

The porch light was on, and a delicious aroma emanated from the kitchen window as she passed by. She was sure she smelled pie. She thought of Cam less than an hour ago, suggesting dessert at the restaurant. Then she hadn't wanted it, or rather, she hadn't wanted to have it with Cam. If she'd been on that patio with Ben and he'd suggested the cheesecake, she would have said, *yes let's*. But all she could think of, when she was with Cam, is how soon can I go home?

She had not yet reached the far side of Alice's woodlot when the door opened, and Ben called out to her. "Hey Felicity. Want company?"

Oh yes, please, she thought. But she called back, "I don't want to interfere with your plans." She met him halfway along the path. "I have to ask. What are you baking in there? It smells divine."

"Cherry pie." He shrugged. "It's a weakness of mine. And I'm not baking it. Only warming it up. It's from that little shop in town where I got the butter tarts. I ate the rest of those for lunch and then went back for more. I cannot eat a whole pie by myself. I can paddle from here to Toronto, and I won't wear it all off."

Felicity smiled. "Cherry is one of my favourites too."

"Good." He rubbed his hands together. "Maybe when we get back, you'll join me. Now, where are we headed?"

"Well, I was just going to the end of the beach, but if you're game, there's a place I sometimes like to watch the sunset. It's about a mile or so up the road. By the time we get there, it'll be perfect."

"Let's do it."

They turned left onto the ring road and began the climb over the first of three hills before they came to Lookout Point. After bumping shoulders and arms two or three times, apologizing for it and laughing at the awkwardness of it, Ben took her hand in his. "Is this okay?" he asked, his eyes searching hers.

"It is very okay," she said simply, as a warm sensation drifted up her arm and into her heart. To the left, the lake shimmered in the evening glow, the pine trees on their right whispered their approval.

"If it's not prying," Felicity said, after a time. "Did you talk to Emma today? Weren't you supposed to have dinner?"

"Huh! A sore spot right now."

"Oh no. She didn't stand you up, did she?"

"No. She came. She was all dressed up. Had done her hair and spent money at a nail bar, she told me. She looked so grown up, so beautiful. It made me feel old."

"We are all getting older, one day at a time." Felicity placed her other hand on his arm and urged him to tell her more.

"I was an idiot. I was flattered that she'd gone to all that trouble to look nice just for me, and I told her so. But it seems she had a date afterwards, so it wasn't me she'd dressed up for. It was someone else."

There was no mistaking the look of disappointment on his face, and Felicity felt a pang of sympathy rush through her. "But she came. What did she say?"

He shrugged and tears brimmed his eyes. He could hardly speak. In a moment or two he said, "She's angry. I don't blame her. She's just learned that her mother and aunt have been lying to her all these years. She also knows that I'm not her real father, and that has come as a real shock. But most of all, she can't come to terms with why I left and if I'm honest, neither can I. I've been harbouring a lot of guilt over it for a long time. I can't help thinking if I'd stayed and fought harder, done something more, things would be different now. I mean, it never mattered that she wasn't mine. I always treated her as if she was, anyway. I still think of her as mine."

"What else could you have done?"

"I don't know. Something, I suppose. But I didn't. So, I'll never know. I just left. I had an opportunity to go, and I took it." He stopped then and looked down at her, swiping his tears with the back of his hand. "Sorry, I'm such an old fool."

"Not a fool." She gave his hand a squeeze. "A softie, maybe. But not a fool."

"She's so angry, Felicity. I don't know if she'll ever forgive any of us. She says her mother doesn't remember any of this. And with her aunt gone now, I'm all she has left. I won't give up trying this time. In her head, she knows what's right. It's her heart that won't accept it."

"Oh Ben. I'm so sorry. Do you think she'll come around?"

He shrugged again, and they continued walking. "Maybe. I hope so. I invited her to come out this weekend. She said no at first, then later she said she'd think about it. So, I'm hopeful, but I'm also not counting on it. I hope you don't mind, but I mentioned my neighbour's family would be here. Young people her own age. I hoped it might be the clincher that would bring her out."

"I don't mind at all, and I'm sure they will all get along famously. The others will be up tomorrow, after work. Did you mention the risotto challenge? Maybe that would entice her."

"I did. But then she informed me she doesn't eat carbs, so I don't know."

"Oh, I know those frustrations. Olivia went through a vegetarian phase. Thank goodness she got over that, but her boyfriend is keto-friendly, and Melody is lactose intolerant. So much for the old Bailey family tradition of meat, potatoes and two veg."

He laughed. "Poor Grandma Bailey."

Felicity groaned. "She'd be rolling over in her grave if she knew her grandchildren were such fussy eaters."

They rounded a bend in the road and came upon the place Felicity wanted. "Here. See, there are steps carved into the side of the hill. There's no cottage on top, but someone must have built these. There's even a handrail part way up."

They climbed the fifty-three steps carved into the dirt and rock at the side of the cliff and came out on a ridge topside where on the flat surface someone had put a bench. A canopy of leaves overhead whispered secrets in the night air as Felicity led Ben to the bench. The view of the lake and the sunsetting was breathtaking. They were just in time.

"This is new," she said, settling onto the bench. Ben sat down beside her, so close their shoulders and thighs touched. She smiled at the pleasant smell of his aftershave, the spice of it reminding her of the kind her father used to wear. "Isn't this amazing?" she said, turning to the view below them.

"It is," he said, sighing softly as the sky became a brilliant spectacle of lavender and deepest purples and bounced off the water, sending shimmering ripples to every curve of their little cove. And in the not too far off distance, they heard the scattering of small creatures beneath the underbrush. A chipmunk skittered into the clearing, stopped when it saw unexpected humans, and dashed off in the other direction as if in a hurry to warn the others of his kind.

"I used to tell the kids that if they used their imagination just a little, they might see fairies dancing across the water." She rested her head on Ben's shoulder. "There is nothing like a Ril Lake sunset," she said.

His arm went around her, pulling her into the crook of his shoulder, and there they stayed until the only light they could see were the specs of porch lights in the distance below. And then he lifted her chin and their eyes met. "Can I kiss you?" he asked.

"Oh, I wish you would," she answered.

It felt as natural as taking a breath and required no thought at all. Ben cupped her face between his oh, so gentle hands, and held her gaze until the very last moment. Their lips touched. And that touch was sweet and tender and perfectly and uniquely theirs. The intimacy in that kiss, in his touch on her cheeks, sent a shiver of wonder down Felicity's spine. She bent her head shyly, till he kissed her a second time, and this time she wanted more. She wanted to know this man who was so gentle and kind, who could turn her anger into laughter, and her pain into joy. Who are you, Ben Pierce, she wondered? And where have you been all my life?

They parted, lips lingering there a moment before he whispered. "I knew that would be nice." And then he pulled her into his arms and kissed again, stirring a long-forgotten passion within Felicity that she could not deny. They broke apart breathless and rested their foreheads against each other's.

"Wow," she said.

"Double wow."

She rested her head on his shoulder, content to be in his arms, silent in the darkness, while their hearts began to beat in tandem, like two kayakers paddling in unison across the lake. Felicity held her breath and counted her heartbeats, still not quite sure she was living this. Or was this a dream? But she was very much alive and awake, and enjoying the intimacy of that moment.

A moment later and she found herself wanting to tell Ben about what she'd done that day. "I went for a paddle this afternoon. I took your advice and opened my suitcases and dumped out the baggage."

He smiled and squeezed her shoulder. "I thought there was something different about you tonight. You seem lighter, somehow. Not so burdened."

"Can I tell you something?" she asked.

"Anything. You know that."

"It's about that big rock. Abby's rock. You might have noticed a little blond girl in the pictures on the mantel in the living room. Abby was Tom's twin sister, born right just minutes after him."

"Was?"

"She drowned, out there in the lake."

"Oh Felicity. I'm so sorry."

"Thank you. It was years ago, now. We were here for our usual family Christmas. We spent a week up here every year, from Boxing Day to New Year's Day. The kids all got new skates that year. We had them sharpened so they could use them right away. The lake always freezes over in December and when they opened their presents, Tom put on his skates and took off. Abby was never far behind her brother, but she was not as fast as he was at tying them up. She was impatient and just couldn't get her skates on fast enough. And Tom wouldn't wait. He hit the ice before her and was halfway around the cove when she stepped onto the ice. He stuck to the rule we have about skating close to the shoreline in case…" Felicity hiccupped a huge sigh and lowered her head. This was the first time she'd told this story in years.

"But Abby didn't?"

Felicity shook her head as tears welled in her eyes. "She was too impatient. She wanted to catch up to Tom. She headed straight across the bay to cut him off at the rock. But before she got there…" Felicity took another big breath. "The sound of ice cracking and Abby's screams still haunt my dreams, even after all this time." She gave a little shudder. "I'm sorry. It's just so…"

Ben pulled her closer and held her until Felicity's sobs lessened.

"I'm so sorry. No one should ever have to go through that," he whispered softly.

"Oh Ben, it was the most horrific sound I've ever heard. A sound so ominous and creepy. It was like the worst crack of thunder you can imagine, and it came out of nowhere. Then Abby's screams, piercing the air, like a knife piercing my heart. And then she was gone. Just gone. She came up twice, arms flailing. We flew down the beach, stumbling over rocks under the snow and docks that hadn't been taken out for the winter. Tom raced to the shoreline and grabbed a stick. He screamed at her to grab it, but there was nothing he could do. She didn't come up again. And we... Richard and I just couldn't get there fast enough. By the time we made our way around the shoreline, there was nothing left but her hat floating on the surface. Abby was nowhere to be seen. We were helpless. Our little girl just disappeared."

Ben pulled her closer, resting his chin on her head. He stroked her hair and cooed in her ear. "I'm so sorry. I'm so sorry. When she looked up at him, there were tears in his eyes, too.

Felicity swiped at her tears. "A neighbour called 911 and the search and rescue team brought out diving equipment. They searched all that day with no results. Finally, she turned up across the lake. She'd drifted under the ice with the current. There was nothing anyone could do." Felicity sighed. "There will always be a hallow in my heart where Abby used to be. But the worst of it was that I have spent the last fourteen years blaming Richard. They wanted him to go too, and I kept thinking if he'd just put down that damned drink and put on his skates, Abby wouldn't have drowned and we'd all be together, still. And then I felt guilty for blaming him, guilty that I might have done something differently that could have changed him, changed us, so he would change his ways. I felt guilty that I'm married him and thought maybe he would have been happier with someone else."

"You can't know that, though, Felicity."

"I know. But it took his death for me to realize it. So, that's what I dumped in the lake today. I let go of the guilt and the blame we both dumped on each other, and I let go of the bitterness between us when our already suffering marriage did a complete nosedive."

"Oh Felicity. What a horrible thing to carry with you all this time. And now he's gone and can't speak to any of it."

"That's it exactly. I think coming up here now, after his death, has dredged it all up again, but this time for a good reason. This time, I have to find a way to let it go." She turned to face him. "And I have you to thank for that. You encouraged me to unpack the suitcases and get rid of the baggage. I will never forget the years Richard and I spent together, but at least I don't hate him anymore for them anymore."

Ben smiled. "And you did all this today?"

"Yes. This afternoon. I went out for a long paddle and got some things straight in my head. Why do you ask?"

His lips worked themselves into a mischievous grin when he said, "Because I could swear there was an old duffle bag floating in the water when I came back to the dock this afternoon. Must have been one of yours."

She laughed then and punched him playfully on the arm. "Funny," she said, softly. And then she began to feel the chill of the night air and the rustle of the leaves overhead seemed to agree when she said maybe it was time to leave.

"Still want some pie?" he asked.

"I certainly do."

Ben pulled his phone from his pocket, switched on the flashlight app, and took her hand in his. "Here's the handrail," he said, reaching out to it. "Let me go first. That way, if you stumble, you'll fall into me."

"And knock you all the way down the cliff," she said, laughing. "What happens if you fall?"

"I won't. I'm as sure-footed as a mountain goat."

"Alright Billy," she teased. "Remember, I've done this a hundred times before, on my own, without a hero to rescue me."

"Yes, but I didn't know you then."

"I wish you had," she whispered to herself. What if she'd met Ben instead of Richard that last year of university? They might have married, and Richard might have married someone else; someone who made him happy. How different would all their lives have been? But nothing could change what had happened and, she reminded herself, she'd tossed all that stuff into the lake earlier. There was only today and the future, and the prospect that Ben just might be a part of that delighted her.

Back at his cottage, they enjoyed a sumptuous piece of still-warm cherry pie with vanilla ice-cream on top, and several cups of coffee while Felicity told Ben more about Richard and the difficulties of her marriage. It was easy to talk to Ben once she got started. She even told him about the wreckage she'd left on Slim Meyers' beach. She did not mention her dinner with Cam, however. It didn't seem necessary to tell him, and besides, there was nothing to it. Nothing at all.

Ben told her that he had never married, even after he'd left Nancy and Emma, because he'd moved around too much, and an absentee husband would cause difficulties. And he was already absent from one child's life. The last thing he wanted to do was miss out on raising another.

When they walked back to her cottage, and lingered on the lower deck, to kiss and whisper goodnight, Felicity wondered if Tom and Melody hadn't been there, would she have invited Ben to come inside, or would she have stayed with him, if he'd asked? It was warm and safe in his arms, and the desire he ignited in her was undeniable. She felt like a teenager again and the feeling was wonderful. It was so long since she'd felt this way about someone, she was sure she'd suppressed these emotions forever. Apparently not.

She kept watch as he made his way back through the stretch of woods that separated their properties until she could no longer see the light from his phone bobbing up and down. And then she heard the slap of his door against the frame and saw the porch light flick off. Only then did she reach for the handrail to climb the stairs to the top deck, and only then did she realize Melody was standing on it, looking out over the lake.

How long had she been there and what had she seen? Felicity was certain she and Ben had been alone when they first arrived. And when they'd kissed, it was under the canopy of the gazebo. She hadn't heard her patio door slide open, or footsteps cross the deck above them. So, it made sense that Melody must have been there the entire time, alone in the darkness.

She did not want to have to provide explanations to Tom—and eventually her other children, because he would tell them. How could she possibly explain that when she was in Ben's arms, years of loneliness faded away and she felt safe and cared for?

When she came to the top step, Melody was bathed in the soft light of her phone, reading something or sending a message. She glanced her way. "Beautiful night, isn't it?" Melody said, flashing her an approving smile. It seemed to say, *'I'm happy for you and your secret is safe with me.'*

14

Felicity slept late the following morning and, having no plans other than preparing for her other children to arrive, she lounged in her pyjamas, enjoying the misty morning view from the Muskoka room, and her second cup of coffee. Mac came to sit on her lap and pushed at the pages of the book she was not really reading, demanding attention and not stopping even when she got it.

"You're a pest, you know," Felicity laughed, stroking her back. "But a pest of the nicest kind." As she settled Mac in her lap, she heard footsteps coming up the stairs from the lower deck. She gathered the kitten closer to her, hoping it was Tom or Melody, but remembering even before the top of Ben's head came into view, that they had gone to *Yummies in a Jar*, in search of some maple syrup for their pancakes.

Ben reached the top deck and raised a hand to knock on the door until he noticed her watching him. "Oh, you're here?" he said in a surprised tone. "I thought I should have gone around the front but, I remembered you like to sit here with your coffee. Oh. You're not dressed yet." He glanced at his watch. "Really? It's nearly ten. Are you feeling alright?"

She knew he was teasing by the way his mouth curved into a smile and his eyes sparkled in the morning light. "Come in," she said. "I'll get you a coffee."

He settled into a chair that faced her and not the lake. "Nice view," he said as she pushed out of her chair.

"Flirt," she teased as she headed for the kitchen.

"And don't bother to get dressed," he called after her. "At least not on my account."

She did dress though, hastily, into jeans and a fresh summer top, and came back moments later, a coffee in each hand, and found him on the loveseat with Mac curled up on his lap. "She'll love you forever if you aren't careful."

"Who is this and where did she come from? I didn't know you had a cat."

"It's a bit of a story, really. My dog died. She ran into the street, chasing after me, the day I left home and was hit by a car."

"Oh Felicity. I am so sorry. Are you alright?" He squeezed her hand.

"I'm okay now."

"I had to leave Bruno when I came home. He's my boxer. He didn't die, mind you, but I left him behind all the same. He was such a comfort to me, helped me through a lot of lonely nights. I miss him. When I get settled, wherever I settle, I'll get another one. They're such great companions."

"Well, the kids thought I needed company, so that's why they bought me the cat. Also, they thought she would be less work than a dog."

"Cats are usually pretty independent."

"But you're not fond of them?" She detected a little dislike in his tone.

"Don't get me wrong. I like them, but they just do their own thing. A dog gives you innocent and unconditional love, always. You'll never get that from a cat."

"Oh, I don't know about that. Mac is pretty affectionate. I loved Hope. She was a great comfort to me, but she was getting on and I didn't think I'd have another pet but if I'm going to have one, a cat's independent nature makes it ideal, really. And I must confess, Mac is cute, and we liked each other instantly."

"Well, she certainly is cute. I can't argue with that." Mac squinted blissfully when Ben petted her, contented just as Felicity was last night, by his caresses. I know just how you feel, Mac, she thought. He's stable and safe and warm and…

"Felicity?" Ben was talking, and she hadn't heard him.

"Hmm?"

He grinned. "You were somewhere else just then. I said that Emma called earlier. She's coming out on Saturday, but just for the day."

"Oh, Ben, that's wonderful news. I'll tell Tom. You guys can always do the risotto challenge another time. Do you want to plan something together, with all my gang, or would you prefer to be alone with her?"

"Oh, I think safety in numbers applies here." Ben grinned. "If you don't mind."

"Well then. We can barbeque and have a campfire later."

"I told her to bring a bathing suit, and I mentioned kayaks and canoes. That was presumptuous, but so I hope it's okay."

"It's perfectly fine. You know it is. And I ordered a couple of paddle boards after I trashed the wooden kayak yesterday. I should be able to pick them up before she comes."

"So, this is all okay, then."

"Of course it is. This will be wonderful. Will and Olivia and Eric will be here tonight. Why don't you join us for supper and meet them before Emma comes?"

"I would love to, but I have something on in town. A supper engagement of sorts."

It was impossible to keep the disappointment and a twinge of jealousy from her face. Felicity knew instantly that she had no right to feel that way, but it was too late. Ben saw her reaction and was already reaching out to take her hand.

"I made these arrangements ages ago," he explained. "Before I met you."

"I'm sorry," she said. "I just thought… I mean… Ben, I have no right…" Her words spilled unchecked out of her mouth, while she reminded herself she just had dinner with Cam, and there was no real commitment between them.

He took her hand in his and kissed her palm. "It's just a work thing, I promise. Someone Alice knows bought a lot on Echo Lake and wants to build a house. We arranged this through emails before I came up here. And if you weren't expecting the rest of your family, I'd say join us. But then we'd be talking shop and that might be boring for you."

"Ben. I'm sorry," Felicity finally blurted out. "We've just met and really a few kisses in the moonlight doesn't give me the right to have thoughts or opinions about anything you do."

"I'm glad you do. It's nice to know someone cares where I go and what I do. I know we don't know each other well and it's early in this… friendship or whatever this is, but believe me, those weren't just a few nonchalant kisses. At least not for me. I care for you very much, Felicity. I hope there are more kisses to come and walks along the beach, and beautiful sunsets and wonderful talks under the moonlight."

She smiled at him. "Me too, Ben. I just…"

"Hey, I'm not asking you to limit your social calendar, if that's what you're thinking."

Felicity took a big gulp. Should she tell him how comfortable she felt with him, how much her dinner with Cam last night had made her realize that there was no one else she wanted to be with? But it was early days, as Ben said; too soon to make a bold statement about who they were together.

"I haven't much of a social calendar. It's a bit of work, the kids. And hopefully some time with you."

He smiled. "Good. And since that's settled, we can just say we're neighbours for now, if you'd rather not put this relationship in a category. For now."

"I like that," she said.

"Me too. So, neighbour, the reason I came over this morning was this besides telling you about Emma, is that I'm hoping you'll come to Algonquin Park today, if you don't have anything pressing. I want to put up some canvas photos to spruce up Alice's cottage a little. Why not take some local shots? Are you in?"

"I'd love to, but I must be back in time for the kids. They'll be here around four."

Ben pulled out his phone. "I mapped it out. It's forty minutes to get there. If we leave now, we can be back in plenty of time."

"I'll just leave a note for Tom and Melody."

Algonquin Park was always on Felicity's to-do list when she was at the cottage, no matter what the season. The magnificent colour in autumn was her favourite and driving up highway 60, with every imaginable shade of orange and rust, gold and red, was breathtaking. But now, in the middle of June, when everything was green and spring had already brought new life to the park, and the streams burbled and trickled along, the park was a hiker's dream.

"If we are lucky, we might spot a moose or two," Felicity told Ben as they turned onto the highway.

"Just as long as we're a good distance away. I don't want any moose thinking I'm going to be his next meal. I've had too many narrow escapes with lions and elephants. I know better than to get too close to wildlife."

"Moose don't eat meat," she said with a grin. "Besides, you've brought that ginormous lens." She jerked her thumb over her shoulder to where Ben's camera equipment lay on the back seat. "You could probably be a mile away and still get a great shot."

Ben laughed. "Maybe not a mile, but it is a good lens. I got some great shots of in Africa."

"I'd love to see them sometime."

"Would you, really? Most people say they would and then, after the first few, they're bored. I don't want to bore you."

"No, honestly. I would like to see them. I wish I knew how to take decent pictures. But then I'd have to have a proper camera, and I'd have to learn how to use it. My phone doesn't really cut it. I'll bet you've taken a few magazine-worthy shots with that equipment."

He grinned. "I have had a few in the National Geographic and Orion Magazine."

"That's amazing! I can't wait to see them."

"I could teach you what I know about photography, if you'd like."

"Oh yes, please. I'd like that, but I'll warn you, you'll find me an impatient student. I get frustrated with myself when I can't work things out."

"That surprises me, considering the amount of time it must take you to research someone's family tree. That's hours of focused work. I know because I spent two hours using some of those free genealogy sites you recommended. It's a never-ending rabbit hole."

"You should have said something. I would have helped you."

Ben shrugged. "It was fun, really. I was hoping I could find something more about Emma's mother's family, to pass along to her, something to show her the entire clan isn't like her mother and her aunt."

"Did you find anything?"

"Not much. Just a few old census records from somewhere near Windsor. Nancy's family came from that way, but these records are for 1911 and 1921, so I don't know for sure."

"I'd be glad to help if you like and exchange for helping me with photography. I don't know anything beyond aim and click."

"Point and shoot."

"Sorry?"

"Never mind." Ben patted her hand. "You'll get the hang of it. Oh look, there's the information centre. Let's ask where the best trails are."

15

It was nearing four o'clock when Olivia's charcoal grey sedan pulled into the driveway, followed by a bright red sports car Felicity did not recognize. When Will got out of it, Felicity let out a deep sigh. Will didn't own a car unless he'd just bought one, which she hoped was not the case. He did not need to add a car payment to his already accumulating debts.

She went out to greet them, propping the door open so they could bring in their cases. "Why didn't you come up together? The price of gas alone would be reason enough." Eric rolled suitcases onto the porch and Olivia pushed past him to give Felicity a hug. Will followed closely behind them, lugging an obviously heavy cooler with two small boxes stacked on top.

"Hi Mum." He kissed her cheek. "Doing some gardening?" He nodded toward the still unplanted pots and stack of soil.

"Yes, want to help?" Felicity asked, relieving him of some of his burden. "Whose car is that, by the way?"

"Don't worry," Will said, plunking the cooler down on the kitchen floor. He stood up and stretched, getting the long drive kinks out of his limbs. "It isn't mine. I borrowed it from Luke. He's fine taking the bus for a couple of weeks."

"A couple of weeks? What about work?" Instantly, Will's shoulders sagged, and his gaze fell to the floor the way they always did when his life was spinning out of control.

Felicity's heart sank for him. "Oh no. Not again."

Will said nothing, his eyes darting everywhere, avoiding hers. He scratched his head and pulled at the collar of his hoodie. "Yeah, I need to sort a few things out."

Tom came from the living room to help and to greet his siblings, or perhaps to ride Will. "I thought it was your dream job." He said sarcastically, drawing air quotes around the words. "If I recall, you said you were going straight to the top to take over from what's-his-face who runs it now."

Felicity looked at Will. "Never mind him. What happened?"

"It wasn't as good as I thought, okay? Can we drop it?" Will's face flushed red, his voice raised in defensive anger. His voice softened when he looked at his mother. "For now, at least?"

"Don't yell at Mum," Tom hissed. "It isn't her fault you can't keep a job."

"I wasn't yelling at her. I was yelling at you. And I could keep a job, if I could find one I liked." Will retorted. "Sorry, I don't have a university degree behind my name like you do."

"Whose fault is that?" Tom said, nudging closer to Will, towering over his brother with a challenging look on his face.

Both of them towered over Felicity, but she stepped between them and put a hand on each of their chests. "Alright boys, enough. This is supposed to be a nice relaxing weekend for all of us. This is something Will and I can talk about later." She patted Will's chest as Tom grunted, pushed past them, and went to help unload the cars.

Will looked at his mother. "I'm sorry, Mum. And I promise I'll find something else. I just need some time."

"Come here." Felicity pulled him into a hug. "I know you will, sweetheart." It was his fifth job in the two years since he'd dropped out of university. Each job brought another complaint about something. He didn't like the people. He'd fudged his resume to get the job and then couldn't do the work. The position didn't pay enough, or it was beneath him. It was always something. And every time, Felicity had bailed him out. Tom and Olivia didn't know she was paying Will's portion of the bills at the apartment he shared with his friend Luke. Richard had been hard on Will, but Tom was even tougher. Olivia would have smothered him with platitudes. Will needed neither of these to help him get on.

She knew that at some point, Will had to figure it out. Something had to give, and this lackadaisical attitude toward work had to stop. She understood his frustration, but it didn't soothe the disappointment she felt with him, and with herself for letting it go this far. She saw the despair in Will's eyes and rubbed a soothing hand up and down his arm. "We'll figure this out, okay?"

He nodded and collapsed against her again, sobbing until her shoulder was wet from his tears. "I'm sorry, Mum. I really am. I'm such a failure."

"You're not a failure, Will." She held him at arm's length to look him in the eye. "Let's just chill. You're here now and if there is any place to relax and get your head on straight, this is it, right? That's what Grandpa Bailey always said. So, let's worry about it later. Alright?" She brushed a hand over the beautiful face of her youngest. So, like her mother, with his sandy coloured hair, and fine features and that smile that played at the corners of his mouth.

Olivia joined them and put her arms around them both and reached for Tom as he passed by. "Family hug," she said, laughing, as Tom tried to squiggle away. "Come on. We made this a thing when Dad died, remember? None of us knows how long we'll be here, so while we can, we hug. And we appreciate each other for who we are, not who we expect them to be." She thumped Tom on the shoulder as the group broke apart. "Right, big brother?"

"Yeah, I guess." Reluctance laced Tom's words until Melody came into the room too, and put her arm around Tom's waist and poked a finger in his ribs. "Sorry Will," Tom said, finally.

Felicity turned around, as if looking for someone. "Where's Eric? Ah, there you are." He set down the things he was carrying. "Come here and join this family hug."

"We don't do this in my family," Eric said as Felicity pulled him into the group. "But I kinda like it."

"I'm glad all of you are here," Felicity said with tears in her eyes as they separated. And then she rubbed her hands together and surveyed her children. "Goodness, you all look starved. When did you last eat?"

"Yesterday, wasn't it?" Eric teased, taking Olivia's hand.

"Pfft. You ate two big macs, an extra-large fry and a large coke on the way up. Don't give him anything, Mum."

"Hey a man's gotta eat. Don't stifle my growth spurt." Eric began unpacking the grocery bags they brought. "How about this? Olivia brought everything for Shepherd's Pie. It's my favourite."

"I thought you were doing the keto diet?" Felicity asked.

"That didn't last," Olivia told her. "A man needs his carbs, or so he says." She sent a flippant look at Eric. "Right honey?"

"You always are, my dear." Eric kissed Olivia on the cheek as he accepted a beer from Tom.

"Oh, brother!" Will said. "Get a room, you two."

Eric's light-hearted mood broke the tension, and everyone spoke at once about the drive up, the traffic, the weather to come over the weekend, and the best recipe for Shepherd's Pie. The boys went to fix drinks and put the extend the dining room table and to set it, while the girls got to work on supper. Felicity chopped onions. Melody peeled potatoes, and Olivia fried the meat and opened tins of corn.

Later, when they gathered around the table, Felicity watched the faces of her children glowing in the candlelight and was overcome with the warmth of their presence. Their laughter and gentle kibbitzing felt familiar and comfortable and it warmed her heart. Will's situation still loomed over them, but for now, it was forgotten. This was what being at the cottage was all about, she thought. Here was where you left the worries of day-to-day life at the end of the laneway and let the serenity of cottage life take you away. She wondered, for a moment, if that same sense of tranquility would still be here if she made this her permanent home? Or would the novelty of it wear off? Grandpa Bailey's words came back to her. *'Home is not the four walls you're in, Felicity, but the people you are with.'*

Grandpa Bailey was a wise man, she thought as Olivia set a bowl of moose track ice-cream in front of her. "My favourite," Felicity said. "It was good of you to remember."

Later, when the table was cleared, Eric and Melody offered to do dishes, leaving Felicity alone with her children. "I've ordered some paddle boards and a few other things," she told them. "I have to go into town to pick them up tomorrow. I could use some help, Will, if you don't mind."

"We were going to take the kayaks out tomorrow," Olivia said. Felicity knew Olivia was doing her best to keep her brother from being subjected to a maternal lecture.

"Well, one kayak and one canoe, actually," Felicity said. "I smashed The Old Gal on some rocks the other day. That reminds me, you should avoid the channel. Someone bought the Keating place and shifted all the big boulders out of the front and dumped them in the lake."

"Can they do that?" Will asked.

Felicity shook her head. "I don't think so, but they did it, and if you don't avoid them, you'll be in trouble. There's no marker. Best to stay out of the channel altogether or, if you do go in, use the McGregor side and steer clear of Keating's dock."

"Someone can share the canoe with me," Will said, his tone hopeful. Obviously, he thought the same as Olivia and wanted to avoid his mother's lecture.

Tom nudged his elbow. "Don't argue, bud. Just do what you're told for once." Felicity shot Tom a warning glance, which he ignored, his words jabbing away at the last of Will's pride. "You can't always get out of doing what's expected of you. Not at work and not with Mum. She asked for help. She's bought stuff for us. Can't you just be grateful, for once?"

Felicity watched the colour deepen in Will's face and gave him silent credit for not pushing back at Tom. It was she who did that. "I appreciate what you're trying to do, Tom, but could you leave this between Will and I please?"

"You're too soft on him. You always have been. He needs a kick in the ass and if you won't do it, who will?" Tom argued.

"Not you!" Felicity shot back. "You're his brother, not his father. You should be supporting him, not criticizing his every move."

"Geez Mum. Now who's being harsh? I was just trying to help," Tom retorted, pushing back from the table.

"Okay. Okay. Everyone, just cool down," Olivia stood up, her hands raised in a surrender mode. "Tom, why don't you pick out a board game or something?"

"I don't feel much like playing games," Tom sneered. "But I'm sure Will does. He's great at games."

Before anyone could respond, Tom stomped away, throwing his hands in the air as he did. He was taking his role as the man of the family far too seriously for Felicity's liking. Olivia was the peacemaker, Tom was the authority figure, and Will just trailed along after them, trying not to screw up in anyone's eyes.

Will fished for the keys in his pocket. "I need to get out of here."

"Wait, Will," Felicity said. "Don't go away angry. It'll be dark before long and there are no lights on the roads back here. And if you're angry and you drive too fast, you'll spin out on the gravel. And then you might go crashing down a ravine or something. Just go for a walk if you really need to let off steam. It's what I do. Please."

He left his keys on the table and nodded. "Yeah, alright. I'm so mad I'd probably miss a turn and end up in the lake." He bent to kiss her cheek. "I'll help you tomorrow, Mum." He shot a glance over his shoulder in the direction Tom had gone. "It's like he's trying to replace Dad or something. Where does he get off?"

Felicity wondered the same thing. And when she heard Tom grumble at Olivia about something, in the other room, she grabbed her hoodie from the hook by the door, ducked her head into the living room to say she was going for a walk too and left.

She spotted the light of Will's phone from halfway up the laneway, so she went down by the beach to walk along the shoreline, to give him some space and to give her some time to think, too. There was just enough of a sandy strip there for her to walk half a mile or so, sit on a rock at the end of it and watch the sunset. And that's what she intended to do.

She wanted to sort things out in her own mind so that when she sat down with Will over the next day or two, she came at the problem from a positive and supportive side. Will could be cocky and sound full of youthful assurance, but the truth was, he'd always walked in the shadow of his siblings, never quite living up to anyone's expectations, especially his own. And now he suffered for it. No confidence, low self-esteem, no one to give him a nudge when he needed it, had all led to what he called failures. Perhaps she'd spoiled him too much, let him get away with more than the others. Tom made good points, but bullying his brother was not going to stir him into action; at least, nothing constructive. Why had Tom gone way overboard with Will, pushing him far more than he needed to? It was cruel, and that wasn't like Tom. He strove for the best in himself, and at work, he was known for encouraging others to find that in themselves. But his reactions with Will told her something was eating at him; something she would get to eventually. But first, she needed to help Will learn to accept his responsibilities, pay his own bills, and stick with something even if it wasn't his dream, until something better came along. She thought about Carleton University and the disappointment he'd shown at his failure to complete the course. And then it hit her. She had an idea and just maybe something better for Will was right around the corner.

16

The sunset had been a brilliant display of colour, as it almost always was, but, like the hint of grey still lingering in the night sky, a hint of frustration still lingered in Felicity's thoughts. Was Olivia her only happy child right now? They say a parent is only as happy as their saddest child and just then, Felicity felt pretty downtrodden.

"Penny for your thoughts, neighbour?"

Felicity was passing Ben's cottage on her way back, and he was sitting on the deck with a steaming mug of something in his hand, silhouetted by the porch light. He wore a contented smile when he looked down at her.

"I think it's a dime now. Inflation being what it is."

"You're probably right." He patted the chair beside him. "Want to join me? It's nice and quiet over here."

Felicity winced. "You didn't hear us earlier, did you?"

Ben cocked his head to one side. "While you were gone, it was a little rowdy. A bit of shouting, a couple of doors slammed. Just sibling stuff, I'm guessing. It didn't warrant getting the police out here, though."

He was teasing, and she knew it, but still she was mortified that he'd had to put up with the noise. "I'm sorry. I'll speak to them about that. Wait… You saw me walk by but didn't say anything?"

"I didn't want to interfere. You seemed pretty focused on your feet."

She laughed. "Yeah, sometimes it feels like they are the only thing holding me up."

"Come on up. I'll get you something hot and we can listen to the crickets sing."

"That sounds lovely. And there's something I want to talk to you about. I'm hoping you'll help me with it." She sat in the chair next to him and lifted the lid of his teapot, sitting on the warmer. The dancing flames cast flickers of light off the metal of the warmer. "That's smells great."

"I'll just get another cup." He pushed out of his chair. "It's ginger. Is that okay?"

"I can't think of anything better to soothe my nerves," she said softly.

"I can," he grinned mischievously. "But we don't know each other that well." He leaned down to whisper. "Yet."

Felicity felt a flush of heat rush from her belly and burst up her neck and into her cheeks. She was about to offer some witty quip, but by the time she'd thought of something, he was inside, rummaging around in the dishwasher for a clean cup.

Neighbours with benefits, she thought as Ben's whistling carried through the open kitchen window. Was it too soon? When did people do those things nowadays? It had been so long since she'd dated anyone, since she'd been intimate with anyone, she was not just out of practice, she was out of touch. Still, she couldn't deny the thought had crossed her mind.

He came from the cottage, wearing a wheat coloured homespun cardigan, with an empty cup in one hand, a thick knitted shawl in the other. "I'm guessing this belongs to Alice. I thought you might want it. It's getting a little chilly. Or we could sit inside, if you'd rather."

"It's lovely out here," she said. It wasn't really a fib. The damp was settling in, and an evening mist swirled across the lake. But she loved sitting outside and this chill of a June evening was the promise of the hot summer nights to come. "But the shawl would be nice." He draped it over her shoulders and poured her a cup of hot tea. "Mmm," she said, savoring the aroma.

He refilled his own cup, too. "I was wondering about a restaurant. The Pub by the Dock in Huntsville. You've been there, I assume?"

She shot him a questioning look. Did he know about her dinner with Cam? Was this his way of questioning her about it? She flinched, feeling Richard's familiar interrogation coming from Ben. She bit back an instinctive retort and kept her voice even. "The food is always good there, and the patio is nice this time of year."

"Good to know." He nodded and sipped his tea. "I was thinking of asking Emma to go there sometime."

Felicity sighed. Not an accusation, she realized.

Ben continued. "I ran into Cameron Meyers outside the library. It was his suggestion to try it."

Felicity's face burned. "How do you know Cam?"

"Oh, that's an odd thing, actually. He was part of a volunteer group of teachers on one of builds in Africa a few years ago. They came to help set up a secondary school and promote education among the natives. He took a one-year sabbatical to help. And he wrote a book about his time there."

"*A Year in the Wilds of Africa*," she said. Maybe she should give the book to Ben, if Cam hadn't given him one already.

"Yes. That's the title, he told me."

An image of Cam and Ben standing outside the library, talking about her, jumped into her head. Were they and, if so, what had Cam told Ben about her? Had he mentioned that he'd tried to kiss her, but she avoided him? Or worse, had he told Ben there was something between them that there was not? And why were they talking about her in the first place?

"It's a small world, isn't it?" she managed to say.

Ben gave a little grunt. "Small world is right. I never imagined I'd see him again, let alone find out his father owns a cottage around the corner. Crazy really. Neither of us could believe it. Or that we both know you."

So they had been talking about her.

"Crazy isn't the word I'd choose," she mumbled. Felicity couldn't keep the anger from her voice, though she regretted it the moment she'd spoken. "While you and Cam had this little reunion, how was it that my name came up? Did you toss a coin to see who would have dibs on the widow on Ril Cove Road?"

"What? No!" Ben shifted in his chair to face her, his eyes locking with hers though she wanted to look away. "Felicity, it wasn't like that. I literally bumped into him outside the library. He'd gone to drop off some more copies of his book, and I was there looking for something to read. He said he'd like to reminisce over a drink sometime, so I suggested then was as good a time as any."

He reached up to rub the scar just above his brow, which Felicity now knew he did when something upset him. He's angry with me, she thought, and rightly so. She was being ridiculous.

"I'm sorry," she said. "My nerves are on edge. You didn't deserve that."

"No, I didn't and quite frankly, I don't know why I'm explaining myself to you. It was a chance meeting. And your name only came up in the conversation because when I said where I was staying, he said he'd brought my neighbour home after a kayaking incident. In fact, he suggested I look in on you. He thought you were more shaken up than you let on."

She was less shaken from the boating accident than she was from her dinner with Cam. But now she was regretting taking it out on Ben. Why had she jumped to such ridiculous conclusions? "You're right. And it was nice of Cam to suggest that. It's been… Well, it's been a bit of a rough day."

"Oh no," he said, reaching for her hand. "You're not getting off that easy." He paused and while he waited in patient silence, she caught her breath. She needed to settle herself but wanted to shrink against the way he looked at her, as if he could read her mind.

"Can I ask you something?" he said, when she let the silence linger too long.

"I guess."

"Why would you assume we'd been gossiping about you? That's what you thought, wasn't it?"

Felicity sucked in air and stiffened in her chair. "Wow! You missed your calling, Ben. You should have been a shrink." She set her cup down on the table and stood up. She was two steps from the stairs before he caught her arm and pulled her back.

"Don't go," he said softly. His face was caught in the shadows of the porch light, and she saw the sincerity in his eyes. She opened her mouth to speak, though what she was going to say she did not know. "Please stay," he said again. "If I've offended you or done something wrong, please tell me. Don't run away from this, from me."

She turned from him and waved a hand toward her cottage. "The kids will wonder where I've got to." She knew full well they were probably absorbed in a movie or a game and likely hadn't given her whereabouts a second thought.

"They can wait. They're doing their own thing. Please, don't leave now. Not like this."

He reached for her hand, and she let him lead her back to her chair. When they were settled again, he refilled their cups and handed her one. "I didn't ask you up here to pick a fight or to analyze either of our pasts. I was hoping to help take your mind off whatever is troubling you. Not make things worse."

Felicity felt tears burning her eyes, and a lump swelled in her throat. "No," she said, with a catch in her voice. "It's my fault." And then she lowered her head. She didn't want to cry, tried desperately to stop the tears, but something inside her ached and at that moment there was nothing she could do now but let them flow.

Ben reached for her hand. "I'm sorry, Felicity. I'm sorry. I'm sorry. Please forgive me."

Between sobs, she said, "It's not you. It's… It's everything, Ben. I wouldn't even know where to start. I thought I'd dumped all this in the lake, but I guess there's still stuff I haven't gotten rid of. I've been bottling all this inside me for so long."

"You don't have to tell me anything, you know, but I'm here if you want to. I'd like to listen, if it will help."

She brushed at the tears. "I'd like that, Ben. I really would. But one thing at a time. There's too much and I can't…" she sighed. "I can't deal with it all at once."

Ben nodded. "In your own time," he said. And then he gave a shiver. "But let's go inside. It's freezing out here." He held his hands out to help her out of the chair. "You grab the cups. I'll bring the tea and the warmer and I'll put on another pot. Or would you like something stronger? Coffee with a little something in it?"

"Sounds perfect."

They settled in what Alice had always called her breakfast room, a smaller version of Felicity's Muskoka room on the east side of the cottage. Like Felicity's Muskoka room, the sunrise views were breathtaking over the lake, but it missed the evening splendor and for that, Alice had always been envious of Felicity's view. Still, the room was cozy and inviting, with two comfy recliners that faced the windows. Between them was a space heater, which Ben turned on to rid the room of the evening damp.

When they were comfortable, with brandy-laced coffee, Ben reached for her hand. "You don't have to say anything, you know. It's just nice to sit here and enjoy the quiet, but if you want to, I'm here. No judgement, remember? No advice, unless you want it. Just an ear." After a minute of silence broken only by the crickets' chirping, he grinned and said, "Or we can just enjoy the sounds of nature." His smile was infectious, and Felicity felt instantly warmed by it. She was sorry she'd started this argument, sorry she'd jumped to unfounded conclusions.

She thought of Richard moping about their cottage, wishing he'd stayed at home and constantly complaining about the lousy internet service. He couldn't stand the quiet or the crickets. She looked at Ben and laughed as a frog croaked in the distance.

"This tranquility, this serenity, this quiet, is exactly what I'd been longing for when I came up on Monday. A few days of quiet before the kids arrived. And without Richard's moaning, about everything and anything, I thought I would have it. But then..."

"But then I came on the scene and messed things up," he said.

"Oh no. Not at all. You have been the one good thing that's happened since I arrived. No, it was everything else. Tom and his overprotectiveness, pushing his way in here days ahead of schedule. My dog dying and no one telling me. Smashing up my favourite kayak. And then Cam…" She looked at Ben then, searching for the forgiveness she knew she didn't need, but wanting it anyway. She lowered her gaze. "I had dinner with Cam the other night, Ben. At that restaurant you asked about. I was afraid when the two of you met, he'd made up some kind of story that we were a thing or something. He… He tried to kiss me. And I didn't want him to, so I avoided it."

"Felicity, he didn't mention it."

"I was so sure that's why you were asking about the restaurant we went to."

"All he told me about you was that he'd brought you home after your mishap on the lake."

She nodded. "I should have known he wouldn't brag about a kiss he never got. Goddess, you'd think we were all in high school. I feel so childish about all this. But what really bothers me is that I felt as if it was a betrayal."

"To your husband?"

"No. To you."

"Me?"

"Well, yes. And yet I kept telling myself we aren't, or at least we weren't… Well, you know. But it still felt like I was doing something wrong. It was a debt paid for him fixing my tire and for bringing me home the other day. I don't even like the man." She threw her hands up in the air. "He suggested dinner and reluctantly I went. I guess I was just a little curious. But I think he had something more in mind. And then when I got out of the car and he…" She was talking fast, rushing over her words, defending what she knew she didn't have to, but doing it anyway.

"Felicity…"

"I really didn't want…"

"Felicity." She turned to look at him. "You have nothing to feel guilty about. You did nothing wrong."

"I just… I…"

He took her hands in his and kissed them. "Why do you think you betrayed me? I mean, I'm flattered, really, but until a few days ago, we didn't even know each other. And we still haven't said anything beyond enjoying each other's company. Neighbours, remember?"

"But it still felt wrong. He felt wrong. The dinner felt wrong. I kept comparing him to you, and both of you to Richard. Is that what I'm going to do from now on, measure everyone by my dead husband?"

"For a while, you probably will. I think that's normal. We all weigh our relationships from what we know of others. That's just part of the baggage we carry around. But sweetheart, having dinner with someone else is not a betrayal to me, or to anything we have now or might have in the future. It was just dinner."

Sweetheart. Had he just called her that?

"I think Cam wanted it to be more than dinner. And that's just not going to happen."

"Are you sure?"

"Of course, I'm sure. I would never… We…"

"Before you went for dinner with him, you and I shared a coffee and a breakfast and some conversation, great conversation mind you, but it wasn't as if either of us had voiced anything more. In fact, if anyone was betrayed it might be Cam. You went for dinner with him and then went to Lookout Point with me." He laughed then and wiped her tears with his thumb. "Poor Cam," he said, "But lucky me."

"And he didn't say anything about this when you met?"

Ben shook his head. "Not a word."

Felicity wiped the rest of her tears away and reached for her coffee. "I'm sorry that I assumed there was more to you and me than there is. All I could think of was Richard and all the other women there'd been, and the last thing I wanted to do was hurt anyone, especially you."

"What a jerk he must have been." Ben said, a sharpness in his tone Felicity had not heard before.

"Who, Cam?"

"No, Richard. How could he be married to someone as special as you and treat you like that?"

"Oh, Ben. Don't put me up on some pedestal." She bent her head and gazed into her coffee. "I have a great many faults."

"We all have vaults, Felicity. But no one deserves a partner who cheats on them. It's wrong, ethically, morally, in every way possible. It's wrong. If you fall out of love with someone, then you deal with that, but you don't run off to someone else."

"You sound like someone who's lived through it."

"There was someone once. A few years ago. We weren't married, but we were together, and we had an understanding. So, I know how it feels. I thought the same as you, I'm sure. What did I do wrong? How could I have been a better partner? Could I have been more supportive, taken on more responsibility in the relationship, spent more time with her? I went through it all. I even asked her, point blank, what did I do wrong? You know what she said?"

Felicity shook her head.

"She said I smothered her with too much kindness. And then she confessed that she just didn't love me anymore. She went her way with another guy. But I know now that I didn't do anything wrong. And neither did you. Richard, if you'll pardon me, was an ass."

They sat a long while, listening to the crickets chirping in the woods and the hoot of the resident owl who lived in the trees between their cottages. The brandy in her coffee sent a soothing sensation through Felicity's body.

After a while, she turned to Ben. "I know this is very forward of me, but I'm going to say it, anyway."

"I'm listening."

"Ben, I don't want to be just neighbours. Two people who share coffee on the deck or watch the sunset at Lookout Point. I don't know what's in the future for either of us, but I would like to share this time, right now, with you. I put my life on hold, for my kids, for Richard, for everyone else, but I don't want to do that anymore. I'm forty-eight years old. It's time I did what I want to do. It's time I lived."

He was smiling at her, grinning in fact, and she worried she'd said the wrong thing again. "Well, say something," she blurted out, laughing at his silly grin. "Or I'll think I've just made an even bigger fool of myself than I did before."

"I'm sorry. I just can't believe you said that. Now. Tonight, when I've been thinking the same thing myself since the day we met. I never believed in love at first sight, but I have to tell you, Felicity. When I pulled into Wally's gas station the other day, I thought to myself, who is this lovely creature? And then I saw you, distressed and worrying over that flat tire, and when you turned me away, I was even more infatuated. I love your spunk, the tenacity, the determination I see in you. You know, I went back. I didn't want to leave you alone to tackle that tire."

"Why didn't you stop or say something?"

"By the time I got turned around and back to you, you had help, so I let it go. I knew you weren't on your own and that's what mattered. And then later, you seemed a little put out with me, so I thought I should give you some space."

"I thought I'd said something wrong. When I asked about children, and you were distant."

"No, you didn't. I just wasn't ready then to talk about her." He cupped her chin with his hand. "So, neighbour. Shall we call ourselves *a thing*, or exclusive or what is it the kids call it these days?"

"I don't know, but whatever it is, you're more than just a neighbour to me."

Ben leaned across the arms of their chairs to kiss her. "Settled then," he said afterwards. "Anything else you want to get off your chest tonight?"

"Like what?"

"Like why your boys were ready to knock each other's blocks off a while ago?" He grinned. "I'm glad I only had Alice growing up. By the time I was old enough to scrap about something, she was hardly ever around. Fighting with yourself is no fun at all."

"I know what you mean. I'm an only child, so I didn't have this rivalry they have. But since you asked. There is something you could really help me with, I think." She told Ben the plan that she had formulated on her walk to see the sunset, before he'd stopped her, before they'd nearly had their own first big row. Ben nodded and agreed and suggested one or two things and finally, when she finished, she said, "So, you'll help me?"

"Of course. I think it's a great idea. When will you talk to him about it?"

"Tomorrow morning. First thing."

He reached onto a shelf behind him and retrieved the file folder she'd left him with the ancestral charts in them. "I haven't forgotten these. I hope it's enough to get started."

Felicity looked at the lines neatly filled in with meticulously neat printing. Spaces here and there, but a good number of names and even some dates. "This is a great start. Many people don't know more than their parents and grandparents."

"I confess I cheated a little. I called Alice to get some of them. She's always been interested in this, just never really did much about it. She remembered that you and she had talked about it. And I signed up for your workshop next week. It will give me a chance to see you in action."

"In action?" she laughed. "I wouldn't really call it that."

"I would. When you talk about your work, I can see the light in your eyes. I can imagine you leading a class of similarly minded people. I'll bet you just shine in front of a group like that."

"Stop it! You're making me blush," she said with a laugh.

"Am I? Good. It's about time somebody did." He kissed her again, then smiled. "I won't hurt you like he did, Felicity. Not ever."

It was after midnight when they heard footsteps coming up the back steps of Ben's cottage. "It's Tom," she said, looking toward the door. "What time is it?"

"Later than we realized," Ben said. "Come on." He was already on his feet, reaching down to help her out of the chair, when Tom knocked on the door.

While Felicity unwrapped herself from Alice's shawl and laid it over the back of the chair, Ben answered the door. "Hi Tom," Ben said. "Everything okay?"

"Sorry it's so late, but have you seen my…?" Ben held the door open for him and Tom stepped into the shadows of the room. "Where have you been?"

"Here, mostly."

"You should have let us know. We were worried."

"But not too worried if you've just started looking for me now," she teased.

"That's not fair. We were watching a movie and Olivia said she thought you'd come in ages ago and had gone to bed."

"Chill. I was kidding. Ben and I have been enjoying the quiet. And really Tom, you don't have to check up on me. I'm not a teenager." She turned to Ben and kissed his cheek. "Thank you," she whispered. "Let's do this again… Soon."

She felt Tom's eyes searing holes into her back as he followed her down the steps and into the woods. She linked her arm in his when he caught up with her. But when he asked for more details about Ben, she kept silent. This was one secret she was determined to keep, for now at least. How the tables had turned, she thought. How many nights had she sat up wondering where her children were, worrying they were in an accident, or had been mugged or any number of things? But that was a parent's job. To worry. To be there when your children needed you.

It wasn't a child's job to smother their parents or to run their lives. And after the way Tom treated Will earlier, she was still a little angry with him. She didn't like the judgement he inflicted on his brother, and he would like the things she had to say about his father, even less. Melody might think a full explanation would answer some questions, but was Tom ready to hear it all? Was she ready to tell it? Knowing all the sordid secrets just might ruin Tom's already marred image of Richard. And Richard wasn't there to offer a defense for anything he'd done or said. Hearing things only from her side wasn't fair. Even a murderer has the right to a fair trial.

In her room, Felicity slipped out of her clothes and draped them over the back of her chair. And then she pulled on summer pyjamas and climbed into bed. She was too tired to take her things to the hamper in the bathroom, too tired, even, to brush her hair or put on hand cream. And most certainly she was too tired to look in the mirror and ask herself what to do about any of this.

At least she had an idea for Will. Ben had been kind and true to his word. No judgement. No advice, unless she'd asked for it. And when she did, he came up with a brilliant idea, one she hoped Will would like, too.

Mac clawed her way up the comforter and circled herself into the crook of Felicity's neck. Instantly, she began to purr. Felicity whispered, stroking the soft spot on the tips of Mac's ears. "I think you and I are going to get along just fine, as long as you promise not to ask me where I've been when I come home late at night."

17

The next morning, Felicity woke late, the memory of last night still lingering in her thoughts. The evening spent with Ben reminded her of the early days of past relationships, when a gentle caress or a kiss was new and sweet and exciting. There was much to learn about one another. Yes, there would be hesitations, just as there had been last night. Somehow, she would have to find a way not to let her past with Richard jade her impressions of Ben. She was not the same person, and Ben certainly was not like Richard.

She pulled back the curtains to let in the morning light, just as Melody, Olivia and Eric in the canoe and Tom in the red kayak were paddling toward Abby's Rock. She watched Tom edge the kayak closer until he was close enough to touch the rock. A tribute to his twin. It always sent a ripple of emotion through her when he did that and she thought him very brave, since that rock held such horrible memories.

As she passed the Muskoka room, she peered in to see Will with his laptop perched on the arm of a chair. From the headings on the screen, she could see he was browsing websites in search of the job listings. In the kitchen, she poured two mugs of coffee, added milk and sugar to his cup and went to join him.

"Morning," she said, cautious of his mood, as she handed him his cup.

"Hey Mum. Thanks." He sipped his coffee and watched her carefully as she settled into the chair beside him. "Wow, that's super sweet. I've been trying to give up sugar. But this is a nice change."

"I didn't know. I can make you another one."

"No. Don't. It's okay." He closed his laptop and set it on the table. "I assume this is where we have our heart to heart, and you chew me out for getting fired again."

"Oh Will. Don't do that. Everybody screws up sometimes."

"Yeah, but me more than anyone else, it seems. I dunno, Mum. I just can't seem to settle into anything."

"I realize that, but the answer isn't to get fired or quit all the time, is it?"

He shrugged. "It's what I do best, I guess. Give up, quit, walk away."

"That's what you've allowed yourself to do. It's a copout, Will. Instead of digging in and looking for ways to fix the problems, you run away from them. I was a little like that when I was young, too." And, she thought, I almost run away from Ben just last night too.

Will shrugged again. "I guess I'm not very good at working that out."

"You're young. You'll have lots of challenges in your lifetime. Gosh, I have them all the time. I can see you're not happy with these jobs you've taken over the past couple of years. So, let's figure out what really makes you happy. What do you really want to do and what will get you on that path instead of in these jobs you end up hating?"

"Well, it's usually my bosses. Like this last one. He was a bast…"

"Language Will. I'm not a prude, but you know I don't like name calling."

"But he was brutal, Mum. I've been working on this website for a client for a couple of weeks now. And the other day, he said if I didn't have it done by five that day, I was done."

"Really? A couple of weeks? Were you waiting on the client for content?"

"No, I had that."

"Okay, did you need video footage or something?"

He shook his head.

"Well, then I might ask the same thing as your boss did. What was taking so long? This isn't new to you. You build websites all the time. I've seen you do it. And even I can put together a basic website with all the do-it-yourself platforms out there today. It won't look as professional as something your company puts out, but it's a couple of day's work and that's sourcing all my content and video footage and photography." She pulled out her phone and showed him the website she'd created for her genealogy business.

"You did that?"

Felicity nodded. "It wasn't hard. I used their stock photos and a few pictures I had of my own from workshops and our family records. Writing the content took the longest, but there are these great places where you can get content relevant to your website for next to nothing. This is a simple one-page site with a link to my blog. That's all I really need, though. Maybe your client needed something more complicated?"

He handed her back her phone. "Not really. I guess my heart wasn't in it."

It was tough to be outsmarted by your mother, Felicity knew. But she also knew he was in the wrong line of work. There were other things Will should build besides websites.

"When I went for my walk last night, I realized something," she said.

"That I'm a failure?"

"You're not a failure, darling. You failed to work at something. There's a difference. You don't really want to build websites or work at a call centre trouble shooting cell phone issues, do you?" He shook his head and picked at the leather piping on the chair until a bit of fluff poked through the stitching. She watched him shove it back with his finger, then put a hand over his. Another day, she might have groaned over the miniscule damage, but today she let it go.

Instead, she put her hand on his and asked, "Why did you give up architecture at Carleton? You loved it?"

"I still do. At least, I think I would, but you know how it is. It was Uni. I started partying too much, missed a couple of deadlines, and before I knew it, I was out."

"But they told you from the beginning it was a tough course with limited enrollment, and that everyone needed to be dedicated."

His face burned red with shame, and Felicity knew from experience he was about to go on the defensive. "Look, I admitted I fucked up, alright? Can't we just drop it and move on? I'll go work in a fucking grocery store if that's what you want."

"Language. Will." Felicity pursed her lips and did her best to stifle her own frustrations. "I don't want you to go stock shelves in a grocery store. You tried that once, remember? But we can't drop this. I can't support you forever. What if I had a heart attack and died, like Dad did? Who's going to foot your bills, then?"

"Inheritance?" There was a little cheekiness in his voice that made her smile, as Will's true nature shined through. And then he became serious again. "I don't mean to be a burden, Mum. Honestly, I don't. I just don't know what else to do. I don't want to stock shelves, or work at a call centre, or stand in a mall flogging cell phones to people."

"You were happiest when you were in the architecture program. Even when it was tough going, you were so excited about it you were practically bursting every time I talked to you. Your work was great. Your teachers were proud of you, and you were getting great marks."

"But it's in the past."

"It doesn't have to be. What if you could give it another shot? You're only 22. Lots of people older than you go back to school to get their degrees."

Will rubbed his forefinger back and forth over his thumb. "There's this little thing called cash, Mum. In case you've forgotten, university costs money and, as you have so blatantly pointed out, I don't have any and I'm already in debt up to my eyeballs to you." He paused and sipped his coffee. "Unless…"

"Oh, no." Will needed to prove it to himself that this was what he wanted to do. It wouldn't mean as much if she dished out the money for him again. "Remember what I said about chores when you were little?"

"Earning our treats makes them taste all the sweeter. I remember, Mum." His head tilted to one side to look at her quizzically. "But this isn't a package of candy or some hockey cards with bubble gum. Not sure how I'd manage it. It would be pretty impossible."

"Nothing is impossible if you want it badly enough. Look. What if we could come to an arrangement? Instead of me paying for your half of the apartment and groceries and your phone and the rest, why don't you move back home with me? Then you don't feel obligated to me, or to Luke or to anyone. And you can find some work. It may not be your dream job, but it's temporary. Something to help you save the money you need for your tuition."

"No offence, Mum, but you might cramp my style." He tilted his chin a little to show off his handsome features.

Felicity laughed. "Hang a sock on the door and I'll stay out," she teased. "But seriously. What do you think? Do you want to try?"

"It'll be years before I have the tuition money, let alone dorm fees and textbooks. I'd need a car to get back and forth from Ottawa on weekends."

"Don't push it. There are busses, and trains that go to Ottawa and a Mum who could pick you up now and again. If I showed you how to budget and helped you stick with it, I'm sure you can do it. I can give you all the support and love and free meals you need. And a place to live while you get it all figured out."

"You know. There's an easier way," he said, his eyes widening a little.

"Win a lottery?"

"You could let me have my inheritance money from Dad."

"Oh Will." Felicity's enthusiasm fell. "I can't. Not because I don't want to. It's because everything is invested and locked up tight until you turn thirty. It's how Dad's will was written."

"Tom got something, though."

"Tom got a small stipend for being one of the executors. It was less than five hundred dollars and it only paid for gas money, meals and a hotel room when he went to Toronto to settle everything."

"Oh, I thought since he got the new pickup truck…"

"No sweetie. He bought that. Well, actually he took out a loan, but in thirty-two more payments, it will be his." She patted his hand, hoping to encourage him. "I know if you worked hard, maybe even took an extra part-time job, you'd have enough money for that tuition by this time next year. A year isn't so long when you have a goal in mind."

"Only a year? Really?"

"Really. Bartending pays well. Maybe you could do that two or three nights a week for the extra cash. You already have your Smart Serve. You like talking to people. You like sports. And how many sports bars are there in St. Catharines? Best of all, they're all right on the bus routes."

Will's eyes widened, and a smile turned up the corners of his mouth. "I'd love to finish that course. A couple of the guys I knew from Carleton have great jobs, and they're getting pretty okay pay, too."

"And so will you." It was refreshing to see a smile on her son's face again. She knew that feeling, too, the hope of new beginnings, things turning around and looking like they were in your favour for once. "There's something else," she said.

"Okay, here it comes. There's a catch to this, isn't there?"

"No. I just thought you might like to get started earning some money now."

"Huh?"

"Remember, I said I wanted to do some renovations here?"

"Yeah, you want to add a second story with a couple of bedrooms and another bathroom upstairs?"

"Exactly. And make that kitchen bigger and a few other things. So, I was thinking maybe you'd like to draw up some plans."

He nodded enthusiastically. "I could do that."

"Of course you can. And when you're finished, I know someone who would look at them for you and help you with any glitches or problems."

"Who?"

"Ben, from next door. He's an architect, and he said he'd be happy to help you. And guess what? He's a Carleton grad."

"Is that right?"

"It is. He and I talked about this last night." She raised a hand to stop him from speaking when he was about to interrupt. "I didn't tell him you got fired or any of that. I didn't even tell him why you left school. I said you left school after your second year. He said the second year was the toughest. After that, it got easier. You should talk to him about it."

"Really? When?"

"Whenever you see he's home, I'm sure he would take time to talk to you."

"Thanks Mum."

"Oh, don't thank me yet. Wait till you see the list of chores you're going to have if you're living with me." She stood up and ruffled his hair. Will swatted her hand away. "Sorry, are you too old for that now?" she teased.

"Yeah, just a little. Wait. Two jobs and chores? Hang on a minute. If you can't afford to pay my tuition, how can you afford to do a renovation on this place?" When she pursed her lips and a frown wrinkled her forehead, he added, "Kidding, Mum. I get it. It's time I stood on my own two feet."

And then she smiled again. "There's my clever boy. I knew he was in there somewhere."

"Are we still picking up those paddle boards today?"

"Yes, but we can do it later. First, I'd like to take a dip. The water looks fantastic. Want to come for a swim with me?"

Will shook his head. "If it's okay with you, I'm going to take some measurements." When he got out of the chair, his posture was straighter, and there was a hint of confidence in the lift of his chin. He bent down to kiss her cheek. "Thanks, Mum. Really. You could have just chewed me out, but this is so much better. I promise I won't let you down."

18

After she'd eaten a bowl of cereal and downed her second cup of coffee, Felicity changed into her bathing suit and a beach wrap and headed toward the dock. The kids were coming in from their paddle around the lake, their faces tinted pink from the morning sun.

"I should have put on sunscreen," Olivia said, helping Eric tip the water out of the canoe.

"The water looks nice," Felicity said. "I was going for a swim. Anyone want to join me?"

"Can't," Tom said. "Eric wants to see wildlife, so we thought we'd head up to Algonquin. You want to come?"

She shook her head. "I'm okay here. But Will might want to go."

Tom groaned. "Really Mum? I'm at the end of my rope with him."

Felicity laid a hand on his arm. "Take him with you? He could use the break. And try not to be so judgmental. He's not you, remember. And honestly Tom. This isn't your problem to worry about."

He lifted his eyes toward the cottage and sighed. "We'll need your car then. We can't fit five in Melody's. At least not comfortably," Tom said. "Oh, but you have stuff to pick up, don't you?"

"I can use Melody's car, if that's okay."

"Sure. But don't you need Will?"

"Maybe Ben is free. I'll ask him if he can help. If not, I'm sure someone at the store will load up the car for me. You know where the keys are," she said.

She watched them troop up the stairs and when the patio door slid closed, she sat on the end of the dock and dangled her feet in the water, trying to decide if she felt adventurous enough to swim to the other side of the lake and back. The width of their little cove was about a quarter of a mile each way. She did it at least once a week every summer, but usually when someone was around in case she struggled on the way back.

"A dime for your thoughts."

She recognized Ben's voice right away as the dock shifted and shimmied under his step. He was wearing a pair of swimming trunks, a towel draped over his shoulders. His skin glistened with a freshly applied layer of sunscreen.

"It's a penny for your thoughts," she corrected.

"You told me I had to account for inflation."

"Oh yes. I forgot." She patted the space beside her. "Join me. The water is cool but refreshing."

He sat down next to her, nudging shoulders as he leaned in to ask, "How did it go with Will?"

"Better than I thought. He was hoping to talk to you about it. Thank you for offering to help."

"Happy to."

Something was worrying him, Felicity thought as Ben reached up to rub the scar above his brow. "What is it?" she asked.

He grinned through his disappointment. "You know me that well already, do you?"

"Anyone could see that something is bothering you."

"Emma called to cancel."

"Oh Ben, I'm sorry."

He shrugged and looked out over the lake, and she could see he was doing his best not to let his disappointment show, but it did. "My fault, really, for letting myself be hopeful. I mean, was I really thinking I could just be her father again, after all this time? You seem to really understand your kids, and this thing you're doing for Will, it's terrific. I suppose I just want to be there for Emma, too."

"I'm not sure I understand them at all sometimes, especially Tom, with this heightened *helicoptering his middle-aged mother, syndrome*. And his need to dominate his younger brother."

"Be grateful he cares."

"I am. It's tough to take when it's coming from your child. And it's been years since anyone looked after me. I've always been Richard's wife, the kids' mother, a smiling face behind a desk when people wanted money. I take care of everyone else."

His arm went around her shoulders, and he gave her a little squeeze. "Maybe it's time you let someone else take care of you."

She grinned and gave him a little nudge. "Alright. How about you help me up?"

"And then we can go for a swim," he said, standing and pulling her up after him. In a smooth motion, without letting go of her hands, he plunged from the dock, taking Felicity into the lake with him.

"You nut," she said, when she surfaced. "You could have warned me and let me take off my wrap."

"Nah. Much more fun when you weren't expecting it," he laughed, treading water. "It's pretty deep here. You were right about that drop-off. And man, is it cccccoooold."

"I believe I said it was refreshing." Felicity reversed herself and floated on her back, looking up at a clear blue sky. A hawk circled in the distance, soaring on an updraft, circling endlessly in search of food on the ground below. That must be amazing, she thought. The feel of the wind in your feathers, arms outstretched to tip and turn you, the rest of the world, a million miles below.

"Ok, I'm refreshed," Ben said, swimming past her to get to the ladder. "Are you staying in?"

"If you swim, you'll warm up, you know." It was a challenge, and he took it up right away.

"Alright then. I'll race you to that rock and back."

"Abby's Rock? Oh, I don't think…"

He was halfway up the ladder, looking over his shoulder at her. "Come on. What do you have to do today that can't wait another hour? Or are you just afraid I might beat you?"

Felicity took off her soaking wrap and tossed it onto the dock. "That does it. You're on!" If Abby could beat Tom to that rock when they were only ten years old, then Felicity couldn't refuse.

Ben climbed the rest of the way onto the dock and held his hand down to help her up. "Get up here Jefferies and put your money where your mouth is. What's your wager?"

"I never bet money," she said, shivering next to him, as water dripped down her body.

"Okay then, dinner on Wednesday after the workshop. Winner pays the tab."

"You're on." She leaned into a diving position. "Ready. Set." But before Felicity could say go, Ben was already off. "Hey, that's cheating," she yelled, diving in after him.

She caught up to him easily, because he let her, and then they were both swimming in long smooth strokes, cutting the water, and gliding easily. She passed him once, then he passed her, and when he effortlessly put a short distance between them, she pushed even harder. Abby's Rock loomed ahead, the top half fully painted in gull droppings, the lower half caked in moss at the waterline. Felicity pushed through the images it invoked, eager to touch the rock ahead of Ben to honour her daughter's memory.

Somewhere nearing the end of the lap, Felicity wavered. She wasn't sure she had the strength to finish the first lap, let alone win this race. Maybe it was too soon after the paddling incident. Suddenly, as her arms ached. There was a sharp twinge in her calf and then it cramped. Hard. Pinching and knotting the back of her leg. Silly nut, she chastised herself. She should never have agreed to this race, at least not until she'd done it a few times for practice. She stopped swimming to massage her calf with one hand and tread water with the other. Relax, she told herself. It will pass.

In the distance, she saw Ben slap its smooth edge above the moss line on the rock. Then he raised an arm in the air. "I win! Dinner is on you," he shouted, and then he saw how far behind she was. "Hey," he called out. "Are you alright?"

"Cramp," she called back to him. "I just need to work it out. And you only won one lap. We were supposed to swim back to the dock, you know." She began edging her way toward the dock, still massaging her calf. When Ben caught up to her, she said, "It's better. Still tender, but not pinching anymore."

He reached out and rotated her onto her back, into a life-saving position, with an arm around her shoulders and neck. "Just relax," he said. "I'll take you back to the dock."

"I'm fine, really."

"Felicity, I will not argue with you. Let me do this. Just lay back and enjoy the ride. We'll take our time." Halfway to the dock, he smiled down at her. "See, it's nice to let someone take care of you, isn't it?"

"It is when it's you. Thanks for rescuing me."

"Glady. And I'd do it again."

"Hopefully, you won't have to."

He gave her shoulder a squeeze. "Like I said, any time. Now be quiet and enjoy the ride."

They were within a few feet of the dock when Ben eased her out of his arms. "I'm touching bottom here, so I think you should be alright. Want to try?"

She nodded, and he released her, but she held onto his arm and pulled him close to her, turning his face to hers. And then she kissed him. "Thank you for rescuing me. Again," she said.

"You're welcome. If that's my reward, I just might have to look for more opportunities."

Felicity laughed as his arms went around her and he kissed her again, longer, more passionately this time. And despite the cold temperature of the water, she felt a warmth flowing within her as they kissed again. The arms that wrapped around her were strong, reassuring, and in them, she felt safe. Safe. She hadn't felt that in such a long time. His kisses were longing, probing, willing her to tell him more, without words. She broke away at last and dipped her chin, letting her head rest against his chest.

And then he nudged her gently toward the ladder. She hadn't wanted it to end, but they were both shivering. She reached up for the ladder and was surprised to see Will waiting for them, arms crossed over his chest, and an annoyed look on his face.

"I thought you went with the others to Algonquin," Felicity said as she reached for her towel.

"Well, you thought wrong." Will did nothing to hide the anger in his voice. He held out her cell phone. "It's been ringing like crazy. I would have answered it, but I don't know your passcode. It's been playing the William Tell overture."

"That's Carrie," Felicity said, easing up the ladder and reaching for the phone. "Thanks, Hun. I'll call her back." She wiggled her fingers at Will for the phone.

Will held onto it stiffly, his gaze flitting between his mother and Ben and back again. "I don't believe you, Mum," he said to her. Then he fixed his gaze on Ben. "You know my dad just died, right?"

"I do. And I'm sorry about that," Ben said. He reached out to shake Will's hand. "I'm Ben. Your mother said you want to talk about architecture with me."

"I doubt that's going to happen. I saw you guys, you know. Everyone else on the lake could see you, too." He shot a dagger at his mother. "Really Mum? Really?"

"Will!" Felicity hissed. "Give me my phone."

Will threw a dangerous glance Ben's when, then threw her phone on the ground. And then he stormed back to the cottage.

Felicity picked it up and dusted off the sand. *Will was right*, she thought.*, What was I thinking? I'm not twenty-something. I'm not a kid. What am I doing?* Ben's hand grasped her elbow, and she whirled around to face him and put her hands in the air to avoid his grasp. "No. Don't. I'm sorry. I shouldn't have… We shouldn't…"

"What are you sorry about? Felicity, come on." His fingers gripped her elbow, but she yanked her arm away.

"No, Will is right. That was a mistake."

She took a single step toward the cottage before Ben, dripping wet, his towel around his shoulders, reached out and gripped both her arms. "A mistake? Last night, you said you were ready to move on. You wanted us to be more than just neighbours. Those were your words. I didn't say them, you did."

Felicity felt his gaze penetrate her thoughts. They were her words and last night, and even this morning, she thought she was ready. But selfishly, she hadn't considered her children or how a relationship with Ben would affect them. Just because Melody thought it was a good thing, didn't mean the others would. "Maybe I was wrong," she said, looking away to avoid the disappointment on his face.

"So, what's the deal here?" he asked. "Is it because *you* don't want this, or is it because your son doesn't?"

Felicity's eyes darted to the cottage, to the lake, and back to Ben again. "I… I can't talk about this right now. I'm sorry, Ben." She left him, dripping water onto the sand, as she hurried off to make peace with her son.

"Felicity," Ben called. He called her twice more, but she refused to acknowledge him. She felt his eyes follow her to the lower deck, up the stairs and inside the cottage. She felt his pain because it hurt her, too. But she'd let herself get caught up in the moment with Ben last night, and again this morning. He was a nice man, a kind man, a wonderful man. But she still had children to think about. They had just lost their father. Maybe that was enough for them right now.

Will's door was closed, and knocking on it brought a series of disgruntled, *go aways*. Felicity went into her bedroom, closed the door, and stripped off her wet things. She put Carrie's phone calls, the cramp in her leg and Ben's oh so sensuous kisses and his confused look out of her thoughts. In the shower, as the water flowed over her, Will's words rolled over her again and again.

You know my dad just died, right?

Will was right. Richard had been in the ground just over three months, yet here she was, flirting with and kissing another man, while her son watched. "What were you thinking?" she asked herself, as her tears flowed, and hot water rushed over her body.

19

After her shower, Felicity felt completely exhausted, and still a little stiff from the cramping in her calf. She was still wrestling with the frustration she felt for what she'd done. Will would tell Olivia and Tom, for sure. They never kept secrets. From her, yes. From each other, never.

She climbed onto her bed and pulled a blanket over her, intending to have a short nap. But she dozed longer than she thought and by the time she woke again, the dim light in the room told her it was later than she would have liked. It must be well into the afternoon, she thought as she sat up. She lingered a moment, hearing voices in the room next door. Will's room. She tiptoed to the wall to listen. He'd undoubtedly told them what had happened.

"Well, I think it's great," Olivia said. "Why shouldn't she

enjoy herself? She's young. She's beautiful, and it's obvious he likes her."

"Seriously, Olivia," Will hissed. "You take her side in everything."

"Not always, but in this I do. Come on, guys. Mum hasn't been happy for years. And this business of faking a happy marriage with Dad? Well, that was just wrong on so many levels."

"Faking a happy marriage? What are you talking about?" Will said. Olivia thumped him, knocking him against the wall. "Ow!" he cried. "What was that for?"

Tom groaned. "Where have you been, Will? Mum and Dad had issues. Wake up."

So, she hadn't been as successful as she'd thought, in hiding the problems of their home-life. That would make things a little easier when she came to talking to them about it. She could go in there right now and do that. It might be the perfect time. They were all together. No need to call a family meeting. But was she ready to tell them everything?

Tom continued. "What's this business about St. Lucia? Why doesn't she want us to have the wedding there?"

"It's not her, dumbass. It's Dad's family," Olivia said. "I don't know all the details, but I remember once, when we all came home after Christmas there. Mum couldn't go for some reason. But I said something about how humid it is in St. Lucia. And she said, '*is it?*', as if she'd never been and had no idea what the weather is like."

Felicity listened more closely. She'd hoped Olivia had forgotten that one slip-up she'd made a few years ago. She had always been careful to shield her children from the nasty parts of her marriage and her relationship with Richard's family. She'd provided plausible excuses for their father's absence for the big events in their lives, got up before anyone else to hide the empty liquor bottles, and clean up any messes Richard had made the night before. And most importantly, she'd invented believable reasons she couldn't attend any of the Jefferies family events, and her absence was always forgiven, understood and, of course, never mentioned by Richard's family. But now, listening to them talk, she wondered if she'd been as successful as she thought.

Olivia's voice was so hushed Felicity had to strain to hear. "And remember when Great Granny died in St. Lucia? I was next door, but I came home to get something, and I heard Mum and Dad arguing. He said they could barely manage the cost of his flight, let alone hers and a hotel bill."

"What? Why couldn't they afford her plane ticket and why would they need a hotel when that place has plenty of room?" Will asked.

"Because she wasn't allowed to stay on the estate," Olivia said. "Dad said it more than once."

Tom said, "And you know, Dad didn't have as much money as we thought he did. The company is doing well now, but it wasn't always. I saw some of the paperwork at the lawyer's office. A few years ago, they had a huge influx of money and when I asked Uncle Ken about it, he said someone had bought the company. Dad was just the managing director. When I asked him who the new owner was, Uncle Ken wouldn't say, or he didn't know."

"That can't be right," Olivia said. "Grandpa Jefferies funded that company when Dad started it. They've argued about it a load of time. I've heard them."

"How is it you hear all these arguments, Olivia? Are you an eavesdropper or something?" Will asked.

Felicity flinched at the word, feeling guilty that she was doing just that to her children.

"Don't know," Olivia retorted. "I guess I'm just in the wrong place at the right time, because no one wants to hear that. So, are you saying all Dad had was a salary?"

"And some investments," Tom said. "But don't look so glum. We'll all get enough for a down payment on a house when we turn thirty. It's just not what I expected it would be. I haven't the heart to ask Mum about any of this. You can see how strained she is."

"Huh! Strained my ass," Will said. "Not after what I saw today."

"Give it a rest, Will. Honestly," Olivia said. "She's lived her whole life for us. It's time she had a life of her own. Don't ya think?"

"Who is he anyway?" Will asked. "What if he's a creep or something?"

"Didn't you say he was going to help you on this project for Mum?" Olivia asked.

"He's around her age. He's staying next door. Why shouldn't they be friends? It's not like they're…" There was a hush and then he said, "Are they?"

No one said anything for a moment, and Felicity imagined the looks on her children's faces as they thought of her and Ben in bed together. *No*, she wanted to scream. *We aren't.*

"You thought he was a stalker," Will said sarcastically. "A crazed lunatic who was going to murder her in her sleep. Isn't that why you and Melody dropped everything to come up here early?"

"Not him. The guy who fixed her tire. And I was wrong. People can be wrong, can't they? I don't think there's anything to this."

"Well, you didn't see them kissing in the lake," Will said. "Gross."

There was the sound of pillow-slapping, and Felicity knew Olivia had had enough of Will's moaning. "I'm telling you both. Let her enjoy herself. If you just let it be, you'll see things have a way of working out. And maybe, just maybe, he's the best thing that's happened to her in a long, long time."

That was when Felicity decided it was time to put an end to this unintended eavesdropping and her children's discussion of her personal affairs. She began thumping around in her room, opening drawers and closing them, turning up the volume on her music, and she closed and opened her curtains, all to let them know she was no longer napping. There was a flurry of hushed mumbling, then footsteps past her bedroom door, and then all was quiet from Will's bedroom.

This, Felicity thought, goes beyond Ben or anyone else who might come into her life. There were things she had to tell her children, things they should know, and eventually, she would have to clarify their suspicions and answer their questions. And she would have to do it soon.

20

Felicity couldn't deny being happy they'd canceled the risotto challenge and though she was sorry for Ben, she was glad Emma wasn't coming and that she would not have to put up any pretenses with someone she hardly knew and with Ben. She and her family ate leftovers in restless silence as Felicity thought how awkward a dinner with Ben would have been, especially with Will's anger still hovering.

She wasn't sure what she would say to Ben the next time she saw him, but he'd want an explanation. He wouldn't leave it, she knew that. She could not deny her feelings for him, or that she longed for the intimacies she had not felt in a long, long time. He'd ignited something in her she thought was dead, but she would not put Ben before Will, or any of her children. They had to be on board, or she would end it with Ben. Maybe when Will was on his own, she could consider a relationship. But now was not the time. Will needed her.

After dinner, Felicity went for a bike ride, the cramp well and truly over and her need to think clearly about what she was going to say to her children nagged at her. As she cycled past Ben's cottage, she noticed a white Volkswagen Beetle in the driveway. Had Emma decided to come, anyway? Or maybe Alice bought a new car? On the way back, the car was gone, which meant it was a brief visit from whoever had dropped by.

In the kitchen, she found Eric and Melody mixing drinks while the others hovered over the folding table in the living room, sorting puzzle pieces.

"Nice picture. Two thousand pieces," Felicity said, picking up the box lid. "That'll take the rest of the summer."

"Not with all of us working on it," Olivia said. "How was your bike ride?"

"Good, thanks. You know there's a garage full of bikes if you guys want to go sometime." She directed her comment to Eric, who handed her a glass of white wine. He wouldn't know what was in the garage, though her children certainly did.

"Thought you could use this," he said in a hushed voice.

Did they all know what happened earlier she wondered? Of course, they did. Olivia would have told him. Tom told Melody everything. She probably added fuel to the fire with what she'd seen from the deck. But then, neither Melody nor Olivia would see anything wrong with her mother kissing a man in the lake, or anywhere else.

"Did you see any bears in Algonquin?" Felicity asked, taking a seat on the couch opposite Eric.

"No, but we saw three moose, so I was pretty happy about that." He hovered over his laptop, scrolling through pictures. "Sit here and I'll show you." She shifted to a place beside him and watched with fascination as he flipped through a series of shots.

"Olivia says you paint from your photographs," Felicity said. "Will you do some of these?"

"I will. There are a few I really like. Like this one of the baby moose and the mother."

"He has an exhibit next month, in Toronto, Mum," Olivia said. "You should go. Maybe Auntie Carrie wants to go too?"

Carrie, Felicity thought. She hadn't called her back. Just as she was about to get up, she noticed Olivia looking in her direction. Then she mouthed. "Can we talk?" and nodded toward Felicity's bedroom.

Felicity nodded slowly, wondering if she was ready for the inquisition. "Yes, let's talk," Felicity said. "But not in private. Out here. Eric and Melody are family now, right? So, they may as well hear this too."

Will looked up from sorting pieces as she came to sit next to him. "Mum, you don't have to explain. I'm sorry. I was a jerk."

"You weren't a jerk, Will. It's my fault. It was impulsive. I wasn't thinking. We should never have…" She reached out to touch his arm. "You were right. And I assure you, it won't happen again. Not with Ben or anyone else."

"Oh Mum," Olivia sighed. "Really? Eventually, this was going to happen. You weren't going to be alone forever, were you? And why not now? And why not Ben?"

"It's not that simple, Olivia. I appreciate what you're saying, but Will is right. It's too soon. I wasn't thinking of you guys. In fact, I'm not sure I was thinking at all. This is not fair for you guys or for Ben, either." She sighed.

Olivia slapped Will's arm and pushed her face into a stern grimace. "Tell her," She said. "Tell her or I will."

"Tell me what?" Felicity said, looking from Will to Olivia and back again.

"He was here, earlier, looking for you," Olivia said, when Will refused to speak. "He brought his daughter over to introduce us all. Her name is Emma, and she's drop dead gorgeous, isn't she, Will?" Olivia flung a piece of the puzzle at Will, who was still pouting and refusing to say anything.

"Well, I'm sorry I missed meeting her. I hope she comes back again," Felicity said.

"She will," Olivia continued. "She said she had a work thing this weekend, but maybe next weekend. Will's pretty excited, aren't you, little brother?" Olivia reached out to pinch Will's arm.

"Ow!" He glared at Olivia, and then he admitted. "Well, she is hot."

Olivia crossed her arms over her chest. "So, it's fine if you cozy up to her, but you can't allow Mum the same curtesy?"

"Ah come on. How many times do I have to apologize? I get it alright?"

"I keep telling you, Ben's a nice guy," Tom said. "You should get to know him, Will."

"Okay. Okay. Can we get off the gang-up-on-Will warpath? What's for dessert? I could go for pie and ice-cream if there's any left."

"I'll see," Felicity said, getting out of her chair, glad to leave this conversation behind.

"I'll help," Melody called out from behind the book she was reading.

While they were scooping ice-cream and cutting pie, Felicity said she was sorry they'd had to cancel the cooking challenge. "I was looking forward to Tom's risotto. Maybe he could make it tomorrow for lunch before you guys all head home."

"Don't tell him this, but I hate his risotto," Melody whispered. "He thinks he's a master chef in the kitchen, and usually he comes up with some pretty good meals, but mushroom risotto is not one of his best."

"Then why did you suggest the challenge?" Felicity asked.

Melody shrugged. "I was hoping someone else might tell him his sucks, so I wouldn't have to, I guess. I'm just a chicken."

"You? I can't imagine it. I always took you for a straightforward and upfront kind of person. Was I wrong?"

"Not entirely. But when it comes to Tom's ego, I sometimes walk on eggshells. There's a difference between honesty and being honest, if that makes sense. I would never lie to him, but I also don't see the harm in overlooking some of his shortcomings. He doesn't mention mine unless he thinks I'm going to get into trouble over them. Isn't that what a relationship is all about?"

"Yes. That's just how it should be. Loving someone despite their faults, knowing they aren't perfect in everyone's eyes. Just perfect for you."

Melody smiled. "You're a wise woman, Felicity Jefferies." She leaned on the counter and crossed her arms. "Can I ask you a question?"

"Of course."

"How did someone so wise end up married to a louse like

Richard Jefferies? Between you and me. Nothing has to leave this kitchen."

Felicity's eyebrows shot up. "What do you mean?"

Melody smiled. "Oh, come on Felicity. You know what I'm talking about. The drinking, the affairs. Before I knew Tom, I saw Richard many times when he had meetings with Gerard. He was such a charmer, and all the women doted on him. He hit on and succeeded, with more than a few of them."

Felicity groaned and looked over her shoulder toward the living room, where everyone's head was bent over the puzzle table. "Let's go outside and talk. I don't want Olivia and Will to hear this. We should pass these out and we can have dessert on the porch." Felicity tidied the kitchen while Melody handed desserts to the others. And then they went outside to sit on the garden bench, nestled into the trees where the scent of pine filled the air. Felicity looked at the plants still not potted and the stack of soil. Tomorrow, she thought, after everyone leaves.

"Alright. Richard had affairs," she said to Melody. "Some were one-offs, some lasted a while. But lots of men do, so I'm sure that's not what you wanted to talk about. We've already discussed the prenup and the letter. What else could there possibly be?"

"I know who bought Richard's company."

Felicity's eyes widened. "That's supposed to be private information."

"It is. I assure you. You must know I would never breathe a word of this. Not only would I lose my job, but I couldn't live with myself. You see, when I first started working there, I was asked to transcribe old meeting notes for Gerard. Everyone was going digital, and they wanted to shred a lot of paper. When I met Tom, and of course I recognized Richard as a client, things clicked. The affairs, the family events with the Jefferies that you didn't attend. That dreadful prenup. But Felicity, this is different. If you don't mind me asking, why do your kids think you're scrambling to pay bills when you obviously don't need to worry about money?"

Felicity's sigh was almost inaudible. "Nothing is ever for sure, Melody. At any moment, things can go wrong. Investments can falter. Stocks can plummet. I've always been cautious with my money. And I don't believe in handing things to kids. Tom and Olivia are much better people because they've had to earn what they have mostly, off their own backs. I think they're stronger for it. Will has had a harder struggle, but he'll get there."

Melody nodded. "I can appreciate that. I paid for my education, bought my car, paid all my bills myself, always. My parents struggled all their lives in low-paying jobs. I don't regret having to do what I did. In fact, I think I'm stronger for it, too, and I would raise my own children the same way."

"So, what is the point of our conversation? It isn't that I don't love talking with you, and it's obvious you haven't said anything to Tom. So, what's up?"

Melody put her hand over Felicity's. "Tell them. At least some of this, so they understand why there were problems between you and Richard. Tell the truth about his financial situation. And the prenup. It will explain why you and Richard's family don't get along."

"You want me to tell them that my father could have bought and sold Sid Jefferies twice over and pushing away that prenup bribe letter was like swatting a fly for him? My father was secretive about his wealth. Even I didn't know the extent of his estate until he passed. And I'm sure it was just as well."

"Smart man, who raised a smart daughter."

"I'm not so sure. Maybe you're right. Maybe it is time to tell the kids about some of this, but I don't want to ruin the image they have of their father. And what will they think of me, keeping these secrets all this time?"

"I think you should tell them everything, Felicity. Not for your sake, but for theirs. It would answer a lot of questions for them."

Felicity clasped her hands around her dessert bowl. The ice-cream had melted while they talked, the pie no longer held it's appeal. She grabbed Melody's hand. "Thank you for this. Sometimes we are too close to our own problems. I'll think about this, but for now, let's go back inside. They'll be wondering what's keeping us."

"Just one more thing, if you'll let me."

"Go on."

"Don't let your children come between you and Ben. It's obvious you care for each other. It would be a mistake to walk away from what could be something really beautiful."

Felicity's first thought was to tell Melody to mind her own business, but she saw the sincerity in her face. She wasn't interfering. She was just stating what she thought, and hadn't Felicity encouraged that in her?

"I will give it some thought," she said. But it just might be too late.

21

Sunday morning, after breakfast, Felicity had tackled the plants and spent most of the morning making potted arrangements which she placed strategically around the property. The porches and decks were now dotted with colour and stepping back to look at them, she felt better than she had in days. Next trip into town, she would buy some window boxes and hang them all across the top deck. It would be spectacular.

As she showered and washed the dirt from under her nails, Felicity knew that her family, except for Will, was packing up to go home. She couldn't let them leave without sitting down to settle some things. Melody was right. It was time. She called a family meeting.

"My room in fifteen minutes," she had said when she found each of them.

And now they perched on her bed, staring wide-eyed and curious at her. She sat in the armchair by the window, hands clasped together in her lap. "There are some things I need to tell you," she began. A deep breath. "Your father and I... No, that's wrong. I should start by saying my biggest regret is that your father isn't here to speak for himself, so you'll either trust what I'm telling you, or you won't, but rest assure the version his family will tell you won't be anywhere near mine."

"Geez mum, you're scaring me," Olivia said, encircling Tom's arm with her own.

"Me too. What's this all about?" Tom said.

"Let me start at the beginning. It's the only way to tell you everything. I met your father when we were at university. He was one of those super handsome young men you thought would one day tackle the world. Everyone loved to be around him. He was charming and passionate and so sure of himself. It was contagious. Every girl wanted to be his. And every guy wanted to be just like him. He was handsome and fit, and way too cocky, but no one cared, because he was Richard Jefferies." She smiled, her eyes fixed on the empty place his portrait used to hang over the nightstand. "It was his drive and ambition, his passion for life that struck me the most. He knew exactly what he wanted, and he was going to get it. And one of those things was me. I couldn't believe it. Richard Jefferies wanted

Felicity Bailey. It seemed impossible, like I was living in a dreamworld. We only dated a few weeks before he put a ring on my finger, and we were married by the end of that same summer. He had just started the company with his best friend Jim. Jim Summers, you remember him?"

They nodded. "I didn't know he worked with Dad," Tom said.

"They started the company together, but a few years in and they had a falling out and parted ways. I haven't seen Jim in years. He was a nice guy. Anyway, the company took a while to get off the ground, as companies do, but it was going well. My pay cheque from the bank kept us afloat until you guys came along and most of my pay was going to daycare and babysitters instead of paying the bills. So, we decided I should stay home and let Dad focus on the company.

"Is that when we moved from Toronto to St. Catharines?" Olivia asked.

Felicity nodded. "And I suppose that's when our focus on each other deteriorated. I was no longer the doting wife who threw brilliant dinner parties for his potential clients. I was a stay-at-home-mum, in yoga pants and sweatshirts soaked in baby puke. He was all about work and I was all about babies. I resented the long hours he worked, and he resented coming home to a messy house and an exhausted wife who complained about our finances."

"But every marriage goes through stuff like that, Mum," Tom said.

"Yes, most do, and hopefully, they work it out. But your father's drinking had gotten out of hand and there was no reasoning with him. And I'm sorry to say, I was beyond trying. I was too tired from taking care of you and the house, so I just pushed on and did what I had to do. And… then there was that Christmas up here when Abby…" Felicity's voice hitched, and tears welled in her eyes.

"We blamed each other, for various reasons, but it was easier to think it was someone else's fault than your own. But your dad wouldn't come with me to grief counseling, and he wouldn't ask for help on his own. He masked his sorrow in whisky, instead. He'd already had a series of affairs, but after this we grew even further apart. And who could blame him? I could barely look at him, and why would he look at me? I was overweight, exhausted, didn't care what I looked like."

"Oh Mum," Olivia sighed. "That's no excuse. And you were never that bad. You are so critical of yourself. That was wrong on his part. He shouldn't have done that."

Felicity lifted a hand. "It's alright, Olivia. I've told myself that many time. But you know me, never say never right. So, I held out some hope that maybe one day, he'd get help and we might still work things out." She let her gaze rise to avoid more tears. "That's the problem kids, we always think we'll have more time, but you don't. So don't hold back on things. I didn't and the biggest mistake of all was hiding everything from you guys. I can't change the past and I'm also not excusing his behaviour or my own. The truth is, he fell out of love with me, and I did the same."

"Why didn't you leave him? You could have gotten your old job back, couldn't you? Taken us with you. Found an apartment somewhere?" Olivia asked, tears welling in her eyes.

Felicity's heart wrenched at the pain she knew she was causing them. But she had to tell them the rest. She bit her lip and carried on. "Oh, the hours I spent debating exactly that. But I had no confidence in myself to support the three of you. Your father was already struggling financially, so there wouldn't be much coming from him. Taking him to court wouldn't have produced any other results, and I didn't want you to have a poor image of your father or get caught up in the inevitable, he said, she said, banter that divorced couples subject their kids too. And to be honest, I owned the house."

"You mean you both owned the house?" Tom said. "A marriage guarantees that things are fifty-fifty," Tom said.

"Not if there's a prenup."

"You made Dad sign a prenup?" he asked, his eyes wide, his brows lifting in surprise.

"We both did. But it started with his family. They were convinced I was only after their money. Dad, being the eldest, would have inherited his father's fortune, so they made me sign a prenup. I knew little about my parent's finances, but I thought two can play this game, so I had my lawyer amend the prenup to work both ways, which meant that your father was not entitled to my future assets through inheritance, and I was not entitled to his. Whatever he had would go straight to any future children or his brother, if we had none. Later, when you guys were born, he amended his will to divide his assets between you and to put your shares in trust, till you turn thirty."

She glanced at Tom, whose mouth was already open to ask something, but Will intervened. "I don't understand. Why didn't you just kick him out?"

"Because of you. I know that sounds like a copout, but we wanted to keep things intact for you, if we could."

"Well, knock me over with a feather," Olivia said. "I knew there was stuff, but I didn't know it was that weird. What's the deal with Dad's family? Is that why you never came to Christmas dinners or weddings and why you've never been to St. Lucia?"

Felicity nodded again. "I couldn't go within a hundred feet of any Jefferies property. So, we made excuses. I thought you'd just accept it as the way our family did things. I can see now that we should have told you something closer to the truth, rather than make up excuses."

Will edged toward the side of the bed. "Are you done now? Cause I could use a beer."

"Not quite," Felicity said. "Tom, you said Uncle Ken told you there was an influx of cash in the company and someone had bought it a few years ago." Tom nodded, but said nothing more.

Felicity continued. "When Grandpa Bailey died, I inherited his estate. I wanted to invest in your father's company, to give it a kick-start again. My lawyers advised that I buy it and take over rather than just dumping money into what had become a failing venture. For the past fifteen years, I have been the owner and CEO of Dad's company. After he passed, we went public, so now it's being run by a board of directors. I have a place on the board, but I'm no longer running the company."

"I thought Grandad Jefferies was backing Dad?" Olivia asked.

"He refused to put out any more money and I'm not sure he had much left to put into it, anyway. We hit a close up or sell situation and who else would buy a company that was on the brink of bankruptcy? But I still believed in your father's vision. And I knew he could do it if he tried. He just had to change the way he did some things. This gave him the freedom to try new things. But there was already a rift between me and the Jefferies. When they learned I had the money to buy a mid-sized Toronto advertising company, they were speechless. And of course, that's when they realized their mistake in forcing the prenup. They still won't have anything to do with me, but now it's because of their own remorse."

"Geez Mum," Tom said. "How did all this happen without us knowing any of it? Besides Dad's drinking. Everyone saw that. We must have been pretty naïve."

"Not naïve, Tom. Just sheltered from the truth."

"So, are you saying you're rich, Mum?" Will asked hesitantly.

Felicity shook her head. "Far from it. But let's just say I can afford to pay for those renovations, and I can pay you for doing the architectural designs. So, you better make friends with Ben if you still want the contract."

There was a long moment of silence while Felicity watched her children's faces go from shock to confusion to love and back again as they processed what she'd told them.

"There's just one more thing for now. I want to explain about what happened yesterday with Ben. In hindsight, I should have told you that Ben and I were becoming a little more than friends. But please understand that your father and I have not had a proper marriage for years. There were lots of other women in his life over the years, but I never stopped loving the man I married. He just wasn't that man anymore, though I honestly hoped one day things would change and he might come back to me. But in all that time, there was no one else for me, even though we agreed to a legal separation."

"You were legally separated, even though you lived in the same house." It was not a question, but a statement from Tom.

"Yes, that's right."

Will clicked his tongue. "Maybe it would have been better if there had been other men, Mum. We might have been used to it.

Then seeing you kissing the neighbour in the lake wouldn't have been such a shock."

Olivia slapped her brother's arm. "You said you were over it," she hissed. "Go on, Mum. Don't let this twit get on your nerves."

Felicity smiled at her daughter. "Thank you, darling. Look Will, I can't change what happened yesterday. But I can say again that it was impulsive, and it came from a long time of being lonely, but it isn't right. I will end things with Ben. You guys are, and always have been, my priority."

Olivia groaned. "Well, that sucks. For you, Mum. I mean. We're all on our own now, getting on with our lives. Why shouldn't you?"

"Shut up Olivia," Will said. "For cryin' out loud, Dad's only been dead three months."

"Don't you get it Will? Why shouldn't Mum have someone in her life?"

"Wait! Wait!" Felicity held up her hand. "I don't want you arguing about me or my choices. When the time is right, if the time is right, then I will decide if I want someone in my life or not. Clear?"

Solemn heads bobbed around the room and, just as Felicity was about to call an end to it all, Melody knocked lightly on the door.

"I'm sorry to interrupt, but lunch is on the table, and we need to get going Tom." She flashed a hopeful look at Felicity, who nodded and smiled.

"Let's eat," Olivia said, leading the way to the dining room, giving Will another smack on the arm as he passed her.

Later, after waving Olivia and Eric off, Will went back inside, still not entirely friends with his brother and sister again. He did, however, kiss Melody on the cheek and shake hands with Eric before skulking away. Tom pulled Felicity aside and gave her a hug. "Thanks for telling us, Mum. It must be a relief to get all that off your shoulders."

She smiled. "You'd think so, wouldn't you? But I'm not so sure. I feel as if I've just transferred the burden. Now I feel guilty about laying it at your feet."

"Don't. What's done is done and you've answered a lot of questions about things I always wondered about. I'm proud of you. Proud that you stuck it out with him, proud that you made that company work, for him, for us. That must have been tough."

Colour rose in her cheeks. If Tom only knew how tough it had been, of the arguments she and Richard had had, of how low his reputation sank at work. He would never know of the sleepless nights while she poured over the books, the people she'd let go, and the new hires. The list was endless. Not for the first time, she wondered if it would have been better to just let that company go under. But Tom was right. What's done was done.

"There's just one thing I don't understand," Tom said. "Who's the fourth beneficiary in Dad's will?"

Felicity's face fell. Her thoughts raced back in time, pulling and tugging at things she'd pushed beneath the surface.

"Mum?"

"I didn't know there was a fourth."

"Well, it isn't Abby, because he would have changed that. So, who could it be? It's an unnamed person. And Gerard said we didn't have to worry about it. The money was already set up in trust and he would administer everything. All Uncle Ken and I had to do was sign off on it."

"Uncle Ken didn't know?"

Tom shook his head.

"It's as much a surprise to me as it is to you. Let me look into it. But for now, don't mention it to your sister or Will, okay?"

22

Monday morning and with everyone gone but Will, the cottage was quiet. As she pulled back the covers, Felicity heard the distinct chug and gurgle of coffee brewing in the kitchen and the thunderous sound of rain on the roof. Hard rain. A torrential downpour, in fact. Mac was curled up on the pillow beside her. She stretched and yawned, exposing her tiny, but oh-so-sharp baby teeth, and then promptly went back to sleep.

"Some companion you are," Felicity said. "Not even a good morning meow."

She wrapped up in her housecoat and went to the kitchen, where she found the two mugs waiting patiently beside the coffeepot. When the coffee was ready, she poured two cups, remembering not to put sugar in Will's and headed for the Muskoka room, guessing that was where she would find him.

"Have you been up long?" she asked, handing him his cup.

"A little while. It's so quiet here, I couldn't sleep."

"You call this quiet? Listen to that rain!" She smiled and sat down on the loveseat. "But I know what you mean. That's why I love it up here. I've been thinking more and more about moving up here, permanently. And last night, after our talk, I made up my mind to do it. I'm thinking of selling the house. But not until we know you're settled at Carleton."

Will groaned. "What if that doesn't happen?"

"It will. I'm sure of it."

"Thanks for the vote of confidence." He sipped his coffee warily. Felicity knew something was on his mind, but she didn't press. Finally, he said, "I'm glad you told us everything, Mum. It must have been hard keeping it all a secret. And I'm sorry this has been such a shitty weekend. I know a lot of it is my fault."

"Thank you for saying so, Will, but first, the time spent with people I love is never *shitty*. And honestly, the fault is mine, for thinking I needed to keep you all in the dark. But we should think about moving forward, instead of dwelling on it, okay? I hate to see any of this mess up your idea of going back to university. I still want you to draw up plans for the renovations here. But I might change my mind about what to do."

"Why don't you make a list of things you want, and I'll see if I can work it all in and what it will cost."

"Perfect. And do you think you could work with Ben, considering everything that happened on the weekend?"

He shrugged and gave her a wary look. "I feel like a jerk, especially after what you told us. I want you to be happy, Mum. And if Ben makes you happy, then don't listen to me."

Felicity gave his arm a reassuring squeeze. "I'm not worried about Ben and I. What I meant was, given what you said to him, can you work with him?"

"I wasn't very nice to him."

"Well, you can fix that, can't you? An apology goes a long way. You just said you were sorry to me."

"It's easy to say sorry to you. I've been doing it for 22 years. And you're my mum. You have to forgive me."

Felicity laughed. "I suppose there's some truth in that. But we all need forgiveness and to forgive. It's soul cleansing and liberating. And what I know of Ben already is that he's not the kind to hold grudges. He's a nice man, Will. Talk to him."

"Do you think he's home now?"

"If his car is there, he probably is."

Will set down his cup and kissed her cheek. "Wish me luck. I just have to grab my notepad."

"I'm going to do laundry," she called after him. "Leave your stuff by your door."

First, I need to make a call, Felicity thought. She had tried to call Carrie back three times, but her friend was not answering. Felicity's texts had gone unanswered, and an email wasn't even opened. Carrie had left no voicemails, nothing to say why she had tried to call her thirteen times in under three minutes on Saturday morning.

Felicity tried again, hitting the green button on her screen, and waited for the call to connect. On the third ring, Carrie picked up.

"You better be dead," her friend hissed into the phone.

"What? Why? What's your problem? I've tried to return your calls, but you weren't answering. Take a chill pill, girl."

"I'm sorry." Carrie relented. "It's just that there's so much going on and I needed you and I stopped by the house and your neighbour was cutting your grass, telling me you've gone north already. You didn't tell me you were going early." She stopped for a breath of air.

"I wasn't aware I had to report to you," Felicity teased, pretending to be hurt. "Oh, come on, Car. You know, I was planning to come up early. We talked about it at your May two-four barbeque."

"Yeah, okay, we might have. I guess."

"So, what's up? Why are you so anxious?"

"Work. The bane of my existence. Natalie Piper. My boss."

"When are you going to quit that job and start your own company? You hate being told what to do, and you could run that place with your eyes closed. Seriously, Car. You should think about it."

"Okay for some, but I've got a five-star appetite for luxury, remember? I'm not sure I could give up my expensive habits while a company gets off the ground."

"Find an investor, or a partner. Preferably a silent one who has the capital to get you started."

"Say, partner. You looking to make a wise investment?"

"No. Sorry. I'm about to dole out a chunk of money to renovate this place. Why don't you could come and visit? Stay as long as you like. Get yourself sorted out. When was the last time you took a vacation?" Did she really say that? Too much Carrie was more than Felicity could stand. She loved her, but her high energy and high maintenance personality always caused disagreements.

"Bugs, eeww. Not my idea of fun."

Felicity heard a rustling on the other end and pictured her friend fidgeting with things, biting her nails, chewing on the side of her thumb, swirling an auburn lock around and around her finger. The impatient silence told her Carrie had more on her mind than just work problems.

"Okay, now do you want to tell me why you really called?"

"Oh god. You know me too well." Carrie heaved a great sigh and exhaled into the phone. "It's Blain. It's… I can't even get the words out." She broke down in huge sobs, her words coming out in mumbles and moans, so that Felicity had to guess by her tone that Blain was having an affair. When Carrie collected herself, she finished with, "When are you coming home? I really need you."

"I can't, Carrie. I've got workshops planned and clients to see up here. I booked them because I knew I was staying for the entire summer. I can't just cancel everything. Why don't you come up here? I know it's not your favourite place to be, but there aren't many bugs right now and there's always spray, you know. The kids have left, except for Will. So, it's quiet until the July first weekend."

"I don't know. I…"

"Come on. You know you want to. And if you really hate it here, you can book into a bed-and-breakfast in town or something."

"There is that possibility," Carrie mused. "Alright, I'll do it. I'll give the cottage a try, and if I can't stand it, I'll book into a hotel. Not a BNB. Sometimes you don't know what you'll get in those places. Wait, they have hotels up there, right?"

"Goodness girl. Haven't you ever been out of the Niagara Peninsula? Of course, they do. Now get packed. And I'll see you when you get here. Today? Do you think?"

"No. I need to arrange things. Tomorrow or Wednesday at the latest. I suppose I can do some work from there. You have internet, right?"

"No. There's no internet here. Just leave work behind and get your butt up here."

"Okay. Wait. How are you texting and emailing me if there's no internet up there? You were kidding, right? Tell me you were kidding. I'm not sure I can live without the internet."

"Carrie. We have internet. Just pack."

Felicity disconnected the call and got busy rearranging things in her bedroom. She would put Carrie there so she could have her own bathroom and the largest of the bedrooms. It had the best view of the lake, though she wasn't sure that would matter to Carrie. Clean sheets, her own bathroom, a bottle of wine and lots of chocolate were more important to Carrie than the view. Felicity shook her head as she gathered her clothes and shoved them into the dresser in the room Tom and Melody had used. She didn't mind giving up her room for Carrie. To some, she seemed a shallow and material kind of person, but deep down, when you really got to know her, Carrie was always there. In all the anguish she and Richard had gone through, it was always Carrie who'd been there to help her sort it out, and to pick up the pieces of her shattered soul.

She stripped her bed and took her sheets downstairs to add to the rest of the laundry. She changed the wash load to the dryer and put a new one in the washer. One more and she'd be done. The dining room table became her place to fold laundry, when she had lots of it to do. And that certainly described what had accumulated after a weekend with six people. She made neat piles for each room, then carried them off to wherever they belonged and was on the last of the towels when Will came through the front door. He leaned on the door frame, watching her fold the last towel.

"Well, how did it go?" she asked. "You were gone a while."

"Good," he said, a hedge in his voice. "Mum, I brought a friend with me. I hope you don't mind."

She looked up as Ben move out from behind Will and into the doorway, his hands jammed into his blue jean pockets. "He asked me to come, so I came," Ben said. "I can leave if you want."

She shook her head. "No, I don't want you to leave. Let me just clear this away and you guys can have the table."

"No. We don't need it," Will said. "I'm heading to Huntsville. I've got some research to do." Will plucked his keys from the hook and headed for the door.

The spring in his step and his straight back were encouraging to see. Will had a purpose, something to look forward to, and Felicity was happy for him. Their talk had paid off. She might, however, regret talking to Ben.

"He thought we should talk," Ben said with a little shrug and a hopeful raise of his brow. "And I do too, if thaC's okay with you."

"I'll put on some coffee?" she said, ready to slip past him to the kitchen.

He caught her arm on the way by. "I don't want coffee or tea, or anything to eat. I want to talk, Felicity. I think we need to, don't you?"

She looked away from his piercing gaze as, toward the window. Outside, Will's car kicked into life. "I think I made it pretty clear this was a mistake, and I should never have…"

"Are you sure?" he asked. "Because, for me, it's not that simple. I really wish you'd reconsider."

"It's not that simple for me either." She met his gaze then and found his eyes searching hers. "But yes, I'm quite sure." Her heart thumped in her chest, arguing with her.

He held her gaze for a moment, and then he nodded. "Alright then. If you're sure." He turned to leave but stood with his hand on the doorknob. "There's something I want you to know, though, before you break my heart and put an end to this." He came back to her, his hands reaching for hers. "It wasn't a mistake for me. I care for you, Felicity, very much. I don't know how things like this happen so quickly or why, and I can't change the way I feel. I know you feel it too. I know I said, no judgement, and no advice, but you I think you're scared. And I know how that is. I understand it. Like I said before, we all have stuff in our past. I'm trying to put my past behind me and I'm asking you to consider doing the same. Don't throw away a wonderful friendship and whatever else this might become."

"You don't know…," she said.

"But I do." He took her elbows in his hands and pulled her gaze to meet his. "Can you stop thinking about your kids and think of yourself for once? What about your happiness, Felicity? They're moving on with their lives. Where does that leave you?"

"You presume too much, Ben," she snapped. "You hardly know me. You don't know my kids, or anything about me."

"I know enough," he whispered. "And I know I'm falling in love with you."

In love? Impossible. They'd known each other a week. She shook her head. "Don't say things you cannot possibly mean." She didn't dare to look at him, or she might never tear herself away. Her heart thumped a frantic rhythm against her chest, blood rushed to her head, sweat beaded and dripped down her back. Not again. She would not do this love-at-first-sight thing a second time.

Ben pulled her into his arms and held on tight, despite her trying to pull free. "But I can mean it, and I do," he whispered into her hair.

Could she deny what she felt? She would never have kissed him or spent so much time with him if she didn't feel something too. Yet, even setting aside her children's opinions, she wasn't sure this was a good thing. Once before, she'd fallen in love with a man, and hadn't taken the time to really get to know him. The only thing good to come from that was her children. She loved her children, was grateful Richard had given them to her, but she would not go down that road a second time.

Ben lifted her chin, and she saw the look in his eyes, and then she knew. He's not Richard, she told herself. And he's not asking you to marry him or spend the rest of your lives together. At least not yet. Live for today, she thought.

But what if he moved away, back to some third world country, especially if he couldn't work things out with Emma? She'd be heartbroken again, just like when she'd found out Richard had been sleeping around. Ben wasn't Richard, but a broken heart was a broken heart, no matter what or who caused it.

"I can't," she whispered, tears welling in her eyes. "It's too hard. It's too…"

"Wow. What did your husband do to you?" he asked, his arms drawing her even closer. "I'm not letting you go until you talk to me, so stop struggling."

She shook her head and lowered her gaze again And then she let her head rest on his chest. "It's not that. I just…"

"Felicity." It was almost a reprimand. "Look at me." He lifted her chin. "Whatever has happened, it's in the past. I'm not him. He's dead. You're alive. For god's sake, woman, live."

And then he bent his head and kissed her, tenderly, softly, until her worries faded away and her heart eased. It was in that moment that she realized she loved him more than she had ever loved Richard. She gave in to the kiss and melted against him, wondering why she'd been fighting this so hard. His arms felt wonderful around her. Safe and warm. It had been so long since she felt the gentleness of a man's hand on her cheek, the tenderness of a man's lips caressing hers, she'd nearly forgotten what she'd been missing. Now it felt wonderful. He felt wonderful, and, in that moment, nothing else mattered; not the children, not the past, not her overly cautious head. Felicity let go of it all and surrendered her heart to Ben's.

23

It was hours before Will returned from Huntsville and in that time the rain stopped and while thick grey clouds still hovered; it seemed the worst was over. Ben and Felicity talked over a simple lunch of soup and sandwiches and then curled up on the couch to watch a movie. And that is where Will found them when he came home with good news. He flashed an approving smile at Ben, whose arm was around Felicity's shoulders, and set himself down on the opposite couch.

"It looks like this is all possible," he said, laying his notebook down on the table. "I worked in some extras for you, Mum. You want to see?"

"Of course, I do. Show me." She leaned forward, her chin in her hand, and watched his face as Will revealed a rough sketch of the plans he and Ben had discussed.

"What's this?" She asked, pointing to something sketched into what was now woods on the side of the cottage.

"We could clear this land for expansion, and this would be a private suite for you. You'd have your own bathroom with a soaker tub, and your own sitting room so you could get away from the rest of us when you want quiet. And your bedroom would face the lake, so you'll have that magnificent view you love."

"Or," Ben leaned across and drew a thick line across a doorway. "If you wanted to rent this suite out, you could just lock this door here on this side and it becomes self-contained."

"But no kitchen," Felicity pointed out.

Will countered. "But would you rent it out, Mum? I mean, it's an option, sure. But would you? You value your privacy so much, I can't see it."

"I might need to if I'm going to afford all this."

"Well, I suppose we could make the sitting room smaller and put in a little kitchenette."

"And the main kitchen?" Felicity asked.

"Here," Ben said, pointing to the sketches. "An eat-in kitchen with a bay window instead of the small one you have now."

"I like that idea," she said.

"And we'll take down this wall," Will directed her attention to the bedrooms on the main floor. "And make two larger rooms. You could use one for an office or it stays as a bedroom. And none of this will take away from what's already here. The living room, dining room and the Muskoka room stay as they are. But we could upgrade the flooring, put in new windows, or whatever else you want since we'll be buying lots of supplies."

"This is great, Will. And upstairs?"

He flipped to another page filled with lines and numbers and markings she did not understand. "Upstairs you'll have two more bedrooms, a large family sized bathroom, and another room for games or a family room, or whatever. Another chill space."

"I really like this, Will. Thank you. Gee, a soaker tub, I like the sound of that." She grinned. "But what's this going to cost? This can't possibly be within the budget I suggested."

"Mum." Will laid a hand on her arm. "You have to stop living like you're barely scraping by. You deserve to have a few luxuries, don't you think?"

Ben looked at her. "You could just do the upper floor if you wanted, but if you're really considering living here permanently and thinking of the future, what Will is suggesting makes sense."

"Yeah," Will agreed. "Tom and Mel want kids right away and I'm pretty sure Eric is about to ask Olivia if he hasn't already."

"Really? How did I miss that one?"

"Sheesh, are you blind? Didn't you see the way he looks at her and the way he goes along with whatever she does, or says, or wants? He's not going anywhere. And she'd be nuts to let him."

"Alright. Well, weddings and grandkids aside, which, by the way, I'm far too young for… How much is this going to cost me?"

Will turned the paper over and showed her a figure. "I need to add in a fifteen percent for flexibility on both the labour costs and the supplies. Just in case." He flashed a look at Ben, who nodded in agreement.

"It's a contingency cushion. Lumber prices fluctuate, drywall costs, electrical, then what if we get in there and find something we can't see on the surface?" Ben said. "You should probably make it twenty percent, Will. This is an old cottage. We don't want any surprises down the road."

Felicity looked at him curiously. "We?" she laughed. "Who's financing this project, anyway?"

"Hey, sorry. I didn't mean to butt in."

"Teasing. Of course, you're a part of it. A big part. And I have a feeling Will is going to enjoy working with you on this."

"You bet," Will chirped. "Okay, I have to do this up formally. This is all very rough right now, but I didn't want to have to do two sets. That's why I went into town to ask about permits and what's allowed the land variances and all that. We'll need to put in permit applications and all kinds of other stuff. When do you want to start this, Mum?"

"Goodness, I hadn't planned on doing any of this for another year, at least. But there's no time like the present. I suppose clearing for this wing of my new castle will mean getting some heavy equipment in here. It will be noisy. I don't want to mess up anyone's summer with that, so why don't we look at the end of the summer, after Labour Day?"

"That should be plenty of time to get all this organized. Will you let me project manage it for you, too?"

"Are you sure you want to do that?"

"Well, Ben's offered to help, if that's okay with you. It would be great on my resume and my application to Carleton. And not being cheeky or anything, Mum, but you'll notice there's a line item in the budget for that. And you know I could use the money."

Felicity laughed. "Yes, you could, so I suppose you'll stay here for the duration, then?"

"If that's okay, except I'm not sure what do to about Luke's car?"

"Maybe Olivia or Eric could drive it back when they come for the holiday weekend."

"That works."

"And once things are underway here, I'll see about selling the house." Felicity glanced up at Ben. "Wow. This is all happening so fast. I really hadn't thought I'd be doing this now. But," she slapped her thighs. "Yes. Let's do this."

They celebrated with a dinner at the Cast Iron Restaurant in Baysville.

"To new beginnings," Felicity said, raising her glass in a toast.

"Here. Here." Ben leaned over to kiss her softly on the cheek.

Will rolled his eyes. "Geez, you two, get a room."

Felicity flashed him a smile of gratitude. If he hadn't reconciled with Ben and urged him to talk to her, she might have missed out on the best thing in her life. She laid her hand over Ben's, the other over Will's. "Speaking of rooms. I forgot to tell you that Aunt Carrie is coming."

"Oh no," Will cried. He looked at Ben. "Can I stay at your place?"

"Uh, I suppose so. But what's wrong with Aunt Carrie?" He looked at Felicity with raised brows. "Your sister?"

"Best friend. The one who so urgently had to speak to me the other day."

"Ah, the William Tell Overture."

"One and the same," Will said. "I really don't know how you two are best friends. She's nuts."

"She's not nuts. She's eccentric and driven and…"

"Nuts."

24

Carrie arrived the next day amid the second day of torrential downpours. Visibility was difficult even from the windows of the cottage and driving, Felicity knew, must have been awful. She pictured her friend maneuvering the partially flooded side roads around Ril Lake and knew they would spend the first hour hearing Carrie whine about it.

When she pulled in and parked next to Felicity's SUV, Will looked at Ben, who was washing up the last of the dishes after helping Felicity prepare their supper. Will put the tea towel he'd been using over Ben's shoulder and gave him a pat. "Sorry mate. You're on your own."

Felicity groaned as Ben dried his hands on the towel. "Is she that bad?"

"No. She's not." Felicity went to open the door.

"I know I'm more than a couple of hours late," Carrie chirped when she stepped inside. "Where am I? England? It feels like I've been driving that long and the weather's consistent." She slipped off a pair of red pumps and kicked them toward the mat. And then she peeled off her raincoat and handed it, with two fingers on the collar, to Felicity.

Only Carrie would dress to the nines for a three-and-a-half-hour drive to a cottage. She wore a much too tight grey skirt with a pink jersey blouse, also a size too small, that scooped low to reveal her ample cleavage. Felicity cast a disapproving eye over her friend, but apparently, Ben didn't mind at all. She caught him sizing Carrie up and rolled her eyes at him. He lifted his shoulders in a *well-I'm-human* kind of look and grinned.

Carrie closed her umbrella and hung it on the hook by the door. "Damn!" she cried, shaking the rain from herself. "At least the Holiday Inn has a canopy." She pulled Felicity in for a hug. "Come here, you."

"We'll get your stuff later," Felicity assured her. "When this dies down. Want a drink?"

"Oh, yes, please. What have you got? Wine? No, I should have something stronger to settle my nerves. Whisky. No brandy. That'll do it." She pushed back a lock of auburn hair, wet and stringy and dripping rainwater into her eyes. And when she had tucked it safely back into her chignon, she caught sight of Ben.

"Damn!" she said for a second time. "Holiday Inn may have a canopy, but it doesn't have one of you waiting inside the door." She stuck out a hand to shake his. "Hi, there. I'm Carrie. Clarissa, actually, but my friends call me Carrie."

Felicity introduced Ben as her neighbour, which was all she was about to tell Carrie for now. When a friend was having marital problems, the last thing they needed to hear was that their best friend had just met someone special.

"Neighbour, eh? Listen lovely, you can be my neighbour any time you like. Do you live in this godforsaken wilderness permanently, or are you from the city?"

Felicity flashed him a *watch out for this one* kind of look. "Ben, why don't you take Carrie to the living room while I make the drinks? We can watch the storm from there."

"Watch the storm? I'd rather hide under the blankets. Wanna join me, Ben?" Carrie giggled and nudged his elbow. And then she linked her arm under his and turned toward the living room. "In here?"

Felicity let out a little groan and pulled the percolator from the cupboard. Coffee with that brandy, she thought, or Carrie would be sloshed in minutes and not from the rain. Flirting had always been Carrie's way of hiding her nervousness and her troubles. She wondered if she should have given Ben more of a warning about her. Still, he was a grown man. Surely, he'd run into others like Carrie before.

When she brought in the tray of drinks, she found Carrie snuggled up next to Ben, who had worked his way as close to the end of the couch as he could, without sitting on the arm. Will was on the other couch, staring blankly at his Aunt Carrie while she grilled him about work, his love life, his siblings; all the things Will never wanted to discuss with anyone, let alone her.

Felicity cut in and changed the subject as she passed around their drinks. "I've got a chicken pot pie in the oven for supper. I hope that's okay, Carrie. You're not on that no-carb diet again, are you?"

Carrie waved a dismissive hand. "What a crock that was. The instant you eat a single carb again, you gain 10 pounds. I gave up. I am who I am. If that isn't good enough, then tough."

"Forgive me for having an opinion," Ben said, pulling his arm free of hers to accept his cup from Felicity. "But neither of you need to worry about your figures from where I'm sitting." He pushed off the couch and took the armchair, leaving a space open for Felicity beside her friend.

"Well, aren't you sweet for saying that?" Carrie said.

Felicity warned Ben off. "If you start down that road, she'll never let you stop."

"Oh, I'm not that bad." Carrie pushed at Felicity's arm. "But every girl likes a compliment, don't they?"

"Indeed we do," Felicity agreed, raising her glass. "Here's to compliments and summer storms and good friends."

"Cheers!"

When the rain let up, Carrie relinquished her keys to Will, and he and Ben went to gather her things from the car while Felicity showed Carrie where she would sleep.

"Never mind that," she squealed, following Felicity to the bedroom. "You've been holding out on me. Fess up girl."

"There's really not much to tell." Not much that she would tell Carrie, anyway.

"I can see why you enjoy coming up here. Is he a regular neighbour who's lived up here for years, like you?"

Felicity shook her head. "He's just visiting for a few weeks."

"You didn't tell me."

"There's nothing to tell."

"Don't kid a kidder. You two have something going on, or I'm not your kids' Auntie Carrie."

"Don't start."

"Are you saying he's available? Handsome. Good manners. A devilish smile."

"Wait. Wasn't it you who was crying on the phone about her husband having an affair?"

"Tit for tat, I say." Carrie lifted her chin and fingered the lace runner on Felicity's dresser.

"Sounds rather childish to me. Is that really what you want to do?"

Carrie flopped down on the bed. "No, but you know what I'm like. I'm an outrageous flirt. I never really mean anything by it. It's all talk. Sheesh, if Ben walked in here right now and said…" She flicked her eyes toward the door. Her face coloured. "Oh, speak of the devil."

"Where do these go?" Ben held up a suitcase in one hand, make-up bag in the other.

"Over here, please." Carrie went to the dresser and patted the surface. "Just put it all here and I'll sort it out. Listen Ben, I'm sorry, if I was a little forward before. I come on strong, but I don't mean it."

He laughed, his eyes lighting up with mischief. "It's fine, Carrie. I'll consider it a compliment. Besides, you're married and I'm…" He flashed Felicity a question look. "Spoken for." He set down Carrie's cases and went to Felicity, who was by the door. "Will has the rest in the kitchen. It's food. Apparently, Carrie doesn't think we have grocery stores up here. There's enough to feed an army."

"Oh, I googled it. I knew there were grocery stores. But Felicity knows me. I go nowhere empty-handed. It's how we were raised, isn't kiddo?" She linked her arm through Felicity's. "Now, did you say something about a chicken pot pie?"

She released Carrie's hold on her arm. "It won't be ready yet. If you want to take a shower after your long trip, the bathroom is right through that door."

Carrie spun around to look at the ensuite behind her. "Oh. No. This is your room, isn't it, Fel? You can't give up your own room for me."

"I can. Besides, you'd have to share a bathroom with Will if I didn't and something tells me you wouldn't want to do that. You know how boys can be."

"Well, only if you're sure."

"I'm sure." Felicity took Ben's hand. "Want to make a salad?"

"I certainly do," he said, chuckling as he followed her to the kitchen.

When supper was cleared away, and most of the clouds had dispersed to the south, they took their tiramisu and wine, both of which Carrie had brought with her, to the lower deck. Droplets of rain trickled and dripped from the trees all around them, but the roof of the gazebo sheltered them. The air held that rain-fresh scent like it always did after a downpour. Will opted to have his dessert inside as he was hard at work with a software program Ben had loaned him, putting together the reno plans. So, it was Ben, Carrie, and Felicity enjoying the after-rain freshness and their dessert.

"You were right, Fel. Not a bug in sight," Carrie said, dropping her spoon into her empty bowl and downing the last of her wine. "I suppose I can survive here for a day or two."

"Oh stop. It's not that bad. You have everything here that you have at home or in a hotel. It's just not as grand."

"From your pictures, I imagined something much more rustic, but this is actually… nice."

Ben's brow lifted. "You mean you've never been here before? How is that possible? Didn't you say this cottage has been in your family for generations, Felicity?"

"I did. But as you might have guessed, Carrie isn't the cottage type, so she's never wanted to come, despite many invitations." Felicity tossed her napkin at her friend. "But she's here now so we'll make the most of it, won't we, Car? Tomorrow, I've got a workshop in Huntsville. Ben is coming too. He's working on his family tree, too. You want to come? We're going out for dinner afterwards."

"Well, I suppose I could do a little shopping or something while you're doing your thing. I'm not much for digging up the past. Let it lie, is what I say," Carrie said.

Ben's phone, which he'd laid on the table, vibrated and a picture of a curly haired blond flashed on the screen. "I better take this. Excuse me, ladies." Heading toward the dock, they heard him say hello to Emma and then he went quiet.

Felicity carried on with her plans for Carrie's visit. "I thought on Thursday I'd take you to see some sites. There's Dorset, Algonquin Park, lots of fun places to shop in Huntsville. There's a great store called Soapstones with body lotions and soaps they make right there. We also must stop at Yummies in Jar, where they make jams and syrups. The owner is an artist. His paintings are on display, and they have other local artisans' things there too. You'll love it."

"Sounds wonderful. Anything you want to do, Fel. Really. I'm game. I just need to chill and figure out what I'm doing about Blain."

"I'm sorry this is happening. I know exactly how you feel."

"I know you do, and you understand me, so you get what I'm going through. I couldn't spill my guts to just anyone. Is my husband nuts or what? I mean, really," she waved her hands over her body, and scooped a breast in each hand. "Does he really want to give up these?"

Felicity laughed. "He's obviously blind, my dear." She played with the rim of her coffee cup. "If you need somewhere to stay, after you leave here, there's no one at my place all summer. Will might go back and forth a couple of times but mostly, he'll be here with me, and I don't expect to go home until September. We're expanding this place and eventually, I'll sell the house."

"No way! You're going to leave me all alone? What will I do without you?"

"Oh, I'm sure you'll manage. You've got more friends than you know what to do with."

"Yeah, but not real friends. Not like you."

"That's sweet of you to say. But we won't lose touch. And I'll come back once in a while and you'll come up. We'll have a full guest suite by then. But the house is going to be empty all summer and if you need a place to stay while you two sort things out, you might as well stay there. I'd be glad of someone there to keep an eye on the place. And there wouldn't be anyone to bother you. Even the dog is gone."

"Hope? What happened?"

"Hit by a car, silly thing. Nothing the kids could do."

"I'm sorry Fel. I know you loved her."

"Yeah, well, things happen, don't they? But I have Mac."

"And Mac is…?"

"A kitten. She's timid but you'll probably meet her later. She likes hiding under my bed. She'll jump up and play with your toes in the night."

"Cute. I look forward to meeting her. At least you've got someone for company, although I'm sure you didn't need a cat when you've got…" she nodded toward Ben, who was heading back to them. "He seems like a keeper," she whispered.

Felicity felt a flush warming her cheeks. "It's early days," she said softly.

"Good news," Ben said, obviously pleased by the news he'd received on the phone. "Emma is going coming to stay for a few days. Starting tomorrow."

"Oh, but isn't tomorrow your workshop, Felicity?" Carrie asked.

"No worries. She's working till five," Ben clarified. "I'll just have to take a raincheck on that dinner you owe me." He winked at Felicity. "I'm not going to let you out of our agreement. I won that race fair and square."

Felicity lifted her chin. "You did, and I always pay my debts. We'll just do it another time."

25

"What do you think, Felicity?" Ben asked the following morning as he leaned against the doorframe of the second bedroom in Alice's cottage. "Do you think she'll like it?"

"She'll love it. Are these the pictures you took at Algonquin the other day?" she pointed to a collection of three framed photos on the wall.

"They are. You took this one."

"No, I didn't. You lined it up. I just pushed the button. They really look great with the paint colour in this room. As for getting things ready for Emma, I'd stop worrying so much about it. I don't know what else you could do. This bedding is beautiful. And she's got a bathroom to herself, which has every luxury a girl could want from a five-star hotel. She knows she's coming to a cottage, right?"

"Yes, of course she does. She was here the other day, remember?"

"Right, I forgot. I'm sure she won't be expecting all this."

"You're right. I went overboard, didn't I?" He fussed, removing pillows from the bed and shifting things on the dresser.

"Stop." Felicity took the things from him and replaced them all. "Maybe it's a little much, but I can see why. And she probably will too. This is huge for both of you. What time do you expect her?"

"Six. She has to work till five, but she's coming straight here afterwards. I hope I have enough food."

"If she's anything like Olivia was, she'll eat next to nothing."

"I suppose, but she is a vegetarian, and she's carb-free. She made the abundantly clear."

"Have you got eggs?

"Yes, and some of those Beyond Meat burgers?"

"Then you'll be fine, and you can always take her shopping and let her pick out what she wants."

"Good plan. Thanks. What would I do without you?" He caressed her arms and pulled her closer to him.

"I have an idea," Felicity said. "Why don't we take the kayaks out and you can wear off some of that anxious energy? If you don't do something, you'll just sit and stew and move things around. Again."

"Or we could continue with this." He bent his head to kiss her, slowly at first, then with deepening the kiss. And then he gave a great sigh. "I think we better go for a paddle, or I will want you to stay right here," he added with a suggestive smile.

"Well, I suppose, if you really don't want to leave just now, we could…" She snuggled up close to him and kissed him again, running her hands over his chest as he cupped her face in his hands.

The sound of someone knocking jolted them apart. Felicity smiled. "Saved by the door," she whispered. "But maybe we can revisit this idea another time?"

Ben nodded and kissed the tip of her nose. "Definitely."

They went through the kitchen to the back door, where Will was waiting on the deck. "Sorry, Ben. I just need you for one, maybe two minutes."

"Take all the time you need," Felicity said, passing her son on the way out the door. "I've got to see what Carrie's up to. Shall I get the kayaks ready?" She asked Ben.

"Yes, an hour on the lake sounds great."

Felicity found Carrie curled up in one of her deck chairs, reading something on her phone. "From my lawyer," she said as

Felicity settled into the chair across from her. "I wanted to know the process for divorce, if we end up going that route."

"Isn't that a little hasty? You two should talk first. Get things sorted out between you. Is there a chance you're wrong about this?"

"The signs are all there. And I don't want to end up living like you and Richard did." Carrie shook her head and reached out a hand to Felicity. "Sorry, that was a low blow. But I couldn't possibly do what you did, Fel. Live with a man all those years knowing what you knew. I don't know if you're a saint or a fool, but you know I respect your decision. You had kids to think about. I don't. And there will be no argument over custody of the damn dog. I hate that thing. He can have him and good riddance."

"You still owe it to yourselves to talk. Is he even aware of your suspicions?"

"He is now. My lawyer served him with a letter of an intent to separate, or something like that. My inbox will dinge like mad in an hour. Look at this." She passed her phone to Felicity, revealing the Instagram account of a blond-haired, twenty-something in a string bikini, with her barely covered backside sticking up in the air. "This is the latest one," Carrie said.

"Oh, Car. I'm sorry. But you know there's nothing to this, right? This is a mid-life crisis he's having."

Carrie passed her the phone again. "This was the last one."

Felicity looked at a similarly posed brunette with a tattoo of a rose on her left butt cheek. "Where does he find these girls?"

"Dating sites. Where else do people hook up these days? You know. If that man came crawling back to me on his knees, I wouldn't take him back. I'm done, Fel. I'm just done." She slapped her phone onto the table, heaved a long and gasping sigh, and bit her bottom lip. "I gave that asshole the best years of my life."

"There's always Cam, if you want revenge," Felicity teased. She'd told Carrie about him earlier, when she'd asked if there were any eligible bachelors up here. "He seemed ready and willing."

"I don't want your cast-offs. He can stay on the other side of the lake as far as I'm concerned. Or go back to Lakehead or wherever you said he lived." Carrie waved her hands and scrunched up her nose. "Not interested."

"Ben and I are going out on the lake in a couple of minutes. You want to come? We can take the canoe. You can just sit up front and do nothing but enjoy the ride."

Carrie shook her head. "I don't want to be a third wheel. I'll just stick in a movie or maybe work on that puzzle you got going in there."

"You sure? We'll only be about an hour and then we're headed into Huntsville for the workshop."

"I'm sure. You know me and water. I haven't been in it, on it, or under it, except in the bathroom since I was in university. Not my thing. But don't let me stop you guys."

26

The library technician, a proficient looking girl with jet black hair that matched her round rimmed glasses, led Felicity and Ben to the meeting room reserved for her workshop. She flipped on the lights, moved a few chairs around and closed the blinds to ward off the glare from the afternoon sun.

"Here's your roster," she said, pointing to a list of names on the table. "Anything else you need, just see me at the desk." And then she left in a whirl of sharp, precise steps, her high heels clicking on the floor as she closed the door behind her.

"I can set up the computer stuff, if you don't mind putting those workbooks out for everyone," Felicity said to Ben.

"Sure. How many are coming?"

Felicity scanned the list. "Looks like…" she stopped as she came across a familiar name. Could it possibly be the same Jim Summers? Her old boyfriend who became Richard's business partner. She hadn't told her children that she'd dated Jim before she met their father. It had been years since she'd seen Jim.

"Felicity?"

"Oh. Sorry. Twelve, and I'll have one too, for reference." She got busy connecting her laptop with the screen provided and called up her presentation to make sure everything was properly connected. One by one, her attendees began filing into the room; a trio of sisters in their late sixties, a young couple, two middle-aged couples and their friend, and a smattering of others who came on their own. The last to arrive was a tall, sandy-haired man with blue eyes and an infectious smile. Felicity knew instantly that it was the same Jim Summers. He pulled her into him and gave her a warm hug.

"Felicity. It's been far too long." He left his hands on her shoulders when he spoke. His voice was smooth and deep, matured from when they'd known each other years earlier, like the voice of a radio announcer or a TV personality.

"I wondered if it was you when I saw the list," she said. "How are you?"

"I'm well. Thank you for asking. And you look great!" A frown pinched his brows together. "I read about Richard. I'm so sorry. It must have been difficult for you."

Felicity smiled meekly. "Thank you, Jim. That's kind of you to say, all things considered. Where have you been all these years?"

"Here mostly. I took a job in Alberta for a while, met my wife, Eve, and then we moved back here about twenty years ago."

"And you didn't look us up." Felicity raised her hand. "No. I get it. You don't have to explain, Jim. But it's really nice to see you now. The kids were talking about you the other day."

"Really? I'm surprised they remember me."

"They do, a little. You should come out to the cottage sometime. They'll be there on the long weekends. Will is spending the summer with me, but the others have to work."

Jim's face broke into a smile. "I'd like that. I really would."

"Good. You've got my contact details on your booklet. Let's set something up." She glanced around the room. "There's one place left, so maybe we should get started."

Felicity turned to see Ben hovering nearby. "Friend of yours?" he asked quietly, when Jim went to the last vacant chair.

Was he irritated or simply asking a question? "An old friend," she said simply. "Alright. If I could have your attention, ladies and gentlemen, we'll get started."

When the workshop ended, a few people stayed back to ask Felicity questions, which she was happy to answer. When the last of them left, she found Ben and Jim talking quietly outside the room. What on earth would they have to say to each other? She approached them with caution, her laptop case tucked under one arm, her reference material in the other.

"Here, let me help you?" Jim said, reaching out to take something from her.

"I've got it," Ben said, taking her laptop from her. "Ready, sweetheart?" he asked.

Jim flashed a questioning look at her. She smiled and leaned up to plant a kiss on Jim's cheek. "Don't forget my invitation," she said. "The kids will love seeing you and bring your wife, kids, whoever you like."

At the car, Felicity dumped her stuff in the backseat and climbed into the driver's side. "Did you really do that?" she asked Ben.

"Do what?" he asked, pulling his seatbelt on.

"Call me sweetheart to warn off, Jim?"

"It's not the first time I've called you sweetheart, is it?"

"No, but it was obvious why you did."

"Oh, come on. There was nothing to it. I just said it, that's all."

"No, you didn't. You wanted him to know there is something between us. Like you were announcing she's mine and hands off." She didn't give him time to answer before saying, "And what were the two of you talking about after the workshop?"

"Nothing really. Just our common interest in family trees. Why?"

"Are you sure it wasn't something else?"

"What could it possibly be, Felicity?"

"Ben. You saw him give me a hug when he arrived. You saw the two of us talking before the class started. Are you telling me you weren't the least bit jealous?"

"Should I be?"

"Ah ha! I knew it." She pushed the button to start the car, a smug grin on her face as she caught his eye. "Admit it. You were just a little jealous of Jim, weren't you?"

Ben shook his head and smiled. "Okay. I don't know what's going on here. Obviously, you've been accused of things in the past, but not by me, Felicity. So, I don't know why you're so upset. I'll admit I was curious until he said you were old friends."

"Old being the operative word. I haven't seen him in years." She pulled into traffic and maneuvered along the main road until she came to her turn. A frustrated silence filled the car, while they watched the scenery flying by. Finally, she said, "He was Richard's business partner."

"He told me."

"Ah."

He reached for her hand. "Felicity. I'm not jealous and I don't want to argue with you."

She shrugged and relented, just a little. "Well, you'd be right if you thought I had feelings for Jim. I did once. Before I met Richard. Jim is the one who introduced us."

"Do you think he regrets it?"

"If anyone has regrets, it's me. I dumped him for Richard. What a fool I was. But that's all in the past now."

"Yes, it is. And there's something you should know about me. I'm not the jealous type. I trust you and I hope you know you can trust me. You realize you aren't the first woman in my life. Come on Felicity. We've been around the block, but I'm not Richard. If you want someone who plays the jealousy game, then you picked the wrong man. It's just not me. Not because I don't care, but because I believe relationships are built on trust." He kissed her hand.

"I know that, Ben. But it seemed rather weird to find you two talking and then you called me sweetheart, as if you wanted him to know who we are to each other."

"Well, if it sounded that way to you, I'm sorry. I didn't mean it that way. Truly. Are we okay?"

"We're good."

"If you're sure." He flashed her a contented smile and pulled her hand onto his lap. "I'm glad we talked about this, though. I don't like letting things bottle up inside."

"Agreed. I'm just not used to anyone caring about my side of things. So, you're going to have to be patient with me. But I promise to always talk things out with you, even if I sometimes need a minute or two to cool off."

"Most people do," he agreed. "Just don't leave things too long." He pointed toward the side of the road. "Especially when we have to pick up a friend. Isn't that Carrie waving at us?"

Felicity pulled over to the curb and Carrie got in, loaded with bags in each hand. "Wow. Who would have thought I'd find all this great stuff up here?"

Felicity grinned. "I told you, you'd love the shopping in Huntsville."

Later, while Felicity and Carrie were doing the supper dishes and Will was in the living room, Emma's car pulled in and parked next to Ben's Subaru. Felicity craned her neck to watch as a young woman in a pair of high-waisted, ripped-at-the-knees jeans and a pink and white crop top got out of the car. She grabbed an overnight bag out of the back, tossed a mass of blond curls over her shoulder, and headed toward the door.

"Pretty," Carrie said, looking over Felicity's shoulder.

"You guys up for a movie?" Will asked, then crept up behind them to look out the window too. "Pretty? She's a knockout."

"Do people really say knockout anymore?" Felicity teased, then nudge Will's shoulder. "Want to run over for a cup of sugar?"

"Huh?" Will asked, a confused look furrowing his brow.

"Never mind," Carrie said, snapping the tea towel across his backside.

"The plan is a communal barbeque tomorrow. So, we'll all get acquainted," Felicity said, shoving a bag of chips and a bowl into Will's hand and steering him toward the living room.

"What are we watching?" Carrie asked, following with a tray of drinks. "Hope you didn't choose a sappy romance or something." She winked at Will.

"Me? Watch a romance. Only if Olivia insists on it and she's not here. I picked Skyfall. Mum likes that one."

"Good choice."

Will hit play, and they settled in to watch the movie. A few minutes after the opening credits, Felicity's phone vibrated in her pocket. She read the message from Ben.

Going well, but I miss you, followed by a heart emoji.

27

The communal barbeque was a success. Ben took care of cooking the ribs he brought over—and a veggie burger for Emma—while Carrie and Felicity organized salads and kept everyone's drinks filled. Will convinced Emma to join him in the canoe, while they waited for everything to be ready, and she jumped at the chance saying she'd never canoed before.

Felicity watched the two of them, splashing each other as they skimmed the shoreline as far as the Lawson place and back. She thought how remarkable it was that they got on so well. Considering what Ben had told her of Emma, she expected there might be some tension or that Emma would be reserved with them. But she seemed to enjoy herself, especially with Will.

"You were right about the bathroom stuff," Ben confessed. "Emma says I went overboard, and that she brings her own stuff wherever she goes. I should have known." Ben's eyes focused on Will instructing Emma on how to do a jay-stroke. "They're getting along like a house on fire."

"Birds of a feather," Carrie said. "Kids just need a common interest and they're away."

Felicity frowned, watching them in the distance, as Emma's face contorted first into a concentrated frown, then slipped into a grin as she did her best to follow Will's instructions. There was something oddly familiar about the way her jaw lifted and dropped with each attempt to get it right. It was almost as if she had seen that look before. Maybe she'd been in the shop she worked in and didn't realize it.

"What is the name of the shop where Emma works?" she asked as Ben got up to tend the barbeque.

"Soapstones. Hey, better call those kids in," he said. "These are nearly done."

Felicity went to the beach to wave at Will and Emma while Carrie went inside to get the last of the food out of the fridge.

While they ate, Emma and Will moved on from canoe techniques to discussing favourite movies and binge-worthy TV series. Naturally, they shared some favourites, but when they disagreed, they did so with such passion and vehemence the adults went to the dining room to play cards and left the young people on their own.

From where she sat, Felicity had a clear view through to the living room and, more importantly, Emma. Again and again, she watched the girl and was certain she knew her. By the time they were ready to call it a night, she was sure she must have been in her store several times.

"Your dad says you work at Soapstone, in Huntsville, right?" she asked Emma when they were saying goodnight.

"Yes. Do you know it?"

Felicity smiled. "I do. Maybe that's where I've seen you before. You look familiar. Have you worked there long?"

"Since high school. And then when I came back from university, they hired me on full time. I like it there. The people are nice and now I run the front part of the store, so I make the schedule, train the new recruits, get orders ready. I even do most of the online orders. It's not my dream job, but it will do until the right thing comes along."

"I know that feeling," Will said with a smile toward his mother.

Emma perched on the last step of the deck, her hand on the railing. "It's been a great day. Thanks for the barbeque and everything. It was really fun. Ben says the others will be back on the long weekend. I look forward to meeting them."

Felicity noticed, not for the first time, that Emma called him Ben and not Dad, and that each time she did, Ben winced. She felt an empathetic pang pinch her heart. "I'm sure they'll love getting to know you," Felicity said. And then Emma surprised her by reaching out to give her a hug.

"She's great, isn't she?" Will said when Ben and Emma were deep enough into the woods between the cottages not to be heard.

"She seems nice," Felicity said. Then, under her breath, she added, "Great remains to be seen."

28

Spending long weekends at the cottage was a Bailey family tradition that they all took time for every year. It was four days of endless barbeques, swimming, boating, trips to the local sites, and other fun. Treks through the woods in Algonquin Park, a hike up the stairs at Dorset, and at least one shopping trip on the main streets of as many towns and villages as they could squeeze in. Often there were local festivals, or craft shows, antique fairs and a host of other things to do.

Felicity had asked Carrie to stay, but she declined, sighting work and facing the music with Blain, as her reasons. She'd enjoyed her first cottage visit, but by the third day, Felicity had run out of energy to deal with her friend's constant comments about how to improve the place, Carrie was surely tired of Felicity downplaying the importance such luxuries as gold faucets and matching soap dishes. She knew they were a diversion; something to take Carrie's mind off her real problems. So, they waved goodbye to Carrie, who promised to take care of Felicity's house until she returned in the fall.

Felicity surveyed the bedrooms after moving her things back into her own and making all the beds up with fresh linens, laying towels out, adding fans and extra lamps to each room. "I think we're ready," she said as Will brought in the last fan from the garage.

"I'll just do a beer run then, unless you need something else," he said.

"No. Ben and I are going to get groceries, though. Do you want me to get the beer, too?"

Will shook his head. "No. You don't even like beer. You'll get crap stuff that no one will drink."

Felicity raised her hands in defense. "Okay. Okay. I just thought I'd ask." She stuck her cheek out to receive Will's kiss and palmed two fifty-dollar bills into his hand.

He looked down at it. "Thanks Mum."

She smiled. "You'll take care of me when I'm old and grey and can't climb the stairs though, right?"

"You know it! See you later."

He passed Ben on his way to the car, who had a list in one hand, his cell phone in the other. "Emma's coming a day later than she planned. Should we rearrange the menus?"

"Hello to you too," Felicity said, giving him a kiss.

He pulled her into his arms and scanned the room for people. "Hey. We're alone," he said with a contented sigh and then he kissed her again. "Oh, this is nice." He kissed her forehead and breathed deeply. "You smell good. Like a bowl of peaches."

"New shampoo," she said with a laugh, and looked up at him as he kissed her a third time. "Menus?" she asked afterwards, extricating herself from his arms. "Did you say something about menus?"

"I did, but I liked the other conversation better, didn't you?" He pulled her into his grasp again.

"Yes," she laughed, "But it's not getting the grocery shopping done."

"Plenty of time for that. You realize we haven't been alone in a room since… Well, for at least… I don't know, but it's been ages since I've even had a kiss. And as I recall, the last time we were alone, we were debating kayaking or staying in." He pulled back to look at her. "Unless you've changed your mind."

Felicity laced her fingers with his and pulled him toward her freshly made-up room. "I have not changed my mind at all. I think you should come with me and make sure that everything in this room is as it should be after Carrie's visit. Have I got things back where they belong?"

"As if I'd know where anything was before," he teased. "Until I put her bags in here, I'd never been in your bedroom." At the door, he realized her intent was not to check the room, but something else.

"Well, it's about time we fixed that, isn't it?" She crossed the room to pull the drapes. "Get the door, will you? Just in case Will forgot something and comes back."

When she turned back, he was right behind her, his arms open to her, enfolding her into him. "Are you sure?" he asked when she looked up at him.

"I'm sure."

Felicity felt the gentle caress of Ben's lips on her shoulder, then on her neck. She knew she wasn't dreaming, but she had no wish to open her eyes. If she did, she would have to get up, put clothes on again, and the magic of this moment would be over. If she stayed right where she was, kept her eyes closed and her body relaxed and curled into Ben's, there was comfort and peace and, dare she say it, yes, there was love.

There was no point in trying to deny the feelings anymore. And she wondered, not that she believed in such things, if fate or destiny, or maybe even some good karma for all her years of tolerating Richard's nonsense, had played a part in this. God or someone was being kind to her. And to Ben, apparently, since he seemed intent on being together.

He gave her shoulder a soft squeeze and whispered. "We should get going if we want to be back before everyone arrives."

"I don't want to move," she whispered, turning over to face him. "Couldn't we just stay like this, lock the door and tell the kids to fend for themselves this weekend?"

He laughed. "We could, but I think we'd have to fess up to what we've done. Are you ready to tell them that?"

Felicity shook her head. "No. Not yet anyway. This was lovely, but I'd like to keep this our secret for now."

"Right then." He extricated himself from her, swung his legs over the side of the bed and scratched his chin. "I'm not sure where you tossed my shirt."

"Where I tossed it? If I recall, it was you who nearly ripped my blouse off me. Who knows if it's even wearable anymore?" Felicity got up too, pulled the sheet around her body and began gathering clothing from the floor. "Yours," she said, tossing a shirt his way. "Mine." She continued until they had everything they'd been wearing earlier. "Just popping into the bathroom," she said, leaving the sheet on the bed.

When she'd finished and opened the door to her bedroom, she found the bed remade and Ben had disappeared from her room.

As she stood at the mirror brushing her hair, she realized he was talking to someone in the other room. Probably on his phone, she thought as she hurried to get ready.

Moments later, in the living room, she found him, but not on his phone. He was talking to Tom and Melody. "Here she is," Ben said, casting her a reassuring they-know-nothing look her way.

"Hi guys," Felicity said, giving each of them a hug. "We were just going to get some groceries for the weekend. You want to come with us, or have you been driving long enough already?"

"We'll come, if you don't mind," Melody said. "At least I will." She sent an enquiring look Tom's way. "Honey?"

"Yeah sure. I'll just get our stuff out of the car. Where's Will? He can help."

"Beer store," Felicity said.

"Right. Okay then."

"I'll help," Ben offered, and the two disappeared.

When they were gone, Melody produced a legal size, manilla envelope from her purse and handed it to Felicity. "I wanted to give you this while we were alone."

"Is it what I thought?"

Melody nodded. "I got on it as soon as you called. How do you think he'll take it?"

"I haven't a clue. But I know this much. I don't want to spoil our family weekend.

Melody put an arm around Felicity's shoulder. "You don't have to say anything ever, if you don't want to. No one needs to know."

"Oh, I think they do. No more family secrets. But I won't say anything just yet."

Olivia and Eric arrived moments after they returned from shopping, which prompted another round of hugs and lugging in suitcases and coolers. Eventually, everyone made their way to the lower deck with drinks. On the lake, the Lawson sisters were paddling around the shoreline and when Olivia reached up to wave at them, Felicity noticed something sparkling on her hand.

"What is that?" she cried, lifting her daughter's hand to see a diamond ring on her third finger. "When were you going to tell us? Shame on your for keeping it a secret." She kissed Olivia's cheek and smiled at Eric. "Welcome to the family, Eric. I'm glad we didn't scare you off the last time you were here."

"Ach, you haven't met my family yet. If anyone's scary, it's them. Right, Olivia?" Eric lifted her hand and kissed the back of it.

"Don't even joke about that, Eric," Olivia said.

"A toast to the newly engaged," Tom said. "And shame on both of you for beating us to it."

"Whose fault is that?" Melody said with a teasing grin.

"You're the one who said we should wait until we're financially ready," Tom argued good-naturedly.

"I did," Melody answered. "Soon, but we'll let Olivia and Eric go first."

"I heard a car door," Will said, anxiously looking over Ben's shoulder at his place. "Yes, there's Emma." He stood up and headed in her direction. "Everyone's over here," they heard him call out.

When Emma chose a chair next to Will's, Melody nudged Felicity's elbow. "Should we get things ready, inside? I'll come and help you in the kitchen if you like."

"Oh, is it that time already? Is everyone getting hungry?" Felicity asked. When she received a round of cheers and requests for food, she stood up and headed toward the door, with Melody following close behind her.

In the kitchen, Melody cornered Felicity by the fridge. "There's a problem," she said, jerking her thumb toward the group outside. "Will is really taken with her."

"I was afraid of that. I was hoping he was just being friendly when she first started coming a couple of weeks ago, but he left his phone on the counter the other day and I noticed a string of text messages."

"You have to tell him," Melody said.

"Tell who what?" It was Ben coming inside looking for meat for the barbeque.

"Nothing just now," Felicity said. She pulled two trays of chicken, sausages, hamburgers, and veggie burgers out of the fridge. "I know it looks like a lot, but this crew can eat. Trust me."

"I do," Ben laughed. "Explicitly." And then he kissed her, on the mouth, with Melody just a few feet away.

Felicity flushed beet red and smiled up at him when he leaned down for a second kiss. "Get," she teased. "So we can get everything else organized." She turned him around and nudged him toward the door.

"Hmm," Melody said, a finger paused on her lips. "That's progressing nicely."

Felicity flushed. "It's the last thing I expected to happen this summer."

29

The traditional weekend of site-seeing, bear and moose watching, tower climbing and ice-cream at Kawartha Dairy ended far sooner than anyone would have liked. Eric, in his car, and Olivia driving Luke's, left in a spin of gravel. Tom and Melody were not far behind them, and Will and Emma went to Bracebridge to see a movie. That left Felicity and Ben alone with the quiet.

They sat on the dock, watching the sun make its final descent over the water, painting the sky and a cluster of fluffy clouds in brilliant shades of apricot.

"Peace at last," Ben said.

"I know. I love my kids, but I enjoy the quiet after they're gone. I think of my parents when we were younger and how they must have felt when I packed everybody up in the car and took off for home. They must have been overjoyed to see the back of us."

He reached for her hand and kissed the back of it, then pulled her gaze to his. "You seemed a little distracted this weekend. Is everything okay?"

She turned away, knowing what she had to tell him and not wanting to do it yet. She had no way of knowing how he was going to react and didn't want to spoil what was so wonderful between them. He would be angry, she knew, but with her? She wasn't sure she could stand it if he were.

"What is it?" he asked again. "Clearly, something is on your mind. Are you regretting the other day, because if you are…"

"No, Ben. Never. It was wonderful and I'm looking forward to the next time, believe me. But that's not it. Stay here for a minute. I have to get something from inside."

When she returned, Felicity had the envelope in her hand that Melody had brought with her. "Before I give this to you, I have some explaining to do."

"This sounds serious. Go on," he said, watching her set the envelope in her lap as she sat down again.

She took a breath.

"In the early days of our marriage, Richard attended a lot of out-of-town conferences. I was naïve enough to believe him when he said he was building up his client list and schmoozing would-be investors. It took me a while to realize that he could have done most of that locally, since we lived in Toronto at the time and that was the hub of everything. When I confronted him about it, he bit my head off, said I didn't know what I was talking about, and I should stay out of his business. So, I did. I sat on the sidelines and watched while he went off and did his thing. Of course, you know what that was, without me telling you."

"I can guess," he said.

"One day, he came home more uptight than usual. He didn't speak to anyone, just went straight to the bar and poured himself a stiff drink. Tom was excited about something that had happened during the day, but Richard wanted nothing to do with him. He pushed us all away, refused dinner and went to bed early, claiming a headache. It was a week before I found the letter from his lawyer. I thought it was a statement of our account."

"But it wasn't?"

Felicity shook her head. "It was the results of something Gerard was looking into for Richard. In the letter, he referred to a woman who was pressuring Richard for child support."

"Oh Felicity. Was it a legitimate claim?"

She nodded. "Yes. The letter and the other documents confirmed the paternity of the child. Richard was the father."

"What did you do?"

"We argued, of course. I wanted to raise the child, and I think he might have agreed, but the mother was having none of that. So, I borrowed money from my father. On his advice, we set up a system, so that the mother couldn't get her hands on all of it at once. We couldn't take the chance she would blow through it all and the baby would get nothing. In order to get her monthly stipend, she had to show receipts; for rent, diapers, clothes, food, you know, proper expenses. We paid her half of the rent on a shared apartment, and I insisted we give her something for herself too, until the child was school age, and she could find a job."

"That's very generous of you, considering the circumstances. And smart to set it up that way. But I'm confused. What's in this letter? Does the child want to see him now, or something?"

"No. I'm sure she knows nothing about her biological father. I thought this was a long shot, and I prayed I was wrong, but when I first met her, I knew there was something familiar about Emma." Felicity sucked in a great breath of air. "Ben, Nancy was the mother we supported. Emma is Richard's natural daughter, my children's half-sister."

"What? Are you sure?" His face contorted into a grimace. She wasn't sure what to expect.

She handed him the envelope. "It's all in here."

Ben's forehead creased as his eyes scanned the documents. He flipped the pages about, ran a hand through his hair, then scrabbled at the stubble on his chin. And then he looked at her. "I can't believe this. This can't be true."

"I'm afraid it is. The DNA tests prove it."

"Felicity, what am I supposed to do with this information? I don't even know what to think or say or how to react."

"I'm sorry. If I'd known, I..."

"You'd what?" he snapped. "Obviously, you suspected something. Why didn't you say anything sooner?"

"Because it was a such a long shot, Ben. I mean, what are the chances?"

"Pretty good, obviously?" He looked at her, his eyes sinking daggers deep into her heart. Then he shook his head and pushed out of his chair, dropping the envelope into her lap. "I think I need to be alone."

"Ben. I'm sorry. What can I say to fix this? Tell me, please." She pulled on his arm, pleading with him.

"Nothing." He wrenched his arm away, rubbing it as if he'd been stung by a bee. "There is nothing you can say, nothing you can do. I need to be alone, to think, to figure out what to do. Obviously, we're going to have to tell your children. Will especially. You realize they are striking up more than just a friendship." He lifted his hands in the air. "I knew this was all too good to be true."

Felicity watched him make his way through the woods and up the steps to his place. The screen door slamming shut behind him was like a slap her across the face. She could not have been more hurt. When the porch light snapped off, Felicity knew there would be no more conversation that night. By the time she reached the top deck, she was cursing her dead husband and herself for their damned secrets, through a curtain of hot tears.

30

The following day, while she was washing up the lunch dishes, Felicity saw Ben get in his car, and drive off with a spit of gravel beneath his tires and a cloud of dust that seemed to take forever to disperse. She'd been trying to reach him all morning, but he had not answered her text messages or accepted her calls. It was as if the Berlin wall had come to Ril Lake, and Felicity could not shake the feeling of helplessness that hovered every time she cast an eye toward his cottage.

For two days, Felicity wandered about, looking for jobs to occupy her time and take her mind off Ben and Emma, and to stop blaming her dead husband for driving a wedge between herself and the one person who'd brought her happiness, besides her children.

That first night, she had cried like a teenager who'd had their heart broken over some silly crush. The next morning, she'd woken, washed her face and had given herself a stern talking to in the mirror. She wasn't a child. And this was life-changing stuff they were dealing with. Of course, Ben was angry. But did he have to shut her out? Why couldn't they just talk about this? It wasn't her fault. But Ben was avoiding her, and there was little she could do to change that.

She had to think of the conversation she and Will needed to have. She dreaded it, but when they sat down to talk, he was less shocked than she thought he should be. When she asked why; he shrugged his shoulders. "I saw the envelope. I'm sorry. I was looking for something to mail some forms in and it was on your dresser. I didn't realize there was anything in it until I opened it. Sorry. I should have told you."

"Yes, you should have, but that's water under the bridge now."

"There was never going to be anything but friendship between Emma and me, anyway. So, this is actually better. She's my sister. That's cool. You might not have realized this Mum, but she's gay. She has a girlfriend."

"Oh! No, I didn't know. Does Ben know?"

"I don't think she told him. I found out the hard way. I tried to kiss her and nearly got my head chopped off. But she was pretty good about it. I'm not the first guy to get it wrong."

"I'm sorry, kiddo."

"Don't be. Obviously, it wouldn't have worked out, anyway. Besides, I've got a lot of work and school and stuff to do before I think about anything serious."

"Good lad!" Felicity said, patting him on the back.

By the end of the third day, Felicity's worry about Ben's reaction and what may or may not be salvageable of their relationship was gone; replaced by anger at his avoidance. She was so angry she was almost sure she never wanted to speak to him again. What excuse could he possibly have for ignoring her? Yes, it was a shock. But it was her shock, too. And why was he angry with her? She and Richard had done their part to see that Emma was taken care of. It wasn't her fault if Nancy hadn't told him about the money. Obviously, she hadn't told him she was getting it. If Ben was also buying diapers and food and clothes for Emma, it would have been easy enough for Nancy to pass those receipts off as her own expenses.

And then she wondered if he was angry about the money and Nancy, or angry at her for not saying something sooner. How could she? She had to wait for the proof. But if he wouldn't listen to her, how could she get through to him?

She could leave him a voicemail, she thought. At least that way he'd have to listen to what she had to say. She picked up her phone and pressed his number into the keypad. When his voice mail message kicked in, as she knew it would, she said, "Ben. It's me. I wish you'd call me so we can talk. I'm sorry. I don't know what else to say, but avoiding me is childish, and it's unfair. It wasn't my fault. I didn't know." She was crying when she finished with, "Could you just stop being so pig-headed and return my calls?" She hung up, tears streaming down her face, and then she threw her phone onto her dresser and closed the door behind her.

She dove into getting things organized for the renovations. The civic holiday weekend was going to be a bust because Olivia wanted to start looking for a wedding dress and Tom and Melody had plans with friends. There would be no family gathering until Labour Day. A good time to box up stuff she didn't need and store it in the basement, out of the way of workmen, when they came. She had emails from potential clients, the sisters who'd been at her workshop, and a board meeting to prepare for next month.

Will spent his days on the phone, or in zoom calls, talking to builders and tradespeople, getting things booked to begin work mid-September. The permits were approved and, in another week or two, they would be in his hands.

"Time to think about booking my trip to the UK," she said to Will on the fourth morning since she'd talked to Ben.

"Really? When are you planning to go?"

"As soon as things get underway here. I'll go home for a few days, repack my bags with fall clothes and then I'll head out. I've got work for a client, in Scotland and Ireland, and I want to visit some of our ancestral homes, too."

"I'm glad you're going, Mum. You've been talking about this for years. And it's a good time to go. This place will be a disaster. And considering…" He nodded toward Ben's cottage. "Has he called?"

Felicity shook her head. "And I don't expect he will." She put her dishes in the sink. "I'm going into the Baysville library, then on to Bracebridge. Anything I can get for you while I'm in town?"

Will kissed her cheek. "Nope, I'm good. See you later."

Felicity could not say why she turned left onto the ring road instead of right. Neither route was shorter or faster, and both ended up at the same place on the other side of the lake. It was her habit to turn right, but perhaps on that particular morning she wanted a change of scenery, or it might have been her desire to avoid Cam and Slim's cottage. She couldn't say, but just over two miles away from home, when she came to the bend at Lookout Point, where she and Ben had first climbed up to watch the sunset, she came upon Wally's tow truck blocking the road.

She rolled down her window and called out to him. "You going to be long, Wally? I can turn around."

He cocked his head to one side. Tugging off his work gloves, he sauntered to her car and leaned on the roof. "Half an hour, probably. If you're in a hurry, maybe you should turn around."

Just then, Adam came around the side of the truck and handed his father a clear plastic bag and a single golf club. "I found this stuff beside the car, Dad," he said, holding it up for inspection.

"Wait," Felicity cried. "I recognize that sweater. Can I see that?" She got out of the car and stood next to Wally.

"I'm supposed to turn it in to the police," Wally said, reluctant to give her the bag. "I suppose you can look, but don't touch anything. Just in case."

Without removing the contents, Felicity shifted the sweater inside the bag and a few other items until she came to a cell phone. Only one person she knew had a phone cover with a sticker of a boxer dog on it.

"Please Wally. Can I see the car?"

"You might not want to. It's pretty dinged up."

"A royal blue Subaru Impresa? A rental right?"

"Yeah, how'd you know?"

"Oh god, Wally. He's not? He didn't?" She clutched his arm as tears brimmed in her eyes.

"No. I don't think so. It's my understanding they took him to the hospital in Bracebridge."

"How long ago? When did this happen?"

"Two, no, it was three days ago. Another company got the call for the other car. Then he couldn't get back out to get this one."

"Other car?"

"Yeah. See the skid marks. Looks to me like the Subaru was coming down the road and the other one was coming up here where you are. She must have been going too fast and took the turn too wide then kapowee, and over they went. You know this guy?"

"Yes, he's… He's my neighbour," she said finally. "He filled up at your station when I first came up. Remember?"

Wally scratched his head. "Yeah, good-looking guy with a friendly smile. I remember." She started heading toward the cliff. "Stay clear of the lines. Adam's just going down to hook them up."

Gingerly, Felicity picked her way around the front of the tow truck, which was flush with the face of the ridge, for a better view down the hill. This was one of the sharpest turns on the ring road, with a steep hill to on one side and an equally sharp embankment heading down toward the lake. There were perhaps fifty feet before and an out-of-control vehicle would end up in the lake, especially now that most of the trees had been cleared away. The owners of that parcel of land were preparing to build a boathouse next to their dock.

Felicity peered over the side, knowing already what she was going to see. Ben's car sat at the bottom, wedged between the last remaining two oak trees. The hood was buckled against one, the back jammed against the other. The roof was compressed, almost down to the seats, and the driver's side door was torn off and laying against a tree stump a few feet away. Every window was smashed and tiny circles of glass glistening from the ground.

Her hand flew to her mouth, and then her throat as tears welled in her eyes. "He rolled?"

"Looks like it."

She reached out for the support of his arm as her body crumbled. Adam came to her other side. "Mrs. Jefferies, sit in the truck a minute. Are you alright, Ma'am?"

"Do you want Adam to run you home in your car? He can walk back."

"No. No." She leaned against the seat of the truck. "I'm alright. You said. Two days ago?"

"Three. I just got the call yesterday. But I've been crazy busy, and it was obvious the guy wasn't going to use it any time soon. But the property owners have been chomping to get it out of here so they can finish working on that boathouse."

"I'll go to the hospital. I don't suppose you'd let me take his things to him, would you?" She nodded toward the bag that now lay on the seat of the truck. "I can't imagine the police would need them for anything. They aren't evidence of the crash, are they?"

Wally's mouth worked itself into a grimace. "I'm not supposed to do that."

"His cellphone at least. He might want to check his messages or make calls."

Wally shook his head. "Sorry, I'm sure the police will take it to him."

Felicity nodded. "Alright. I understand. I wouldn't want you to get into trouble over it."

"Dad!" It was Adam calling from down the hill where he'd gone to hook up the winch cable.

Wally waved toward him. "I just gotta see to the boy. You sit there as long as you need to, alright." His gaze flipped to the bag on the seat and back to Felicity again. She frowned, and he did it again. And then she knew. He was giving her the chance to take the phone. But she didn't need to. She only wanted to delete one message. She worked the phone through the bag, just in case the police dusted it for prints. Though why they would do that, she had no idea.

She found the 'on' button on the top and pressed it. Nothing. She tried again. Still nothing. She swiped the front, tapped the sides, flipped it over and back. Battery's dead, she thought. Of course, it was lying on the ground for three days. She'd just have to face the music when Ben got his phone back. How much worse could this possibly be? She shouted goodbyes down the embankment, and Wally and Adam both looked up, shielded their eyes from the sun, and waved to her.

A three-point turn became a six on that narrow stretch of road, but eventually, Felicity got her car turned around and was off in the other direction. Thirty minutes later, breaking every speed limit along the way, she was standing at the reception desk at the hospital, watching a pink-cheeked blond tap Ben's name into her computer.

"Third floor. Room 308," she said, looking up at Felicity. "But there's a notation." She frowned at her screen and gave Felicity a sympathetic look. "Family only, so unless…"

"I'm his sister, Alice," Felicity lied, the fib slipping from her mouth so easily she almost believed it herself. "We've been so worried about him."

The nurse at the third-floor station was not as easily swayed as the blond downstairs and demanded to see her identification. Felicity stared into her steel-grey eyes and begged the sergeant major of a head nurse to let her see him.

"You are not family," the woman insisted. "And the files say family only."

"Indirectly, I am," Felicity said with hesitation. "We share a child. Does that count?" She glanced at the woman's name tag. "Rhonda", she added for a personal note.

Rhonda's eyebrows shot up. She jammed a hand onto her hip and cocked her head to one side. "Really? You want to play that card?"

"No, I suppose not," Felicity said.

Rhonda's features softened when Felicity started to walk away. "Wait." She came out from behind the desk with a clipboard in hand and led Felicity down the hall to where several straight-back chairs lined either side of the corridor. The place smelled of antiseptic pine cleaners and Felicity's stomach threatened to heave at the combination.

Rhonda waved her into a chair and sat down next to her. She set her clipboard in her lap and folded her hands on top of it. "I can tell you this, honey," Rhonda said, when Felicity looked at her, doing her best to hold back her tears. "He hasn't regained consciousness. So, even if I let you in there, you could sit there all day and it won't do you any good."

"He's unconscious? But why? How bad is it? What's the prognosis? How long will he be like that?"

Rhonda put a hand on Felicity's arm. Her compassionate touch brought more tears, and Felicity fished for tissues in her purse. "I'm sorry, I just have so many questions."

"I'm sure you do. But I have a couple for you too, since you obviously know him. His wallet was in his pocket, so we know who he is, and his next of kin. We've been trying to reach the sister, but the number is out of service. There is a picture of a young girl about ten or so, but it looks old. You know those school pictures?"

"Emma," she said. "At least that's probably who it is. She's the shared child. It's a long and complicated story."

Rhonda's brows raised. "I've heard it all, honey. But do you know how to reach her? Maybe she knows the sister and can help."

Felicity nodded. "She works at Soapstones in Huntsville. You could try her there. I don't have a cell phone number for her." She thought of Will and Emma's messages back and forth. "But I could get it for you, if I message my son. He has it."

"That would be a help, but we'll try her workplace first. You wouldn't happen to have another number for the sister or know where she works. Anything else that might help?"

"Alice teaches piano for the Royal Conservatory. In Burlington, I think." Felicity wracked her brain, trying to recall the evenings spent with Alice around the fire. They'd talked of so many things, but discussed very little about work. "Maybe it's not Burlington. It might be Hamilton, or Oakville." Felicity threw up her hands. "I'm sorry. I wish I'd paid more attention when we talked. We're neighbours on Ril Lake. Our cottages are next to each other."

"But you and Alice's brother share a child?"

"Like I said, it's complicated. I wouldn't have believed it either. Coincidences, you know?"

"I don't believe in those," Rhonda said, matter-of-factly. "No such thing. Everything happens for a reason."

"Seriously? You mean Ben being run off the road, crashing into the woods and ending up in the hospital was for a purpose? What could that possibly be? People make their own choices and fate has nothing to do with it. Karma is just something people say when things happen, good, bad or indifferent," she said.

"If you say so," Rhonda said. "But experience tells me different." Her attention was drawn to another nurse at the station, looking for instructions, which left a matter of seconds for Felicity to glance at Ben's chart. She'd never been good at reading upside down, but she deciphered the words body cast and paraplegia, which she did not need Google to know was paralysis from a spinal cord injury.

Felicity sucked in air and bit back her tears. All this time she'd been cursing Ben for not returning her calls, thinking terrible things, selfish things, first worried, then fearful, then angry. She'd run the gamut of emotions in the past three days, when all the while, if she'd just gone up the road on one of her walks, she would have known what was going on with Ben.

Rhonda was watching her, she realized, with great interest, and an awareness of emotion, Felicity had not given the woman credit for. Apparently, she wasn't as rigid as her first impression had seemed.

"Look, Ma'am, I can see this man is more than just a neighbour's brother and you may or may not share a child in some peculiar and hard to explain way. But here's the thing. You aren't going to get in to see him. Not today, at least. So, why don't you see this girl, Emma, and ask her if she knows how to get in touch with the sister? Are there other siblings and what about his parents? Someone needs to sign off on things and his family should know his condition. Is he married?" Rhonda's brow lifted in a way that showed she'd already worked out Felicity's connection to Ben.

Felicity ran her hands over her thighs and sighed. "No, he's not married. Alright. I'll do what I can. But will you take my name and phone number? And call me if there's any change."

"We can't do that, Ma'am," Rhonda said. "Unless he gives his permission."

"I know, but under the circumstances, couldn't you…"

Rhonda's sigh was exhaustive. "You're not a relative, by your own admission." She shook her head. "Unless he wakes up and says he wants to see you, my hands are tied. I'm sorry. I really am."

Felicity nodded. "I see. Okay then." She rose.

Rhonda nodded and gave Felicity's shoulder a squeeze. She didn't have to, Felicity thought. She could have walked back down the hall and left her standing there, cold and alone, to wallow in her worry and fear. And then Rhonda pulled a pen out of her uniform pocket and held it ready to write. "Go on then. Give me your number. I'm not promising anything, but if he regains consciousness, and he gives his permission, I'll call you."

"Oh, thank you! Thank you," Felicity cried. And then rhymed off her cell number as Rhonda recorded it in the margin below the next of kin line. "Will you tell him? If he wakes. Will you tell him I was here?"

Rhonda nodded. "I will. I promise."

Felicity took the stairs instead of waiting for a rambling, slow elevator. It felt good to move, to make use of her limbs, as if in doing so, she was moving for both of them. She imagined Ben lying in bed, his body covered in white plaster, nothing more than eyes, toes and fingers poking out of it. She had to stop halfway down a flight of stairs to sit and cover her face with her hands, because tears blurred her vision so badly, she could not see. Eventually, she stood up again and made her way toward the exit door and the parking lot.

The minute she was in the car, she put in a call to Will. No answer. It went straight to voicemail. She tried again, and again, and kept on trying until she arrived at Soapstones where Emma worked. To her disappointment, Emma was not there, and the owner refused to provide her address or her cell number.

"If you can't give me the number, could you call the hospital and tell them what it is? Her father's been in an accident, and they want to reach her." Felicity bit back more hot tears as the man's face softened.

He nodded. "I can do that, yes."

What more could she do? Felicity thought. She needed to go home. She was worried about Will now, since he wasn't answering her calls. Her phone chirped as she pulled out of the public parking lot. She didn't recognize the number but wondered if it was the hospital calling.

"Hello. This is Felicity Jefferies?"

"Mum?" Will said. "Where are you? I've been trying to call you."

"I'm in Huntsville. I was looking for Emma. I didn't see any calls from you?"

"My phone is dead. I dropped it in the lake. I've been using Emma's. Mum, there's been an accident."

"I know. That's why I've been trying to call you. To get Emma's number. This is a mess. I've been at the hospital, but they won't let me see him. Wait, if you used her phone, that means she's there with you?"

"Yes, and she's a wreck. Mum, please come home."

31

"Tea," Felicity said to Will, as she came through the door and Emma fell into her arms. "And put a little something in it, Will," she added. And then she steered Emma toward the living room and lowered her onto a couch.

Emma sobbed into her shoulder and blubbered, unrecognizable words until she managed to calm herself enough to speak. "It's all my fault. We got into a huge argument, and I told him I never wanted to see him again and then… I felt bad. So, I came out here to talk."

"And she saw the tow truck guy up the road," Will said, settling into the couch opposite, waiting for the kettle to boil.

"You didn't see the car, did you?" Felicity asked.

Emma shook her head. "No. The guy said it was bad. Said he rolled and then smashed into the trees." The sobs came on twice as hard. "I called the hospital, but they said I couldn't see him, and they couldn't give me any information. They said I'm not on the list as next of kin or family."

"I got the same," Felicity said. "I told them about you. A charge nurse, named Rhonda."

Emma shook her head. "No, Cathy was the name of the nurse I spoke with."

"Did you tell her you were his daughter?"

"She said the only person who could see him was Alice. Who is Alice?"

"Ben's sister. It's her cottage he's staying in. Didn't he tell you that?"

Emma shook her head and buried her face in Felicity's shoulder. "I'm such an idiot. I finally got him back and then I..." She hiccoughed and reached for a tissue.

"Oh sweetheart. I'm sorry. I'm sure the doctors are doing everything they can for him."

"But he's unconscious, Felicity. Has been for days. That can't be good, can it? What if he doesn't remember anything when he wakes up? What if he does, and he hates me for being so angry with him? What if..."

"Stop," Felicity eased. "Just take a deep breath. We can't live by what ifs. What's done is done. What's been said, has been said. We'll deal with the consequences as and when we must." And that nasty phone message too, she thought as she felt Emma's body ease against her.

"They let me leave my number," Felicity said. "But I was told that unless he specifically asked to speak to me or see me, they wouldn't call."

"They told me the same thing. Do you know how to contact this Alice person?"

"I told them what I could remember, but it's not much to go on."

The kettle clicked off and Will got up to brew the tea. Emma watched him leave the room, then turned to Felicity. "Is it true? What my father said. That Will's father is my biological father."

Felicity nodded. "It would seem so."

"But Will doesn't know, does he?"

"Will knows. I told him yesterday. But the others don't. I haven't seen them and it's not exactly something you say over the phone. I only found out for certain, a few days ago. I told Ben and…" she gulped in air. "That's the last time we talked. He walked away from me, refusing to talk about it. The next morning, he was off in the car somewhere and I haven't seen him since. He didn't answer my calls, or messages, but of course I know why, now."

"He went to see my mother. She's in a nursing home in Huntsville. I don't know what he thought he was going to get out of her. She's practically comatose herself. I don't blame him for being angry, if everything he told me was true. You and your husband paid child support to my mother for me? Is that right?"

Felicity nodded. "We had no idea there was someone else taking care of you. We believed she was destitute and had no support other than a little government supplement. We knew nothing about Ben, only that she shared an apartment with someone. We assumed it was another woman, another single mother, possibly. To be honest, I didn't give that much thought at all. But there's something else you should know. When we first learned of this, I wanted to bring you to live with us, instead of paying out money to someone we didn't know. But your mother refused. We couldn't even see you. But to be honest, Emma, you had a better father in Ben than you would have had in Richard. Even if it wasn't as long as you both would have liked."

"For as long as I can remember, he was there. But every time I tried to call him Daddy, Mum said I shouldn't, and that he wasn't really my father. But he's the only father I knew. And then, when he went away, it was like," she gulped air. "A big blank void. Mum was already nutso by then. Aunt Sarah took me to live at her place. She was a miserable old cow of a woman. And then Ben left. My world fell apart. It was like everyone I ever loved just vanished from my life. I wrote a hundred letters at least. Aunt Sarah put stamps on them and said she posted them, but I doubt she ever did, because he said he never got them. Finally, I gave up. I heard nothing. I thought he didn't want to see me. So, I just got on with my life."

"And now that he's back and you know everything, do you feel differently?"

"I never stopped loving him, Felicity. He was my father. I didn't know my mother and my aunt were bleeding him dry and I certainly didn't know about…" her gaze flitted to Will and back again. "… any of you."

"You can say what you like," Will said. "I know you're our half-sister. Mum told me."

A momentary silence fell among them as they sipped the tea Will had brewed, laced with brandy, to take the edge off. There was nothing any of them could do but wait. Wait for Ben to regain consciousness. Wait for Alice and Stan to be notified. Wait for whatever was going to happen, to happen.

Emma's hand slipped to Felicity's and tightened around it, but her eyes did not shift from staring at the lake. It glistened in the waning light of the afternoon; the sun creating dazzling lights twinkling off the ripples like fairies dancing across the water. She wished Ben was here. He would have loved that view.

Some things will always remain the same, Felicity thought, as she watched the sky darken into a magnificent display of orange, apricot, and finally lavender. Thank goodness for the constants in our lives that keep us grounded and remind us of the important things. We are here. We are alive. And we have each other, she thought.

"I could warm up leftovers," Felicity said when Emma's stomach grumbled.

"Maybe some soup," Emma said. "If there is any. I don't really have much of an appetite, but I could eat something."

"Soup it is," Felicity said, pushing herself off the couch. And then she went to the kitchen to make them all a light supper. She was just about to call them in to the dining room when she heard the familiar crunch of gravel in the drive. But it wasn't her driveway. It was next door. A red convertible pulled up and Alice got out from the driver's side. There was no mistaking the woman's tall, and lean stature, or her white hair tucked beneath a scarf. It was one of the things Felicity had admired about her, wishing that when her hair turned, it would be white like that.

Alice took an overnight back out of the back seat, closed the door again, and went inside the cottage. The small garage blocked the front entrance, but when the porch light flipped on, Felicity knew she was inside.

Felicity decided not to tell Emma that Alice was next door, at least until she'd had time to speak with her. Alice would already be upset, and Emma had had enough upset for one day. And meeting another stranger was probably not the best thing right now. Instead, she told Will and Emma she was going for a walk and their supper was on the table. And then she slipped out the patio door and across the deck to Alice's cottage

Alice sat on the deck with her hands wrapped around a crystal tumbler of something amber. Whiskey had been her drink of choice, Felicity knew. She approached the bottom step and called up, as they used to, "Permission to come aboard, captain."

Alice called back. "Granted. Did you bring booze?"

Felicity shook her head when she reached the deck and took up a chair on the other side of the patio table. The white-haired woman looked at her. "They told me you tried to see him. They should have let you. Not that you could have done anything for him."

"Alice I... Ben..."

Alice lifted her hand. "You don't have to tell me anything. Ben already did."

"He's conscious?"

Alice shook her head. "No, before. He called me several times over the past few weeks. He was like a teenager, a kid in a candy store, and he didn't know what to do first."

"Oh, I knew you were helping him with names for the family tree, but I didn't know…"

Alice leaned forward. "Felicity, you know he's in love with you, don't you? Or has my brother been stupid enough to hide his feelings?" She pushed an envelope toward Felicity and several pictures fell out of it. Pictures they'd taken on their trip to Algonquin Park. Some he'd taken from the deck, she realized, when she had been unaware. In some she was reading, in others just coming into the dock after a paddle around the lake and in others, her head thrown back in a laugh at something one of her children said.

"Ah, well we… ah," Felicity hedged.

"Goodness woman. Look at you. You're as bad as he was. You're like a couple of school kids. Well, good for you, I say. Both of you. I read about your husband's death in the paper, but I have to say I never liked the man. And my brother hasn't had anyone for a long time. Oh, probably a woman here or there to warm his bed and take away his memories for a while, but that's not the same thing as really loving someone, is it?"

"I don't know what to say, Alice. I've only known him a few weeks."

"Oh, don't give me that crap. I can see it in your eyes, and I heard it in his voice. If you want to deny it, go right ahead, but you're not fooling anyone."

"I won't deny it. I care for him very much. But love? It's a little soon for that. But how is he? What did they tell you at the hospital? How did they finally track you down?"

"The hospital told me it was you who told them where I work. Thank you for doing that. Otherwise, who knows how long it might have been? They also said that Emma tried to see him. I don't know how to reach her to tell her it's okay to come now."

"She's right next door, Alice. She's worried. As we all are. What did they tell you?"

"Not a lot. They really don't know. His body is mending. The body cast is just a precaution. They thought his spinal cord had been severed, but they can't see anything on the ex-rays. So that's good news at least. They wanted him immobilized while the rest of his limbs heal, and just in case there's a hairline fracture or something they can't see right now."

"Will he regain consciousness?"

"Remains to be seen. No one can say for sure."

They were silent for a moment, then Alice lit a cigarette and blew a thick stream of smoke into the air. "Stupid, stupid girl," she hissed. "No one in their right mind would drive these roads at such ridiculous speeds. And she's got barely a scratch." Alice turned sharply, her jaw stiff, her chin lifted. "I saw her, you know. She was in the room across the hall. They were watching her for some internal injuries, but there was nothing more than a few scratches on that girl. Seventeen if she's a day and probably just got her license. Driving Daddy's new SUV into town, all by herself for the first time. Her parents told me. Oh, they were sorry. They were beside themselves with worry about Ben. Afraid he'll sue is what they're worried about." Alice flitted ash on the ground and took another deep drag.

"But she tried to help though, didn't she? I saw the golf club. She smashed his car windows trying to get him out."

Alice frowned. "No one told me that. Ben didn't golf. Where did the clubs come from?"

"Hers, I suspect." She was right. It was the younger sister of the girl at the secondhand shop. The one she'd dropped the golf clubs off for. "Are you pressing charges? Are the police?"

Alice nodded. "The police have charged her with reckless driving. They'll up it if Ben doesn't pull through. But there is a chance to launch a civil suit. I've seen this before." Alice butted her cigarette after only a second drag. "I quit smoking six years ago," she said, pushing the package away from her. "I have no idea why I bought these. Damn it, Felicity. What if he never wakes up?" Alice dropped her head in her hands and began to sob. Icy Alice's cold exterior melted away as her emotions caught up with her bravado. "And just when he finally came home again."

Felicity sat forward and reached for Alice's hand. "You have Emma? Do you want to meet her?"

"Not tonight, Felicity. This is all too raw. I can't. Not now. And she won't remember me. I haven't seen her since she was a toddler. But you'll come with me in the morning, won't you? In case he wakes up. I know he'll want to see you."

"I'll come, but I'm not so sure he will. We haven't spoken in days."

"Well, whatever it was, he'll get over it. He's never been one to hold grudges and if he's wrong about something, he usually comes around. Was it about the girl?"

Felicity nodded. "It's a little complicated, and it's a lot to take in and stupidly, I left him a less than supportive message on his phone. I thought he was ignoring my calls. I had no idea he was…" she paused, "in an accident." Should she tell Alice about Emma's real father, or should Ben do that? And would he? "I feel awful."

32

This time, when Felicity went to the hospital and she and Alice passed the third-floor nurse's station, Rhonda nodded to them both, but did nothing to stop Felicity from entering Ben's room.

"She knows better," Alice explained. "I told her that last night. She should have let you in to see him, but I guess hospitals have policies for a reason."

Felicity hung back by the door, while Alice went immediately to Ben's side to look for evidence of any change. And then she waved Felicity forward. "Come here and talk to him, Felicity. Ben. Ben. It's Alice. Felicity is here too. Can you hear me?" She shrugged and pulled a chair close to the bed.

Felicity did the same on the other side, her face filled with shock as she took in the amount of white plaster covering Ben's body. The arms she'd laid in where she'd felt so safe were now immobilized and stuck out like the arms of a scarecrow in a cornfield. Machines hissed and ticked and beeped around his head and wavey lines squiggled across a monitor reporting his vital signs. The smell of stringent antiseptic cleaners stung her nose. Felicity sucked in a breath as she reached out to touch his cheek as tears slipped down her own.

"Oh Ben," she sighed. "Come back to us." Nothing but the hiss of machines and the squeaking of someone's shoes on the floor in the hall. She reached for the chair to sit down again.

"His eyes are twitching," Alice said.

Felicity jumped up again. "Ben? It's Felicity and Alice. Can you hear us?"

Alice shot out of her chair. "I'm going to get the nurse. Keep talking to him, Felicity."

Felicity lay a cool hand on his cheek and then across his forehead. And then she pleaded with him. "Ben. Wake up, Ben. Can you hear me? Blink or wiggle your fingers, if you can." She held her breath, watching for movement, listening for a sound, anything that might suggest he knew she was there. "Ben," she tried again. "Ben, it's Felicity. Please, please if you're hearing me, please move something, a finger, an eye, something."

Felicity put her forehead next to his and whispered. "Please Ben. Please. Emma needs her father. Alice needs you. I need you, too. I never thought I needed anyone until I met you. Come back to us." She watched his face for movement, a twitch, a flick of his eyelash, anything.

There was no response, and when Alice returned, Rhonda was right behind her. She checked all the dials and gauges and then watched Ben's face for movement. "Could be reflexes," she said, finally. "Just the once?"

Felicity nodded.

"Well, keep trying. It's good to have familiar voices around him. What kind of music does he like? He might respond to that."

"I have a playlist we made together." Felicity pulled out her phone. "I teased him about his taste in old country music, because my father used to play it all the time." She turned up the volume and put the phone on his nightstand as Hank Williams Jr. came on signing *All My Rowdy Friends Are Coming Over Tonight*. "Come on Ben. It's no party without you."

"What if we just sat here and talked?" Alice suggested. "Maybe just the sound of our voices will bring him around." Alice looked at Rhonda, who nodded.

"It can't hurt." She patted Alice's shoulder. "Call me if there's any change."

Rhonda went back to her duties on the floor, and Alice and Felicity settled into their chairs. "Okay. Why don't you tell me about these renovations you're doing in your cottage? When are you starting?"

"Sometime after Labour Day. Will's been working on things with Ben's help. He's been struggling to figure out his life, so I suggested he work with Ben on my renovations." She filled Alice in on the details of what the cottage would look like when everything was done.

"And you're going to stay there while they do all that work?"

"No. I've been thinking about going to England and Scotland. For a month or maybe six weeks. But now I'm not so sure." She nodded toward Ben, then dropped her gaze to her hands. "I'm so glad I haven't booked anything yet."

"Why not?"

Felicity looked up from her lap. It wasn't Alice who spoke.

Both turned their heads toward the bed where Ben's eyes flickered open, once, then again, and then he was looking from one to the other.

"Ben!" Alice cried, getting out of her chair. "Geez Louise, brother, you sure know how to scare a girl. What the heck?"

His eyes filled with tears as he looked from Alice to Felicity and back again. "Sorry," he said. "I didn't mean to worry either of you."

"Do you know where you are and what happened?" Alice asked.

"The last thing I remember is a white SUV barreling down on me." He tried to move, but when it was impossible, he groaned. "What is all this?"

"You're in a body cast," Alice told him. "It's just a precaution. I'll get the nurse and she can explain everything."

Felicity bent closer to kiss his lips. "I'm so sorry," she said. "I'm so very sorry."

"Whatever for?" he said, his voice cracking through a dry throat. "Can I have some water?"

Felicity fumbled with the straw and finally got it into Ben's mouth so he could sip it. "This mess. It's all my fault," she said. "I'm so sorry."

"No." Ben said. "You did nothing wrong. If you need to blame someone, blame me for flying off the handle and going off in a rage."

Nurse Rhonda pushed open the door and made room for a doctor in a white lab coat, a stethoscope dangling around his neck. "Well, it's good to see you awake, sir," he said. "Can you tell me your name?"

"Ben Pierce."

"Good. And do you know who this lady is beside you?"

"Felicity Jefferies."

"And this one?"

"Alice Styles, my sister."

"Good, and what's the last thing you remember?"

"Swerving to miss a white SUV and then feeling like I was flying. I'm pretty sure the car rolled at least once, then everything went black."

"Are you in any pain?"

"The only thing that doesn't hurt is the tip of my right index finger," Ben said, then laughed a little. "Am I going to live, Doc?"

The man nodded. "I think there's a good chance of that. We'll take you down for some further x-rays and probably get you out of this cast. There are fractures in both your legs, though, so we will recast them. You also have two broken ribs, and your shoulder was dislocated. But let's see where we are, shall we?" He turned to Rhonda and ran off a list of instructions. And then he turned back. "If you ladies would like to come back in a couple of hours, we'll have the answers we need, and Mr. Pierce will be able to start his recovery."

33

It was the start of a long recovery for Ben, physically and emotionally. And it was a time for reconciliation for all of them, of words thought but not spoken, of fears suffered, but not uttered, of loves felt and not declared.

Emma learned more truths about all her aunt had done, including the money that was supposed to have gone for her care, was what has paid her mother's bills in the nursing home facility. It was her eighteenth birthday, and the end of Richard and Felicity's payments that began the compilation of unpaid bills. When Emma learned that she was the fourth beneficiary in Richard's will, she vowed to pay her mother's unpaid bills. Ben assured her it had been taken care of and she was not to give it another thought.

Emma eased into the family and became one of Felicity's children as if she'd carried for nine months, like the rest. She spent all her spare time at Ben's side learning to love the man again, with the childlike fondness she'd had years ago. She and Will became inseparable friends, arguing like siblings over petty things. They teased and cajoled sometimes, and others Felicity would find them on the couch, watching movies with Mac curled up between them. Emma had taken an instant liking to Mac and offered to take care of her while Felicity went on her holiday.

In the hours of his recuperation, Felicity sat at Ben's beside and listened as he told her what had happened the day of the accident.

"I went to see Nancy, thinking I was going to have it out with her. I was going to challenge her to deny she'd been getting all that money from you and Richard. Tell her what I thought of her scheme to use me like she did. But…"

"But she isn't well, is she? Emma told me."

He shook his head. "Nancy doesn't speak. She didn't even know who I was, and there was not even a flicker of recognition at the mention of Emma's name. It's sad, Felicity. I'm glad Emma has you and now Alice. A girl needs a mother figure, especially as she navigates through everything she's learned. She doesn't want to see her mother, now that she knows the truth."

"And who's paying the bills for Nancy?"

"Alice kicked in for the overdue bills. Her husband left her well off and they had no kids, so what was she going to do with it all? My lawyer did all the paperwork to get her on government assistance and I'll work something out to subsidize what that doesn't cover. It really isn't a lot."

"Generosity runs in your family, I think."

He took her hand in his and looked toward his phone, lying on the night table. "I heard your message." She flinched and tried to make excuses, but he calmed her and held her gaze. "No. Don't. It was my fault. I should have at least sent a text. Pigheaded and stubborn was exactly what I was. And inconsiderate. And a lot of other things. I don't blame you. None of this is your fault. You and I have been the pawns in this crazy, mixed-up scheme. I don't ever want anything like that to happen again between us. Can we promise to always talk things through?"

She nodded. "I think we did, once before. But we also agreed to give each other space when we need it?"

"I took too much space. I don't want to be very far away from you, ever."

"Except for my trip? I wish you were coming with me."

"Next year," he said. "After all, someone has to supervise these renovations, and I can't leave it all to Will."

Once Ben was released from the hospital, Alice had returned to Burlington, assured that her brother had the best of care from the nurse and the physiotherapist who both came daily, and Felicity, who hovered closely with a watchful and loving eye.

"I'll be back for Labour Day weekend," Alice had said, when she was leaving. "You've got a month to get out of that wheelchair and start barbequing. I like my steak medium rare, and a baked potato with all the fixings." She bent to kiss her brother's cheek, then turned to Felicity. "I'll bring the fixings."

Ben made significant progress, determined to regain the muscle loss from weeks spent in bed with no exercise. By the end of August, his casts were all removed, except for one walking cast on his left foot, which suffered the most damage. He'd gone from wheelchair to crutches to two canes and, of course, Felicity hovering nearby wherever he went.

The heat of summer was gone when the early days of September began to unfold. Labour Day weekend brought the rest of Felicity's family north for their last weekend of the summer and Ben was appointed chief barbequer. He sat on her deck, pale after the walk from his cottage to hers, balancing on one cane. She'd offered to drive him around, but he'd refused. "It's less than a hundred feet. Surely, I can manage that," he'd said.

"But it's through the woods. The ground is uneven. There's a slope."

"Stop fussing, woman!" he'd said with a grin. "You can drive me home afterwards, if you insist on it. But for now, I'm going to walk under my own steam."

And there he was, flipper and a long-handled fork at the ready. "I heard car doors," he said as sounds echoed off the pines and out across the water.

"It's Olivia and Eric," Felicity said, setting down her phone. "She just text me that they've arrived. She knows we're out here."

Felicity fussed with pillows at Ben's back, pushed his drink a little closer to him, adjusted the snack bowl so he could reach it. And then he grabbed her wrist and turned it so that he could kiss her palm. "Sit, my darling woman. And don't fuss. I'm fine. We are all fine."

"I don't know what to do if I'm not doing something," she said.

Olivia and Eric came through the Muskoka room. "Hey everyone. Tom and Melody just pulled in. So, we are all here." Olivia came to give her mother a hug and leaned down to kiss Ben on the cheek. "So glad to hear you're on the mend," she said.

He patted her hand. "Thanks," he said. "Me too. But we aren't quite all here. Have you met my sister, Alice? She's never been on time for anything in her life. But rest assured, by the time the food is on the table, she'll be here. She enjoys eating it, just not making it."

"What's that, little brother?" A voice called from the lower deck as Alice appeared, a bottle of wine in one hand, a grocery store bag in the other. "The fixings," she said, as she reached the top and handed the bag to Felicity.

"You're in trouble now, Ben," Tom said, stepping out from Muskoka room.

"Aren't I always, though?" Ben said, with a wink at Felicity who brought pulled more chairs around the table.

She looked at Will. "I think we better build a bigger deck. This one isn't going to hold us all."

"Especially if there are grandchildren in a few years," Will said, casting looks at his brother and sister.

Emma appeared at the door in a wet suit. "Paddle board anyone?" She addressed them all, but her eyes fell to Will.

"Yeah, I'm coming," he said. "She's relentless."

Ben laughed and flicked a glance at Felicity. "I know the type."

"Well, Mum," Olivia said, settling onto a chair. "We've set a date. I know I should have run it by you first, but we thought you'd be okay with it. We booked the little chapel at Balls' Falls. May fifteenth. Is that okay?"

"My birthday? Well, of course it's okay. I'll never have to ask when your anniversary is, will I? Not that I'd forget."

"And we have some more news," Eric said. "At least, something we want to ask." Olivia nudged his elbow and frowned at him. "Now is as good a time as any, isn't it? We want to buy your house. Olivia loves it and I do, too. And we thought it would be nice if it could stay in the family. We can talk about the details later, but we're hoping you'll say yes."

"Of course, I'll say yes. That's wonderful. And I'm relieved. The idea of strangers living there was worrisome."

"Aunt Carrie will be happy. If we buy it, she can stay until she gets herself settled. She's made herself pretty comfortable there, the past couple of months."

"As a matter of fact, she called yesterday. She and Blain are going to try to make things work. She's moving back in with him at the end of the month and he's going to put up the money for her to start her own business."

"That's amazing!" Olivia cried. "She'll be the best wedding planner. I'm going to set up an appointment with her right away. But what about Will? He's not living with us. No way am I going to pick up after two men."

"He'll stay here for now. And this time next year, he'll be in Ottawa. He's been accepted back into the program at Carleton. All he has to do is save the tuition money."

"And what are your plans, Ben?" Melody asked. "Are you going to stay in the area once you've fully recuperated, or are you planning to head off to parts unknown again?"

Ben cast a *will-you-tell-them-or-me* look at Felicity, who smiled. "He'll stay at Alice's until the renovations are done and then, when I get back from my trip, he'll move in here," Felicity said.

"With me." Her face flushed, and she held her breath, waiting for someone to tell her it was wrong, or too soon or something. She'd run over it all in her mind a hundred times. The questions they'd ask, the protests they'd make.

But there were none. Only congratulations when Ben grinned and kissed her.

Epilogue

Later, when she thought about how her summer had transpired, Felicity found it interesting how the death of one person could affect so many lives. If Richard hadn't died, she would not have gone to the cottage early that year. Felicity and Ben might never have met. Ben would probably have driven straight on to Alice's cottage, caught up with Emma and might have given up after her first refusal to see him. He might have gone back to the city to lick his wounds, and Emma would not have met her half siblings, all of whom adored their new sister. Of course, Hope might still be alive, but somehow, Felicity knew that her life was coming to an end sooner rather than later. She knew Hope was in a better place now, just as Richard was. Just as they all were.

Maybe there was something to this idea that all things happen for a reason. Was it karma or fate or destiny who'd played a hand in all that transpired that one summer at Ril Lake?

The end

Afterword

The cottage we used to visit on Ril Lake, which is not as described in this story, was owned by Stuart and Beverly Bradley. They were kind enough to give me wonderful rates during the month of December, when I would go, alone, to write and to explore the neighbouring communities. Many of my stories were inspired there, in the beautiful Muskoka room that overlooked Ril Lake. Sadly, they sold the cottage and my days of vising there are now over, though I visit the Muskoka area as often as I can.

Baysville is a lovely little town that is the epitome of cottage country life, with lakes and rivers running around and through it. It sits midway between several inviting destinations; approximately forty minutes from Algonquin Park, half an hour (or less) to Bracebridge, forty minutes to Dorset where you'll find Robinson's General Store and the look-out tower, and forty minutes from Huntsville. Lookout Point is purely factious, although the winding and hilly roads, with narrow slippery slopes toward the lake, are not. There is a garage in Baysville, but it isn't run by Wally. He, like all the characters in this novel, is purely from my imagination.

I have used the names of some of the businesses in Huntsville, with their expressed permission; specifically, That Place by The Lights, which has amazing food and wonderful staff, Soapstones, which is a regular stop on my visits to Huntsville where they make amazing lotions and bath products in enticing aromas, and Yummies in a Jar, which is not to be missed if you are traveling in that area. Their jams, jellies and sauces are out of this world. And they really do display the art of owner John Murden and other local artisans' items. Other businesses mentioned in and around the area are, at the time of writing this, up and running and if you're planning a trip in that area, you will want to include them in your adventures.

No author completes a book on their own. The writing might be theirs, but others contribute to the finished product. I would be remiss if I didn't take a moment to thank a few people who have helped me along the way, not only in writing this book, but in writing in general. First, my beta readers, without whom I would finish nothing. To my sister, Judy, to whom this book is dedicated, for her endless patience with brainstorming ideas, her developmental and copyediting skills, gleaned from 40+ years of teaching and reading more books per year than I can count. I must also thank Brian Henry for imparting his vast knowledge of writing, editing and the publishing industry through the many classes, workshops and retreats I attended. And in that vein, a shout out to all my writing classmates who have had some part in helping me hone my craft. I learned a great deal about writing and critiquing in Brian's classes, and for that, I am eternally grateful. To Mark Baker, for his help with all my formatting questions, and his constant critique of my work, a simple thank you doesn't seem enough, but I think he knows how much I appreciate all the help he's given me.

And lastly, I thank you for reading One Summer at Ril Lake, the first in the Muskoka Cottage Read Series. I sincerely hope you enjoyed it. And please watch for more books to follow in the near future.

About the author

Margery Reynolds retired from working life in 2016, when she closed her Niagara Falls bookstore, *Novel-teas*, and started her writing career. She took creative writing classes for a number of years, produced several manuscripts in historical fiction and the cozy mystery genres, before embarking on light romance. She currently lives with her son and grandchildren, in the Niagara Peninsula and when she's not reading or researching her family tree, she loves to read, go to movies and do jig-saw puzzles. On a bright day, you might even find her combing the conservation areas for great nature photos. She also loves blending herbal teas and still sells them under the Novel-teas label.

Margery Reynolds is also an editor and the owner of *The Golden Pencil*, an editing and story consulting company, and a small publisher. For more information about editing services visit www.goldenpencil.ca or follow Margery on Facebook to keep up with pub dates on future books at: https://www.facebook.com/authouroffiction

Manufactured by Amazon.ca
Bolton, ON